SWAMP SWEETS

A Miss Fortune Mystery

NEW YORK TIMES BESTSELLING AUTHOR

JANA DELEON

Design and composite cover art by Janet Holmes using images from
Shutterstock and DepositPhotos.

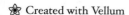 Created with Vellum

MISS FORTUNE SERIES INFORMATION

If you've never read a Miss Fortune mystery, you can start with LOUISIANA LONGSHOT, the first book in the series. If you prefer to start with this book, here are a few things you need to know.

Fortune Redding – a CIA assassin with a price on her head from one of the world's most deadly arms dealers. Because her boss suspects that a leak at the CIA blew her cover, he sends her to hide out in Sinful, Louisiana, posing as his niece, a librarian and ex–beauty queen named Sandy-Sue Morrow. The situation was resolved in Change of Fortune and Fortune is now a full-time resident of Sinful and has opened her own detective agency.

Ida Belle and Gertie – served in the military in Vietnam as spies, but no one in the town is aware of that fact except Fortune and Deputy LeBlanc.

Sinful Ladies Society – local group founded by Ida Belle, Gertie, and deceased member Marge. In order to gain membership, women must never have married or if widowed, their husband must have been deceased for at least ten years.

Sinful Ladies Cough Syrup – sold as an herbal medicine in Sinful, which is dry, but it's actually moonshine manufactured by the Sinful Ladies Society.

CHAPTER ONE

I STOOD IN THE MIDDLE OF THE DARK, DIRTY ROOM THAT smelled like stagnant water and enzymatic cleaner and listened as Ally explained her vision for her new bakery. Ida Belle and Gertie were there with me, and I was pretty sure none of us could remove the smiles from our faces, even if someone were pointing a missile at us.

"Oh, it's going to be so great!" Gertie said and started clapping.

Francis, who was perched on Gertie's shoulder, flapped his wings and started singing

"How Great Thou Art."

I gave him a nod as Gertie pulled a grape from her pocket and popped it in his mouth to shut him up.

"Probably appropriate, since everything sold in here will be heavenly," I said.

"Got that right," Ida Belle said. "It's going to be the perfect space and location for your shop, and I can't wait to see it when you're done. You've painted a pretty picture in my mind."

"Bet it smells and tastes even better than it looks," Gertie said.

Ally beamed at us. "I just can't believe it's finally happening. I know I always said I was working toward it, but sometimes I never thought I'd get here."

Her smile faltered a little and she rubbed her nose.

Gertie put her hand on Ally's arm and squeezed. "Are you doing all right, honey?"

Ally's mom, who'd been in a facility in New Orleans for longer than I'd been in Sinful, had finally succumbed to the cancer that had swept through her body. It had been so long in coming that everything had already been prepared as far as funeral services went, and Ally had taken power of attorney over her mother's estate years ago, which made everything easier. At least, as easy as it could get when you were saying goodbye to your last living parent.

"I'm fine," Ally said. "The reality is the physical degeneration and pain medication took Mama from me a good while back. I'm just glad she doesn't have to live that way anymore. I've had plenty of time to prepare..."

"But sometimes it hits you like it was new," I said.

Ally looked at me, her expression one of gratitude and empathy. I'd buried my mom when I was still a kid. And according to the CIA, my dad had officially died twice now, but I had a feeling I'd be called up for at least one more set of paperwork down the line.

"I think it's the insurance policy that really got to me," Ally said. "I knew she had one. She'd always told me she'd set something up to cover final costs and such, and the payment was drafted out of her checking account. So between what she had said and the amount drafted being so minimal, I never would have guessed that she had a hundred thousand dollars in life insurance."

"She must have gotten the policy years ago," Ida Belle said.

Ally nodded. "That's what the insurance agent told me. I was still in elementary school and Mama was healthy as a horse back then, so it didn't cost much and the rate was locked in as long as she kept paying."

"She loved you very much," Gertie said. "I know things were hard with her these last few years. That disease can really do a number on people, but I think she's looking down on you now and she's thrilled that this is finally happening."

Ally sniffed. "I hope so."

"So when does construction start?" I asked.

"Monday," she said. "They told me they'd let me be the first to hit that wall with a sledgehammer."

"That's incredible," I said. "I can't tell you how happy I am for you, Ally."

Ally threw her arms around me and squeezed me so tightly my ribs hurt. "I'm so glad you came to Sinful."

I grinned. "I'm the ecstatic one. I've had the good fortune —no pun intended—of being your extremely willing baked goods test subject for over a year now. And not only am I looking forward to many years of service in that position, but soon I will have the option to double down on my favorites."

"You're going to have to double down on your running," Ida Belle said.

"Some things are worth going the extra mile," I said. "Or ten."

Gertie shook her head. "I'm glad I'm at the elastic-waist-pants stage and don't care to be skinny anymore."

Ida Belle grinned. "At what point did you care to be skinny? Because I've known you since diapers, and you were wearing the plus-size Pampers."

"See, everyone knows you're making stuff up because Pampers wasn't even around in our mothers' day," Gertie said.

"And if they were, I would have been wearing the Future Sex Goddess line."

Ida Belle gave her a dismayed look as Ally laughed.

"It's really something how the timing all worked out," Ida Belle said. "It was meant to be."

Ally nodded. "I can't believe Miles decided to retire and sell the building the day Mama passed. I thought he was going to still be standing here wrapping clothes in plastic long after the rest of us had gone over yonder."

"Miles Broussard was so cheap, he never would hire someone to help," Gertie said. "He spent so much time with all those chemicals, there's a good chance he passed years ago and has been moving around in a semi-embalmed state."

"Broussard? Any relation to Molly?" I asked. I'd met Molly Broussard, a caterer, on a recent case.

Ida Belle shook her head.

"Why didn't Miles sell the business as well?" I asked. "Not that I'm complaining that he just sold the building and high-tailed it out of dodge with a check. But why not make the extra dollars?"

"It couldn't have been worth anything," Ida Belle said. "Sinful's not big enough to support a dry cleaner anymore, and the equipment is all old and likely needs to be upgraded at this point. But beyond that, style has changed so much. Clothes are far more casual, even at church."

Gertie nodded. "And most everything worth having is wash-and-wear. I haven't dry-cleaned something since that horrible shower curtain I bought that I couldn't return. Remember that?"

Ida Belle shook her head. "I never understood why someone would make a shower curtain that's dry-clean only."

"That explains why it wasn't returnable," I said. "I can't imagine paying to dry-clean a shower curtain and go through the trouble of keeping it from getting wet. How long did that last?"

Ida Belle started laughing and Gertie glared at her.

"There was an accident," Gertie said.

"Uh-oh." I knew exactly how Gertie's 'accidents' went.

"When I took it out of the package, it had deep creases in it where it had been folded," Gertie said. "I ironed the heck out of it, but they weren't coming out. So I took it to be dry-cleaned, per the instructions."

"And that didn't work?" I asked.

"It worked fine until she stepped outside," Ida Belle said. "A storm kicked up while we were inside and when we went out of the cleaner's with the newly pressed shower curtain, Gertie walked too close to the street and the wind blew that plastic wrap up like a parachute. It got caught on the tailgate of a truck passing by, and the guy had his radio up so loud he didn't even realize he was dragging Gertie until he was halfway down Main Street."

I smiled at the visual and Ally giggled.

"I remember that," Ally said. "He drove right by the café, singing Garth Brooks at the top of his lungs while Ida Belle ran behind him yelling and Gertie rode that shower curtain like a magic carpet."

"Yeah, it was hilarious," Gertie groused. "I paid fifty bucks for that shower curtain and another ten to dry-clean it."

"So it got torn up, I presume?" I asked.

"Not exactly," Ida Belle said and started chuckling. "Surprisingly enough, the curtain wasn't damaged by the dragging, although it was a little dirty, but when the plastic finally tore loose, it got rained on."

"Oh no," I said.

Gertie shook her head. "By the time I got home, the darn thing wasn't big enough for a place mat."

"Place Matt's body in the cooler," Francis said. "We'll come back for it later."

We all stared.

"Why the police didn't hang on to that bird, I have no idea," I said. "They could just run through a list of missing persons and probably wipe out half of their cold cases."

"I hate touching them before they're cold," Francis said.

"That bird would give me nightmares," Ally said.

"Well, at least you don't have a cooler in here yet," I said.

Ally laughed. "Is that your idea of a silver lining?"

I shrugged. "Just trying to help. Well, if there's nothing we can assist with, we have a hunting trip to pack for. You sure you don't want to come?"

Ally shook her head. "I appreciate the invitation, but I have to meet with the contractor tomorrow and go over everything. And I prefer to get my dinner from the grocery store or the café."

We all congratulated her again and made our way across the road to the General Store to pick up supplies. Unfortunately, everyone's least favorite citizen was already in the store. Celia was at the counter, probably giving Walter a hard time about something, based on the exasperated look on his face. When she heard the door chime, she turned around. As soon as she caught sight of us, she frowned, then she zeroed in on Francis and her face turned red.

"You are *not* supposed to have that bird in public places," Celia said.

"This isn't a public place," Gertie said. "It's a private business, and the only person who can ban Francis is Walter."

Since Francis's last visit to the General Store had resulted in two destroyed displays, the theft of some fruit, and an unfortunate pooping accident, I wasn't convinced that he was going to back Gertie up on this one. But apparently, his dislike for Celia was far stronger than his dislike for cleaning up bird poop.

"The *bird* is welcome," Walter said, his tone implying that Celia was not.

But Celia wasn't giving up. "I see Ida Belle's SUV parked right out front, which means you walked on a public street and sidewalk to get in here. That's illegal."

"So call Carter and tell him to come arrest me when I leave the store," Gertie said. "We'll see if he can get the cuffs on before I get in the SUV. It will be like a game."

"Let's play a game," Francis said. "It's called Russian roulette."

Celia's eyes widened and I grinned.

"Just finish up your business, Celia," Ida Belle said. "The only one keeping you in the presence of Francis is you."

"No one likes Celia or her big panties," Francis said.

I didn't think Celia could get any redder, but she managed to. Then she grabbed a loaf of bread on the counter and swung it at Francis. She missed and got Gertie right across the face. The tie fell off the bag and slices of bread flew all over the store.

"She's been bitch-slapped!" Francis cried, flapping his wings.

I sank onto the floor, laughing so hard I couldn't even stand upright anymore. Ida Belle and Walter were both clutching the counter and gasping for air. Gertie stared at Celia in disbelief, then grabbed a container of dish soap off the counter and dumped the entire thing over Celia's head.

"You crazy old crow!" Celia yelled and launched, her hands reaching for Gertie's throat.

I didn't have time to jump up and intervene, so I did the one thing I could do and lie about later on—I stuck my foot out.

Celia hit my foot and yelled as she slammed into Gertie, and they both tumbled into a fruit display. Francis took off from Gertie's shoulder as she fell, but he was connected by the leash on his foot and was just flapping around in a circle, yelling 'Just kill them all!' as loud as possible. As I jumped up, Ida Belle pulled out her knife and cut the leash, and Francis took off for a high shelf.

But not before depositing a show of his supreme displeasure right on Celia's forehead.

I reached down to help Gertie up as Celia grabbed her forehead, then drew her hand away, screaming as though we'd just doused her with acid.

"You'd think we threw holy water on her," Gertie said.

The door chimed and I looked over to see Carter stroll in. Celia was sitting upright now, the bird poo mixed with dish soap starting to run down her nose. The rest, she'd smeared into her hair. Gertie had two slices of bread hanging out of the top of her shirt, which had gotten yanked down in the fray and would have been exposing entirely too much cleavage if it weren't for the bread coverage. Francis had spotted the fruit on the floor and was now sitting in the middle of what had to be the best buffet ever from a bird's perspective.

"Maybe I'll just pick up my groceries later," Carter said.

"That's probably a really good idea," I said.

"Oh no, you don't!" Celia managed to crawl up the counter and pointed her finger at Carter. "I want that woman arrested. She has that bird in here and look at all this damage. He attacked me and took out the display."

Carter looked at the rest of us. "Is that how it happened?"

"Not even remotely close," I said. "In fact, Celia took the first swing."

"With a loaf of bread," Ida Belle said, shaking her head.

"That doesn't count," Celia said. "I was trying to hit the bird."

"Maybe you could all finish up your business here and leave Walter with some remaining displays," Carter said.

Celia glared at Carter. "Marie is not going to be the mayor forever. And when someone with some decorum takes office, they'll be getting rid of you."

Carter smiled. "Guess we'll just have to see, right? Walter, you done ringing up Ms. Arceneaux's goods?"

"I ring her up as she shops to save time," Walter said, and pushed the bags across the counter.

Celia put her hands on her hips and glared at Walter. "I guess you're not going to take them to my car?"

"Nope," Walter said. "My wife's a better shot than you."

We all started laughing again, and Celia grabbed her groceries and stomped out of the store.

Walter shook his head. "I keep thinking that she'll get tired of my being rude and do her shopping up the road, but so far, no luck."

"She'll never stop because she knows it annoys you," I said.

"What are you three troublemakers doing here anyway?" Carter asked. "I thought you were going hunting?"

"You say that like you don't believe us," Gertie said. "We happen to be here picking up supplies for our turkey hunting weekend. Ida Belle called ahead and Walter has them ready to go."

"Sure do," Walter said and put the bags on the counter.

Carter peered inside them. "If you guys eat all this junk along with the bathtub worth of alcohol I figure you've already got in the SUV, you'll never leave the cabin."

"We're going to pace ourselves," I said.

"If you're hunting, what's this for?" Carter pulled two paperbacks out of the bags.

"Those are for me," I said. "Ida Belle and Gertie are hunting. I'm along for a girls' weekend."

"You're not going to hunt?" Walter asked.

I shook my head. "I only shoot things I don't have to dress and eat."

"Not helping," Carter said. "How did you get a license for turkeys this time of year anyway?"

"It's one of those lottery things," Gertie said. "The population is out of control in some places and one happens to be here. So Wildlife and Fisheries opened up some extra hunting slots for certain groups of people. I qualify under the disabled veteran category. Ida Belle refused to go through the approval process, so we're limited to only two turkeys."

"You mean Ida Belle refused to lie on the application?" Carter asked.

Ida Belle wisely remained quiet.

Walter frowned at Gertie. "What's your disability?"

Carter laughed. "You have to ask?"

"My disability is private information between me and Wildlife and Fisheries," Gertie said.

Carter put his hands up. "I don't even want to know."

"Yeah, changed my mind," Walter said. "I don't want to know either."

"Is this everything?" Ida Belle asked, and Walter nodded.

"You didn't ask for a turkey call, though," Walter said. "You want me to toss one in there?"

"We have the best turkey call ever," Gertie said and scooped Francis up from the middle of a banana-and-grape-eating session. "Francis, do the turkey."

And darn if that bird didn't gobble just like a turkey.

CHAPTER TWO

GERTIE'S HUNTING CAMP WAS ONLY ACCESSIBLE BY BOAT, AND since we never knew how the landscape of the bayous might change and we had a decent amount of stuff to haul with us, we took my airboat. And if I was being honest, mostly since Ida Belle loved to drive fast. Because Gertie insisted on bringing Francis—even though Ida Belle pointed out that whole turkey call thing wouldn't work so well once they started shooting—we had to make sure his cage was secured well and covered with tarp.

He started complaining as soon as his cage went dark.

"You should be thanking us," I said as I pulled bungee cords around the cage to secure the tarp. "If we didn't do this, you wouldn't have a feather left by the time we got there."

Finally, we got everything loaded and headed out. The camp was across the lake and down one of the lesser bayous, and neither Ida Belle nor I had ever been there. That was because Gertie had surprised us both by secretly acquiring the camp from a former church buddy who needed the money for their new place of worship, the Swamp Bar.

I had a bit of pause about buying something when the

money was going straight for the bottle, but Gertie said he was going to drink anyway and since he had just turned eighty-nine, it was hardly the time to make life changes. She'd kept the purchase from Ida Belle and me, hoping to surprise us with an official hunting camp. Walter had a camp on Number Two, an island appropriately named for its awful-smelling mud, but it was better for short fishing trips. No one wanted to stay on Number Two long enough to hunt.

Gertie indicated the somewhat dilapidated dock, and Ida Belle expertly directed us next to it. I tied it off and stepped onto the dock, then reached back to take the stuff we'd brought from Gertie. Ida Belle jumped up and started carrying it off the dock.

"I'm not sure this thing will hold our weight and all our stuff," Ida Belle said as she moved things onto land. "And none of us wants a trip in the bayou."

"Yeah, I only brought three changes of clothes," I said.

"We're only going to be here two nights, and you're going to sit inside and read a book," Gertie said. "Why would you need more than that?"

"Because I'm here with you?" I suggested.

Finally, we got everything onto land and everyone picked up a load to make the trip up to the camp, which was set back in the trees about twenty yards from the dock. I was carrying Francis, who was still wrapped up and was currently alternating singing "Rescue Me" and reciting the Lord's Prayer. As we approached, I assessed the camp. It was on pilings, and the wood siding looked as weathered as the dock. I hoped it was sturdier.

"Isn't it great?" Gertie asked, practically bouncing with excitement. "I know the outside looks rough but it's strong as heck. I had everything checked out, but I didn't want to fancy up the outside too much. It attracts attention."

"Attention to what?" I asked as we climbed the stairs.

"What might be inside," Gertie said as she swung the front door open.

Ida Belle and I stepped inside and drew up short, staring in shock at the interior.

"This looks like something out of one of those rich-people hunting magazines," I said.

Gertie grinned. "This was the big part of the surprise. I've had contractors in here for a month getting this ready."

"Won't the contractors tell people what they put in here?" I asked.

"I hired them all out of Mudbug," Gertie said.

"You have a big-screen TV," Ida Belle said, and pointed to the giant screen over the fireplace in awe.

"You know we're not going to hunt all day," Gertie said. "Between my lack of conditioning and your corns, I don't figure us for more than a couple hours before we call it quits and order our turkeys from the butcher."

"Oh, I've already done that," Ida Belle said. "I wasn't counting on getting a turkey. I just wanted to get away from my house for a while."

"Don't tell me you're already tired of living with Walter," I said.

"Nothing like that," Ida Belle said. "Well, maybe sometimes. It's just that I've lived alone most of my adult life and now that there's someone else in the house with me, he likes to do things."

"Sexy things?" Gertie perked up.

"Talk," Ida Belle said. "He likes to talk."

I had to laugh. "You need to get away from the man because he likes to talk?"

"I don't see you living with Carter," she said.

"Fair enough," I said.

It wasn't as though it hadn't crossed my mind, but that was mainly because I figured it had crossed Carter's mind. Lord knows, it had crossed Gertie's mind. She asked me weekly if we were going to move in together. But since neither one of us had brought it up, I figured neither of us was ready to take that step. We stayed at each other's homes several times a week. But while I missed his company when he wasn't there, I also enjoyed my time alone. I had a feeling Carter was the same.

Gertie shook her head. "I used to think that Ida Belle was the most stubborn person in the world, but you give her a run for her money. And the fact that Carter is just as bad doesn't bode well for forward progress. At least Walter always made his desire for more perfectly clear. I'm afraid you and Carter will still be having slumber parties when you're eighty."

"Nothing wrong with a long-term slumber party arrangement," Ida Belle said.

"Just how long were you and Walter 'slumbering' before you finally agreed to marry him?" Gertie asked.

"I'll never tell," Ida Belle said.

Gertie sighed and I laughed.

"Let's get the rest of the stuff in," I said. "We've got snacks galore and a ton of booze, and that recliner is calling my name."

It took us a good twenty minutes to get everything in the camp and unpacked. There was only one bedroom but it had two sets of king-size bunk beds, so everyone had their own sleeping space. And if anyone snored, the couch looked cushy enough to spend a couple nights on, so I wasn't worried. I'd definitely slept on worse during my time with the CIA.

Gertie already had a perch set up for Francis in the living room and he was recovering from his life-threatening boat ride by eating grapes. At least he'd stopped singing and praying. We loaded up on snacks and drinks and headed for the living room.

"This is the life," Ida Belle said and kicked her feet up on an ottoman. "I may never leave here."

"You don't have a choice," Gertie said. "If we don't show up on Sunday afternoon, the men will come looking for us. And if they see the inside of this place, they'll want to use it. Then they'll talk and other people will want to use it, and I don't need that kind of grief. I'm not running a free vacation rental here."

Ida Belle frowned. "Good point. Looks like I'll be listening to Walter talk Sunday afternoon."

"You know, you could always suggest doing something that keeps him from talking," Gertie said.

"Woman, do you ever give up?" Ida Belle asked. "I thought for sure when you started dating Jeb regularly, you'd give up this interest in everyone else's love life. Maybe you need to ratchet up your own a little more."

Gertie threw her hands in the air. "Jeb's back keeps us from doing that. The darn thing goes out at the drop of a hat. Talking is all we can manage sometimes. But it's sexy talk. Maybe you should try that."

Ida Belle stared at her as if she'd lost her mind. "You're lucky I left my gun in the bedroom and am too comfortable to go get it."

I laughed. "I think it's time for the movie."

"Is it a love story?" Gertie asked.

"Horror," I said.

Gertie sighed. "I give up."

———

THE NEXT MORNING, Ida Belle and Gertie were headed out to try to get a turkey. I surprised them by agreeing to go with them. I brought my pistol, of course, but not a shotgun. I had no intention of shooting anything unless I didn't have other options. But I'd consumed so much beer and snacks the day before that I needed to walk for a long, long time to burn off even half the calories. Ida Belle had tried to talk Gertie out of bringing Francis, but Gertie was insistent that the bird would be able to attract turkeys better than a turkey call.

"But what about when you need to shoot?" I asked.

"That's why he's on my left shoulder," Gertie said, as if that covered everything that could possibly go wrong with her plan.

I had a backpack with our water supplies and tossed in a crab net I'd found in the camp closet, just in case I needed to capture that bird. Or tie off a compound fracture. It could swing either way. We tromped a good ways into the woods until we reached a nice-sized clearing, and Ida Belle declared it as good a place as any to try this Francis-turkey-call farce.

I found a stump to sit on and waited for the show. I also pulled out my nine, just in case.

Gertie got her shotgun in position and then asked Francis, who'd been remarkably quiet during our trek through the brush, to do the turkey call. I think we were all a bit surprised when he actually complied.

But not nearly as surprised as we were with the result.

We waited, looking around for a couple minutes, and I was just about to assume that Ida Belle was going to have to break out the turkey call she'd let Walter slip her or go target shooting instead, when I heard something moving through the trees. Except it sounded much bigger than a turkey. Heck, it sounded bigger than a bear.

"They don't have dinosaurs in Sinful, right?" I asked, only half joking.

"Alligators aren't close enough for you?" Ida Belle asked. "But that's no gator."

I rose from the stump and got into ready position. The entire situation felt off and the closer the sound got, the more it worried me. If it couldn't be outrun or killed with a nine or a shotgun, we might be in trouble.

Then the sound burst through the trees.

CHAPTER THREE

I HAD NO IDEA WHAT I WAS EXPECTING, BUT THE FLOCK OF turkeys was not it. And not just any flock of turkeys. These were some kind of giant, mutant turkeys. All I could see was huge bodies and claws. I'm not sure who was more surprised, us or them, but I was going with us. I threw my arms up, ready to fire, but with no idea what to fire at. Turns out, arms up was a good position as the birds started landing, diving, and then went on the attack.

Gertie spun around as one of the turkeys went for Francis and for a moment, I was afraid she was going to lift the shotgun and fire, which would have been problematic as one of the birds had just knocked her glasses off. Francis, who was clearly in a panic, did his version of prison break and slipped his lead. He took off into the trees and Gertie set up a howl, running after him.

I figured the trees looked like way better cover than standing in the clearing and bolted in the opposite direction from Gertie. No point in moving in the same direction as the birds. As I ran, a turkey dropped out of the air and whacked me on the back of the neck so hard, it sent me spiraling into a bush. I barely managed to do the tuck, but the roll was out of the question. The bush was so thick that my tuck ended up leaving me shoulders on ground, butt in air, caught in the dense foliage.

I flopped around a bit, trying to contort my body around the limbs, and finally managed to work myself to belly down. I could still hear Gertie yelling and peered out of the bush to assess the situation. That's when I saw Ida Belle leaning calmly against the trunk of a cypress tree and eating an apple where Gertie had entered the woods.

Then the sound of police sirens filled the air, and a voice yelled, "Put your hands up!"

Completely confused, I started to climb out of the bush, but then I heard a gunshot and the giant swarm of turkeys came straight through the clearing again, headed in my direction.

I threw my hands over my head as they passed, then heard Gertie yelling and looked up to see her running after the turkeys, firing her shotgun. Since her glasses were still in the middle of the clearing, I stayed down and prayed that she didn't trip. Turkeys were in an uproar all around me as Gertie ran past my bush. I crawled out and hauled butt across the clearing, picking up Gertie's glasses as I ran, then slid to a stop where Ida Belle was still leaned against the tree.

Gertie fired another shot, and I heard her victory cry.

"She must have gotten one," Ida Belle said. "Guess I lost that bet with Walter."

"Why was Walter so certain she'd get a turkey?"

"He was certain she'd end up killing something if she tromped around the woods for two days. I didn't specify a turkey in our bet."

"That was a lapse on your part, although he'll probably just be happy it wasn't one of us who got shot."

"Why do you think I was on the side of the tree opposite from Gertie?"

"Makes perfect sense. I can't believe the entire flock came down on us like that."

"Francis was doing a mating call," Ida Belle said. "All those turkeys were male. That's why they're so big. Well, part of the reason they're so big. I'm going to reconsider your dinosaur question though, because...wow."

I stared at her in dismay. "A mating call?"

Ida Belle shrugged. "Food and that are what get males to come running and there's not a dinner bell for turkeys."

"Poor Francis. No wonder he pulled the *Shawshank* move."

Ida Belle nodded. "Well, I guess we'd best go make sure Gertie's not getting into more trouble."

"Ta-da!" Gertie stepped out of the clearing, dragging a turkey. "I can barely lift this sucker. But I think we have a problem."

"They're not coming back, are they?" I asked.

Gertie shook her head. "Four of them aren't, anyway."

Ida Belle shook her head. "You're only supposed to shoot two."

"I was under attack," Gertie said. "I had to defend myself."

"You were charging when you shot those turkeys," I said. "You were under attack when you fled."

Gertie waved a hand in dismissal. "Who's going to tell—you two?"

"Francis might," I said.

"Francis!" Gertie dropped the turkey and the shotgun and took off into the woods.

I retrieved the net from my backpack and Ida Belle gave me a nod. "Smart."

We headed into the woods after Gertie and found her peering up into the trees.

"He was right around here when he did the police siren."

"That was Francis?" I asked.

"Where did you think it came from?" she asked.

I shrugged. "I figured you might have something stuffed in your bra."

"Just grapes," she said. "Francis! Wanna grape?"

I heard a squawk in the trees and a couple seconds later, Francis swooped down and plopped himself right on Gertie's shoulder.

I tossed the net over her head. "Time for lunch?"

———

WE DECIDED to take Francis to the camp first and get him squared away with grapes and maybe a Valium. Then we needed to figure out what to do about the turkeys. If we got caught with four of them, it was going to be trouble, but it seemed like a waste to leave them there. And then there was the issue of actually getting them back to the camp. They were all huge and it wasn't as though we could take a four-wheeler through the woods. It was too dense, and we didn't have a four-wheeler anyway. Finally, we decided to put them in a tarp and drag them.

Which proved to be much harder than we'd originally thought it would be. The ground was covered with roots and branches, and we kept having to unhook the tarp from something every couple feet. And it took all three of us to pull the thing. After an hour, we'd made it about fifty yards from where we'd loaded up and had another hundred and fifty to go.

I dropped my end of the tarp. "I have a better idea."

"We get Gertie's purse and blow them all up?" Ida Belle asked.

"We'll make that plan B," I said. "I can see the bayou

through those trees. It's only twenty yards or so away. I say we haul this to the bank and Ida Belle goes to get the boat. Then we can toss these things into the boat and get them back to the camp that way."

Ida Belle raised one eyebrow. "You want to *toss* them into the boat?"

"Okay, maybe toss was an exaggeration," I said. "I'll settle for bowling them over the bank and into the boat."

"I haven't been bowling in a while," Gertie said.

"We still have to get them from the boat to the camp," I said, "but at least there's a nice smooth path."

"Bowling it is," Ida Belle said.

We hauled the birds to the embankment, and Ida Belle set off to get the boat. Gertie and I flopped down on a log. I opened my backpack, hoping I'd stuck some food in there that I had forgotten about, but no such luck. I pulled out my one remaining bottle of water and a pack of breath mints.

I sighed. "I'm afraid this is all I've got."

Gertie pulled a grape out of her bra and offered it to me.

"Why do you still have grapes in your bra?" I asked.

"Because I couldn't fit a sandwich in there."

"Something about that is just totally wrong," I said, and elected for two breath mints instead.

Gertie shrugged and popped the grape into her mouth.

It wasn't long before we heard Ida Belle coming with the boat, and then she appeared around a bend in the bayou. She eased up as close as she could to the embankment and tied the boat off to some cypress roots. It was about a ten-foot drop from the side of the embankment into the boat, and there was only a small gap between the boat and the embankment wall. There was no way those turkeys would fit in the gap, so we were good to go with my bowling plan.

I hefted up the first turkey and dragged it to the side of the embankment, then did a sort of swing thing over the edge and let it go. Then Gertie and I looked over to see it fall right in the middle of the boat in front of the bench where Gertie usually sat.

"My seat cushion is going to be a mess after this," Gertie said.

"It's washable," I said. "Remember, it was designed for you."

"Let me get the next one," Gertie said.

"That sounds like a horrible idea," Ida Belle said.

"You sure you want to try it?" I asked. "Because even that low toss I made was no joke."

"I got those kettlebells we saw on TV and use them while I watch *Supernatural*," she said. "Every time a hot guy comes on the screen, I do a curl."

"The main characters are two hot guys," I said.

Gertie nodded. "I've been getting a *lot* of curls in. Did a marathon watch last weekend and couldn't lift my arms above my waist the next day."

"Is that why you missed church?" Ida Belle asked. "You told me you were sick."

"Sick of not being able to lift my arms," Gertie said. "All my alcohol is on the shelf above my refrigerator. But I've been working out hard, and I'm much more toned now."

Ida Belle didn't look convinced, and neither was I, but what the heck. I waved a hand at the turkeys. "Go for it then."

Gertie grabbed one of the turkeys by the tail feathers and hefted it up better than I thought she would. She inched to the edge of the embankment, then took a big backswing and flung the turkey over the side. Altogether, she had pretty good form.

Except she forgot to let go.

She twisted as she flung the turkey and stumbled to the

side as she started to fall. I leaped forward, trying to grab her before she toppled over the ledge, but I didn't make it. She pitched over the embankment and crashed into the bayou just in front of the boat. I jumped from the embankment into the boat and ran to the front where Ida Belle was leaned over, waiting for Gertie to break the surface.

A couple seconds later, Gertie splashed up, flapping around like a fish on a line. We yelled, and she stopped flapping and started treading, trying to focus on where the boat was, which is hard when your eyes are full of salt water, but she'd also lost her glasses when she fell. She finally located the side of the boat and grabbed it, then Ida Belle and I leaned over and hauled her up. She flopped onto the bottom of the boat, and two grapes rolled out of her shirt.

Ida Belle shook her head. "Somewhere, there is an eyeglass maker who can attribute half their profits to Gertie alone."

"The bigger question is how she still had grapes in her bra," I said.

"They're probably wedged in there with a gun and a po'boy," Ida Belle said.

"Are you okay?" I asked as Gertie struggled to sit up.

"That water is colder than what you'd think," she said.

"It *is* November," Ida Belle said. "The air's not particularly warm either, so we need to get you dry as soon as possible."

"I'm not leaving those turkeys!" Gertie said. "I killed them fair and square and they attacked us. This will not be settled until I have them on my dinner table."

"I'll get the turkeys," I said and scrambled back up the embankment.

I made quick work of the third turkey with no mishaps, but the last one got me. We didn't have another tarp, so we needed the current one to drag the turkeys from the dock to the camp. But instead of tossing the turkey, as I had the others, then following up with the tarp, I got the bright idea that I'd swing the whole shooting match over to save time.

I didn't forget to let go, so I won't say I Gertied.

But I did put a little too much muscle into it.

I knew I'd overthrown the boat as soon as the tarp left my hands. It was almost slow motion as Gertie and Ida Belle leaped from the front and tried to catch the tarp before it crashed into the bayou. Gertie managed to get one hand on it just as it went by but didn't have enough stability to stop the momentum.

And Gertie didn't let go.

Again.

She tipped over the side of the boat and went into the bayou again, and the turkey tarp pulled her under. I jumped back into the boat and leaned over the side with Ida Belle, waiting for the eventual rising of the woman who needed to be voted Sinful's Least Likely to Learn from Experience.

But this time, she didn't pop up right away.

I was about to dive in when she broke the surface and managed to grab hold of the boat with one hand. The other was down in the water, and I assumed it was still grasping the tarp.

"Why is this thing so heavy in water?" she asked.

"Good Lord, woman," Ida Belle said. "Why didn't you just let that thing go? You're over the limit anyway."

"It was a reflex," Gertie said. "I hate wasting food."

"You regularly throw casseroles into the bayou for an alligator," I said.

"That's not wasteful," Gertie said. "That's taking care of a friend. Anyway, I lost my grip when I hit the water and had to feel around for a bit. Man, this thing is getting heavier by the second. I must be getting tired."

"What you're getting is old," Ida Belle said. "Can you pull it up high enough for us to reach it? Because I'm not getting into that bayou to haul out an illegal turkey."

"I think so," Gertie said. "Hold my other arm."

"You're going to pull your arm out of socket," Ida Belle grumbled as we reached down.

As soon as we had Gertie as secure as she was getting, she started pulling up on the tarp, grunting and panting as if she were lifting an elephant instead of a turkey.

"It must have filled with water," Ida Belle said.

I wasn't sure how, when the thing was littered with holes from being dragged across jagged branches and tree roots. More likely, Gertie had some kettlebell work to do before she could haul a turkey tarp up after a full morning of physical activity. Finally, her hand broke the surface and I let go of her arm to grab the tarp. Instantly, it dragged my arm down and I yanked it back up, surprised with how quickly it had pulled me down. I tugged it to the surface and frowned.

"This isn't the tarp," I said. "The tarp is green and this is beige."

"Crap," Gertie said. "I must have grabbed some trash instead of the tarp. Oh well, I've got three turkeys. Let it go."

I was just about to do that when I noticed a tear near the top and what appeared to be a finger poking out. I looked over at them.

"Guys. I think we have a problem."

CHAPTER FOUR

IT TOOK ALL THREE OF US TO HAUL THE BODY INTO THE BOAT and then we all stared down at the bag for a bit. Finally, Ida Belle spoke.

"Do you think we should open it or wait for Carter?" she asked.

"Heck, no, I'm not waiting," Gertie said. "I almost drowned pulling that thing up. I deserve to know who it is and if Carter takes over, we'll be shoved out of everything."

"I can't argue with those points," Ida Belle said. "Fortune? You have to put up with him after this. What do you think?"

"I think that any forensic evidence is long gone, so I can't see what harm it would do. And since I seriously doubt this location is the crime scene, we're not compromising anything if we haul this back to the dock and call from there."

"But first...?" Gertie gave me a hopeful look.

"First, we see if anyone recognizes them," I said. "Be ready. This is probably not going to be pretty, even though the bag might have helped with predation."

I bent over and tugged on the zipper at the top of the bag, but it was stuck. Ida Belle pulled out her knife and handed it to me and I carefully slit down the bag, next to the zipper. When I'd managed a couple feet, I pulled back the bag and we all studied the man inside.

"Water really does a number on people, doesn't it?" Gertie said.

"You sit in my hot tub every week for a couple hours," I said. "And look how that does your skin. Now imagine being at the bottom of the bayou for who knows how long."

"Probably not very long," Ida Belle said. "Something big enough to tear open that bag would have caught scent of it soon enough. But the medical examiner will make a determination, of course."

"A determination that we won't get to know about," Gertie grumbled.

"Do either of you recognize him?" I asked. "I know it's tough, but, anything?"

Ida Belle frowned and gestured to me. "Turn his head to the right a bit, so I can see near his ear."

I moved the head over and Ida Belle nodded and pointed.

"I recognize the scar by his ear," she said. "It's Miles Broussard."

I didn't know Miles but the name rang a bell, and then it hit me. "The guy Ally bought the building from?"

"One and the same," Ida Belle said.

"I thought he'd moved to Florida," Gertie said. "What the heck is he doing dead in a body bag in the bayou?"

"Not a body bag," Ida Belle said. "Look."

She pointed to lettering in the lower corner of the bag that was partially missing. "It's a dry cleaning bag. I can still see part of the business name."

"Did he drown?" Gertie asked.

"I don't think so," I said and cut the bag open a little more, then tapped on his chest. "Bullet hole."

"So someone shot him, stuffed him in a dry cleaning bag, and tossed him in the bayou," Ida Belle said. "That's pretty old-school, even for Sinful."

"We *do* usually get the more creative deaths here," I agreed.

"What's that?" Gertie asked and pointed to something peeking out toward the top of the bag.

I cut the bag open all the way to the top and pulled out a hundred-dollar bill. There was another stuck in the zipper. Ida Belle looked at Gertie and held up her hand.

"Don't say it," she warned.

"Maybe he was laundering money," Gertie said.

Ida Belle shook her head. "You just couldn't help yourself, could you?"

"Are they real?" Gertie asked.

I shrugged. "They look real, but they're waterlogged. And since they're the old design, they were probably already worn from circulation. But who knows? Counterfeiters are top-notch these days."

Ida Belle nodded. "I suppose it would be smart to make older bills and ease them into circulation given all the new security features of money these days."

"But why would someone leave the money behind?" Gertie asked.

"Maybe they were in a hurry and had to," Ida Belle said. "Or maybe they didn't notice when they zipped him up. Maybe it was in his pockets and came out."

I shook my head. "Not the third option. Those bills were zipped up when the bag was closed, but I suppose it's possible they fell out of his pockets at some point during the bag stuffing and they didn't see them."

I pulled out my cell phone.

"You going to call Carter now?" Gertie asked.

"Not just yet," I said and took some pics of the bills. "I

don't want to remove them because we can't without tearing them, but you know we'll never get to see them again. Hey, reach into that storage bench and pass me some gloves."

Given our propensity for coming across things we shouldn't and, well, going into places we shouldn't, I'd gotten in the habit of keeping a box of gloves everywhere. You never knew when Gertie might not have her purse with her or, more accurately, when her purse might be destroyed along with its contents.

I donned the gloves, then cut the bag more and checked the man's pockets. In his right pants pocket I found his wallet, and it confirmed Ida Belle's identification. This was Miles Broussard. Age fifty-two. Brown eyes. Other than his license, the wallet contained a bank card, two credit cards, and his insurance information.

"Now I'll call Carter," I said and dialed.

"Has anyone been shot?" he asked when he answered.

"As a matter of fact—"

"Good God! Is anyone seriously hurt?"

"It wasn't one of us."

"I assume this means you got a turkey? That is not a nice way to tell me, by the way. You *are* hunting with Gertie. You could cut a guy some slack."

"We did get a turkey, but someone also intruded on our girls' weekend."

There was dead silence and I swear I could feel him tensing.

"One of you shot an intruder?" he asked.

"Your confidence is overwhelming."

"Again. You're hunting with Gertie."

"Fair enough, but no. He was already shot. We just found the body."

There was silence again and then he sighed.

"Of course you did. Have you identified him?"

"Miles Broussard."

"Miles? You're sure? He's supposed to be living it up in Florida."

"I know, but it doesn't look like he made it out of Louisiana. His wallet is in his pocket, and Ida Belle ID'd him."

"Text me your coordinates, and I'll get out there with the ME and a forensics team. Have you secured the crime scene?"

"Well, technically, there isn't one. You see, the body was stuffed in a dry cleaning bag, and Gertie accidentally dragged it up from the bottom of the bayou, thinking it was a turkey tarp."

"You know, if anyone else had made that statement, it would make no sense, but it's you and it's Gertie, so I'm just going to roll with it. Secure the body somewhere that it can be easily retrieved and not molested by wildlife—other than the three that hauled it in—and I'll be there as soon as possible."

"Did he refer to us as 'wildlife'?" Gertie asked as I slipped my phone back in my pocket.

"Would you rather be referred to as domesticated?" Ida Belle asked.

"So what do you want to do with our laundry bag problem?" Gertie asked.

"Let's take the boat back to the dock and tie it off," I said. "And I say we leave the body in the boat. It's sturdier than the dock, and I'd prefer not to lift the body again. That can be on Carter and his crew."

"That's my vote," Ida Belle said. "Besides, we still have to deal with these turkeys. Might as well conserve energy where we can."

I looked around my boat and sighed. "When the corpses outnumber the living, you know your boat has taken a hard turn in the wrong direction."

"At least we didn't shoot him," Gertie said cheerfully.

Ida Belle shook her head. "Which leads to the question, who did and why?"

Gertie clapped her hands. "Another murder to solve. Thank God. I was getting bored."

"We just had a head fall off in front of us a few weeks ago at the Halloween festival," Ida Belle said. "How many people need to be murdered to keep you entertained?"

Gertie shrugged. "I guess we'll know when we get there."

"I take it this somewhat indifferent attitude means Miles never won any popularity contests with you two?" I asked.

Ida Belle's brow wrinkled. "It wasn't that we didn't like him. More like we didn't really know him. He wasn't the mingle-with-the-townsfolk type."

"Was he a Sinful native?" I asked.

I could sort of understand the lack of desire to mingle with quite a few of the locals, so the fact that he wasn't a regular around town, outside of running his business, wasn't necessarily a slam to his character. It also explained why I'd never met him, especially as I'd never owned anything that had to be dry-cleaned in my entire life and certainly not in Sinful, where my wardrobe mostly consisted of cotton items purchased online.

"He was a transplant," Ida Belle said. "Been here about five years."

Gertie nodded. "That sounds about right."

I was a bit surprised. "He thought opening a dry cleaner's was a good idea five years ago? I figured he'd been here for way longer."

"The dry cleaner's has been there for a long time," Gertie said. "He bought it from the third owner, who also retired to sit on a beach, like Miles was supposed to do."

I frowned. "But that makes no sense. Why buy a business

that you two have already indicated was on a downturn that wasn't likely to go back up? And then do it close to the time that you were planning on retiring?"

"Maybe he's the worst businessman ever," Gertie said. "Or just plain stupid. He might have thought he could make it work. Or maybe it was a midlife crisis. Or I guess that would be a later-life crisis in his case."

"Looks like a near-death crisis from where I'm standing," Ida Belle said.

"Was he friends with anyone who could give us the scoop?" I asked.

"So you're planning on poking your nose into police business?" Ida Belle asked.

"I wasn't 'planning' on it, per se, but it tends to happen," I said. "I'm just getting things lined up in case I need to do something."

Gertie grinned. "You mean in case you're bored. Admit it— you're more like me than you say."

"Okay, maybe I prefer when there's some action," I said. "But that doesn't mean I necessarily want bodies to keep appearing in front of me. You know, a different person could develop a complex."

"Not in Louisiana," Gertie said. "In Louisiana, they'd just assume they were cursed."

"Well, I won't rule it out," I said. "We better get the boat back to the dock."

Ida Belle sighed. "I guess this means we have to go home early."

I held in a smile. "I don't see why we should. Carter's always telling us to stay out of official police business. Seems like staying here the rest of the weekend is the best thing we could do. It's not like the cabin's a crime scene, so we don't have to clear out."

"And more importantly, no one else has to come in," Gertie said.

Ida Belle untied the boat from the cypress roots. "Then the dock it is."

I hopped into my seat and Gertie looked around, then sat on the bench. "It was either this or the body," she said.

Ida Belle grinned. "I'll take it slow."

———

WHEN WE GOT to the dock, we hauled the turkeys out of the boat and dragged them onto land, then tromped back to the camp to grab something to drink. Since Carter was on his way, and Gertie was treating her new camp like Fort Knox, we took the drinks and some snacks back outside and plopped down on a tree log to eat. We'd only been there ten minutes or so before we heard a boat and then Carter rounded the bend, the ME along with him.

Carter eyeballed the sketchy dock as he approached, then made the smart decision to pull next to my boat and tie off. The ME looked over at us and gave us a half-hearted wave. I couldn't really blame him. We had associations with entirely too many people that landed on his table. We walked up to the edge of the dock as the ME stepped over into my boat and squatted next to the body.

"You pulled it out of the bayou like this?" he asked.

We all nodded.

"What was it caught on?" he asked.

"The bottom," Gertie said. "You see, Fortune overthrew the boat with my turkey tarp and I fell in trying to save it. I lost my grip when I fell but then thought I'd found the tarp again. Instead, I came up with a dead guy."

The ME stared at Gertie for a moment, and I knew he was

trying to process a turkey tarp, coming up with a body, and then getting to the part where we were all sitting on a log eating potato chips like nothing unusual had happened, but I had a feeling he was never going to reconcile all of that. Carter, on the other hand, was all too familiar with the way things seemed to roll with us and looked completely unfazed.

"You cut the bag?" the ME asked as he pulled apart the folds.

"Yes," I said. "I didn't figure there was much forensic evidence left after he'd dragged around on the bottom for however long."

"Yes, well, I won't know time of death until I do my examination," the ME said.

"I can give you *cause* of death," I said. "There's a bullet hole in his chest."

The ME pulled the bag further over and took a closer look. "It does look like a bullet hole, but I can't be sure that's the cause of death until I do my examination."

I laughed. "You guys are all the same. Not admitting to anything until you do your examination. Let me help you with the important parts. That guy was shot, and unless he had the ability to zip himself up in a bag and then dump himself into the bayou, Carter has a murder investigation on his hands."

Carter nodded. "She's right about that. Let's get him over into the sheriff's boat and back to your facility. The sooner you can pin down time of death, the better. Unless the bullet is still in the body, I don't think you're going to get anything else off him that matters."

"Not necessarily off the body," I said. "But look at the top of the bag. There's a couple of hundred-dollar bills caught in the zipper."

"Seriously?" Carter asked and sighed. "Why can't I ever catch a simple bar fight?"

"It does seem like everything lately is over-the-top with drama," Gertie said.

"Which you're enjoying the heck out of," Carter said. "I know I don't have to tell you—"

"To stay out of official police business," we all said at once.

"Don't worry about us," I said. "As soon as you get that body out of my boat, we're headed back for an afternoon of cleaning turkeys, a hot shower, then a night of drinking and television."

"You're not going home?" Carter asked.

"Do you want us to go home?" I asked.

Realizing what I was asking, he shook his head. "Nope. Staying here sounds like a good idea."

"Good," Gertie said, "because I'm not cleaning those turkeys at my house. You remember that disaster when I tried to clean my own chicken."

"The chicken wasn't dead yet," Ida Belle said.

Gertie threw her hands in the air. "Who knew they could pretend for that long?"

Carter winced and glanced past us at the turkeys lying next to the path to the camp, probably making sure they were really dead. "There are three turkeys there."

"Would have been four if I hadn't come up with the dead guy instead," Gertie said.

"But you only have a license for two," Carter said.

"There was a situation," Gertie said.

Carter held his hand up. "The less I know, the better."

"That's what Walter says," Ida Belle agreed.

"Intelligence on certain matters runs in the family," Carter said.

"I'd like to make the counterpoint that Walter married Ida Belle, even after knowing her for a hundred years," Gertie said.

Carter pursed his lips, and I could tell he was thinking how to reply. If he said it was the right decision, then he was going against that 'intelligent man' comment he'd made earlier, the implication being they both avoided our shenanigans. If he accepted Gertie's counterpoint, then that meant marrying me someday was negating his own intelligence.

I had to smile. It was rare to see Carter at a loss for words.

He glanced over and saw me smiling and shook his head. "Try not to find any more dead people," he said. "And for God's sake, don't shoot any more turkeys."

"We're only here another day," I said. "We should be able to manage both."

He nodded but didn't look completely convinced.

Given our track record, neither was I.

CHAPTER FIVE

THE TURKEY CLEANING TURNED OUT TO BE MUCH MORE involved than I figured it would be—mostly because of the size of the turkeys. After Carter and the ME left, we dragged the three birds up to the camp, and then Ida Belle and Gertie began discussing how to attack the problem.

"You can't Cajun fry them without the skin," Ida Belle said. "The skin is the best part on fried turkey."

"I agree, but if we don't skin them, we have to pluck them," Gertie said. "And I don't have a container big enough to soak the turkeys in."

"You soak the turkeys?" I asked.

"In hot water if you expect to get the feathers off," Gertie said. "And we're not using my bathtub."

I held my hand up. "I also vote for not using the bathtub, especially as there's only one."

"We're going to have to skin them," Gertie said.

Ida Belle sighed. "It sucks to lose all that skin, but you're right. At least we can quarter them up and no one will see you carting three full turkeys into your house."

"I can oven-roast them and we can have them for sandwiches," Gertie said. "And I can make casseroles with them. They freeze well."

"If you make casseroles with even one of those, you'll feed Sinful for a month," I said.

"Or Godzilla for a couple days," Ida Belle said.

"As long as she's not doing it in my backyard, I don't care," I said. "Is he still hanging around Francine's camp?"

Gertie shook her head. "I think all the commotion we made scared him a bit. He's relocated since then."

"To where?" I asked.

Gertie put on her blank face. "I might have seen him behind the General Store last week."

Ida Belle narrowed her eyes at Gertie. "Last week when Walter was cooking all that barbecue for Scooter's party?"

"Maybe," Gertie said. "I can't remember exactly."

Ida Belle shook her head. "You can remember. You just don't want to admit it. You've ruined that gator. If he's moving into occupied areas because of the smell of food, he'll be strolling down Main Street before you know it, and someone is going to put a bullet in him."

"I know that," Gertie said. "I've been luring him this way with casseroles. I'm hoping he likes the new territory and decides to stay put."

"This is exactly why you don't feed wild animals," Ida Belle said.

"I can barely handle a house cat," I said. "Just saying."

"Okay, this conversation is going nowhere and neither are those turkeys," Ida Belle said. "And since I'd like to shower and be sitting on the couch with a beer before the sun goes down, we need to get moving."

I nodded. "Where do we do this?"

"I have a fish-cleaning station under the camp," Gertie said. "It's got a sink and stainless steel counter. We can throw the innards in the bayou or if you want to be ambitious, I've got some crab traps we can bait and we can have us a crab boil tomorrow."

"Since we're already going to be handling innards, I vote for the crab boil," I said.

"No use wasting good bait," Ida Belle agreed. "Then let's get these suckers sliced and wrapped. Daylight's burning."

We hauled the turkeys to the fish-cleaning station on the back side of the camp and then Ida Belle proceeded to work her magic with the knife. Gertie helped and I abstained completely, claiming I was going to take notes for next time but didn't want to mess anything up, especially given how much trouble we'd gone through already. I wasn't completely lying. I even filmed it for future reference but ultimately decided I was a Butterball-for-life purchaser. That was entirely too much work. And mess. Lord, the mess. I was really glad there was a place outside for this, but I also had other concerns.

"Won't the smell from the blood and guts attract predators?"

"We'll douse everything with bleach when we're done," Gertie said. "But to answer your question, yes, it can. The small predators aren't the issue, but I definitely don't want bears hanging around here."

I nodded. "I'm pretty sure I've reached my annual limit of running from bears. Between this year and last year, maybe this decade's limit."

"You've still got a lifetime to go," Ida Belle said and grinned.

"Well, if it's all the same, I'd rather not use it up this weekend," I said.

Gertie dumped the last of the guts into a bucket and took a hard look at the last turkey. "You know, this one might be small enough to fit in the pot I have here. I know it's extra work, but we could get one fryer out of this."

Ida Belle nodded. "I'm up for it. There's really nothing better than fried turkey."

As I'd finally gotten to partake of fried turkey the previous year, I had to agree. I'd had turkey a bunch of different ways but fried was definitely the best.

"I'm just along for the ride," I said.

"You're going to be along for the lifting as well," Ida Belle said. "Let's get this sucker up to the camp and get some water heating. We can soak and pluck it on the screened porch. That way, the mess isn't inside the camp but it isn't blowing everywhere either."

Gertie nodded. "I have a shop vac for clean-up."

Ida Belle and I each grabbed a side of the turkey and we started up the steps. Gertie ran ahead of us to get the pot of water on the stove. It was slow going because we had to keep redoing our grip but finally, we made it onto the porch and dropped the bird on a garbage bag that Gertie had tossed out. Then we sat down in patio chairs for a break. Gertie popped out and passed us all a beer.

"The water temp is already headed up," she said. "Should be ready to go in a couple minutes."

"There's no way you can boil water that fast," I said.

"You don't get it to a boil," Gertie said. "You need hotter than your spa but not as hot as a cup of coffee. When it's ready, I'll bring the pot out here and you guys can dump the bird in. Then we'll have another round until it's time to pluck."

"This plucking plan is getting better by the minute," I said and clinked beer cans with Ida Belle.

Gertie finished her beer, then went inside to retrieve the pot of water. Ida Belle and I got up and we positioned ourselves to pick up the bird again. A couple seconds later,

Gertie came out the door, stumbled, and sloshed water onto the porch. At least she was wearing rubber gloves. I looked up and realized the problem—her glasses were fogged over. She lowered her head to look over them and got the pot onto the middle of the tarp. Ida Belle and I lifted the turkey over it and were doing the countdown when Gertie stuck a bare finger in the water and yelled.

"Wait! It's not hot enough."

But it was too late. The countdown hit one and Ida Belle and I let the heavy bird go, then jumped back so we wouldn't get splashed.

And then the unthinkable happened.

The turkey rose from the dead.

As soon as it hit the water, its wings spread open and it shrieked. It flapped twice and lifted right out of the pot, then made an impressive dive through the front door of the camp. I heard Francis yell, "Intruder! Someone grab the tommy gun!"

We ran inside where the turkey flapped around the room at a rate of speed far faster than I'd thought it capable of. It was also in a complete panic. And I learned that turkeys do two things when they panic—sound comes out one end and something else comes out the other. The turkey crashed into a kitchen cabinet door, and the door broke loose from the hinges and hit the floor. Then he flew into the light in the dining alcove and the bulbs shattered before the whole fixture dropped onto the table. That sent the turkey straight for us in the living room.

"Grab him!" Gertie yelled.

Ida Belle and I ducked. It was involuntarily on my end because that's just what I was trained to do when things were flying at my head. Ida Belle's dodge might have been involuntary or might have been from years of hunting but either way, the only one standing was Gertie, who thrust her hands up to grab hold of the bird.

She got a handful of feathers with one hand but lost her grip, and the turkey dived right onto the top of her head, sending her tumbling backward over an ottoman and into an end table. The lamp on the end table started to sway and I did a dive, catching it just before it crashed into the hardwood floor.

Then Francis Gertied.

He did the turkey call. The turkey *mating* call!

It just goes to show how a woman can completely change a man's focus. The turkey, who'd just crash-landed on the kitchen counter, took off straight for Francis. He attempted a landing on Francis's cage, but he was too heavy and carrying far too much speed. The cage tipped over and as I was still holding the lamp, I didn't have time to make a move for the cage. With some quick thinking, Ida Belle yanked a pillow off the back of the couch and threw it on the floor below the cage before it struck the ground. The turkey, not about to be put off of the company of a good woman, stood on top of the bird-cage, stomping his feet like he was trying to break through the bars.

"Francis, do the siren!" Gertie yelled.

Immediately, the sound of police sirens filled the air. The confused and once-again-panicked turkey launched from the cage and flew right at us.

"Duck!" Ida Belle yelled, and Gertie and I hit the floor.

Ida Belle had snagged another couch pillow before calling out her warning and dodged to one side as the turkey flew by, then whacked it on the rear with the pillow and sent it right out the front door. Then she ran to the door, slammed it shut, and sank to the ground, her back against it.

"Down to two," she said.

Gertie jumped up and ran for the birdcage. She righted it and let Francis out and put him on his perch. He was singing "When the Saints Come Marching In."

I laughed. "Appropriate in so many ways."

I stood and surveyed the damage. A screwdriver would probably fix the cabinet door, but the light fixture was going to have to be replaced. And the place was going to need a good cleaning. That turkey had deposited feathers and worse stuff everywhere.

"It's the chicken fiasco all over again," Gertie said.

I shook my head. "I don't ever want to hear the word 'turkey' come out of your mouth again unless 'Butterball' is in front of it."

———

I SUGGESTED we leave and hire someone to come clean the camp. Ida Belle suggested we leave but set it on fire before we go. But ultimately, cleaning turkey poop won out over going home and listening to Walter, apparently, because she donned rubber gloves and we all set to it. With three working, it went faster than I thought it would. It probably helped that Francis continued to sing between grapes.

We hummed along and moved as quickly as possible to get the place back in order. The upside was that the floors were hardwood and Gertie hadn't gotten around to ordering rugs yet, and all the furniture was leather. The throw pillows were the only fabric in the room and somehow, the turkey had missed all of them with his bombs. We stuffed everything damaged into a trash bag and hauled it out to go home with us the next day, and tossed the turkey guts into the bayou. No one was interested in the crab traps at that point. It sounded too much like work.

Finally, the last piece of countertop, furniture, and flooring showed no sign of our uninvited guest, and we all lined up for the shower, each promising not to use all the hot water. When we were all clean and changed, we flopped into the three recliners in the living room with beer and thick sandwiches and a lack of inclination to move for another day or two.

"Hunting is entirely too much work," I said. "I'm never going with you guys again."

"But if we hadn't gone hunting, we wouldn't have found that body," Gertie said.

"Maybe it would have popped up downstream and some fisherman would have caught sight of it," I said.

"I hate to agree with her," Ida Belle said, "but if that body had remained overnight in the bayou, there wouldn't be anything left to pop up but that bag."

"Okay, so we can come out to the camp as often as you'd like because these recliners are the bomb, and I love the big-screen TV and people who like to watch the same things I do. But if hunting is involved, I'm taking a pass."

"What about fishing?" Gertie asked.

"Fishing is okay as long as you repair the dock and do it from there, but I'm still going to read a book instead. And no boat fishing. Not in my boat. You can't ever get the smell of fish out of there."

"You're the only person in Louisiana who has a problem with fish in their boat," Gertie said.

"Then the rest of Louisiana needs to get a clue," I said, "because I can smell their boats when they drive by."

"Might be the people you smell," Ida Belle said.

I cringed.

"It's going to be really hard for tomorrow to top today," Gertie said. "What a ride."

"Good Lord, why would you want to top today?" Ida Belle

said. "It was a year's worth of horror shoved into a matter of hours."

I nodded. "I'm okay with sitting right in this chair until we leave. Except for expected breaks for bathroom and food, of course."

"You guys are no fun," Gertie said. "Good thing I brought my new paintball gun. We can try it out tomorrow."

I glanced over at Ida Belle, who looked as afraid as I felt, but we were too tired to argue. We'd just deal with it tomorrow.

"So? Who's up for a movie?" I asked.

We decided to take things back and settled on a Rambo marathon. At some point, we must have all dozed off because my ringing cell phone startled me out of sleep. I jumped out of the recliner, momentarily confused by my surroundings. Ida Belle sat up and pointed at my hand.

"Are you going to kill an intruder with that or make them a pie?" she asked.

I looked down and realized I was holding the banana I'd brought to the end table with my sandwich. I hadn't gotten around to eating it, but I was clutching it the way I would my nine.

"Good Lord, I left my gun in the bedroom," I said. "I am seriously losing my touch."

"Are you going to check your phone?" Gertie asked, rubbing her eyes.

"Oh yeah," I said and picked it up. Carter. It had already stopped ringing and I noticed the time. Midnight. That probably wasn't good.

"It's Carter," I said.

"Maybe he's missing sexy time," Gertie said, looking hopeful.

"He's probably been dealing with that body all day," I said.

"I doubt sexy time was at the top of his list for things he wanted to do tonight, and he definitely wouldn't call me about it."

My phone pinged, signaling me that he'd left a message. We all looked at one another, now growing concerned. I accessed the message and put it on speaker.

"I'm sorry to call so late, Fortune, but we had a situation tonight and I know you wouldn't appreciate not hearing about it until tomorrow. Ally went back to her new bakery site late tonight to take some measurements, and she was attacked. She's okay, but she took a solid crack on the back of the head and my mom has gone with her to the hospital to get checked out. I don't know much yet because I was more worried about getting her to the hospital than taking a statement. I'm sure she'll fill you in as well. I'll be working the scene probably until early morning."

My hand clenched the phone tighter as we listened, and when the message was done, Gertie jumped up from her recliner.

"We have to get back to Sinful," she said.

"Agreed," Ida Belle said. "Fortune?"

I broke out of my thoughts and nodded. "Definitely."

"What's wrong?" Gertie asked. "I mean, besides the obvious?"

I stared at them. "Do you really think it's a coincidence that we found the dry cleaner's owner dumped in the bayou and then Ally was attacked tonight in that building?"

Gertie's eyes widened. "I hadn't gotten that far."

Ida Belle shook her head, her expression grim. "Looks like things just got complicated."

I nodded. "And looks like we just got in the middle of police business."

CHAPTER SIX

BY THE TIME WE GOT THINGS ORGANIZED AND PACKED, AND made the boat ride back to my house, an hour had passed. We unloaded the boat first, because leaving food out in a docked boat isn't a good idea, then Ida Belle took Gertie home to drop off Francis while I went upstairs to get my guest room in order. By the time Ida Belle and Gertie got back, coffee was ready and I called Emmaline.

"Fortune," she said. "You heard, I assume?"

"Carter called. Are you still at the hospital?"

"Yes. They did some tests and everything is clear. We're just waiting on the doctor to release her, then we'll be headed back."

"Great. Will you bring her to my house instead of her own? If that's okay with Ally, of course."

"Honestly, it would be a big relief to do so. I was going to insist she stay with me, and I expected her to put up a fuss. But she might not be as opposed to spending the rest of the night at your house. And I know I'd feel better. What in the world is going on in this town? This is a safe place for women, and I don't want that to change."

"I don't know what's going on, but we're going to figure it out. In the meantime, we're going to make sure Ally is secure."

"Oh, here comes the doctor. I'll call you when we're close to town."

I took a big sip of coffee and blew out a breath. Gertie patted my hand.

"She's fine," Gertie said. "If she wasn't, the doctor would want to keep her and Emmaline would hog-tie her if she tried to leave."

"I know," I said. "But the fact that this happened is just making me so angry. Ally isn't like us. She doesn't do criminal behavior. She doesn't even like confrontation. She's the last person who should be dealing with this."

Ida Belle nodded. "She is a rare gem of sunshine in an otherwise cloudy world. But trust me, she's tough. You never met her mother, but she wasn't an easy woman, and when she got ill, she got even more difficult. There's a reason Ally left as soon as she graduated from high school."

"That's true," Gertie said. "Don't get us wrong, Ally's mom was a good person, just not the most positive of people to be around."

"What about her dad?" I asked.

"Well, he was Celia's brother," Ida Belle said. "The apple and the tree thing happened with those two. Their parents weren't the most pleasant, and the kids fell even further out."

"Are you sure Ally wasn't adopted?" I asked.

They both smiled.

"That point has been made more times than we can count," Ida Belle said. "But her mom was clearly pregnant and delivered, and Ally looks like her dad did when he was a kid. It's just one of those odd but fortunate things."

Gertie nodded. "This town could use more Allys and fewer Celias for sure. So what's the plan? Beyond tonight, I mean."

"Convince Ally to stay with me until we figure this out, for one thing," I said.

"She still has to deal with everything at the bakery," Ida Belle said. "And my guess is she's not going to stay away, even if there could be a serial killer in the walk-in cooler."

"I know," I said. "And I can't blame her. She's been dreaming about this for a long time and never really thought it would happen."

"And she needs to get up and running and get the profit flowing in," Gertie said. "I'm sure she's got some money to keep her floating for a bit, but it won't last forever. And she can't continue working at the café and get her bakery open at the same time."

"So we'll help get the bakery running," I said.

Ida Belle smiled. "If the mountain will not come to Muhammad..."

"Exactly," I said. "I can't help with the baking, but I can lift things and unpack boxes and paint or something."

"She's going to know why we've suddenly taken up residence in her shop," Gertie said.

I shrugged. "And? She'll have to kick us out if she wants us to go. I think she'll be fine working there during the day. It's right on Main Street and the area is busy. But if she plans on being there after dark, then at least one of us needs to be there with her."

"I agree," Ida Belle said. "The more people, the less chance of the attacker making a move again. Plus, he'll probably figure everyone is on alert."

"Maybe he won't be back," Gertie said. "It might have been someone looking to see if there was anything to steal."

"That's possible," I said. "But you know how I hate coincidence. And finding that body..."

"Yeah, it's not a good look," Ida Belle agreed. "The two

things could be completely unrelated, but the prudent call is to assume they aren't and take the proper precautions. At least until we know otherwise."

I reached for my laptop. "Okay, so tell me what you know about this Miles Broussard."

Ida Belle and Gertie looked at each other and shook their heads.

"What we told you at the camp was about it," Ida Belle said.

"Come on," I said. "The guy was here for five years. He had to have at least one friend."

Ida Belle shrugged. "Not that I ever saw him with. He ran the dry cleaner's himself and was there every day. It closed at noon on Saturday and opened again on Monday morning. According to Myrtle, who used to live across from him, at least once or twice a month, he threw an overnight bag in his car Saturday afternoon and drove out. Didn't come back until late Sunday."

"Anyone know where he went?" I asked.

They both shook their heads.

"Anyone ask?" I asked.

"Of course," Gertie said. "This is Sinful. But he just said he had hobbies in the city and that's all he'd say."

"Hobbies." I considered this. "So probably drinking, gambling, or a woman."

"Maybe all three," Ida Belle said. "Only place to drink socially around Sinful is the Swamp Bar. There's no gambling except for the illegal sort, but you have to know people to get an invite, and I can't imagine Miles would have passed muster. There's plenty of available women here, especially of the type a bit older than Miles, and I'm sure some took a run at him, being a business owner and all, but I'm not aware of any success stories. And the Swamp Bar pickings are fairly slim. Most of the women brave enough to go there are with their man or at least a mean brother."

"But if all his personal interests were in New Orleans, why buy a business in Sinful?" I asked. "Why not buy a business in New Orleans?"

"He probably got a good price on the dry cleaner's," Ida Belle said. "I think it had been on a downturn for a while, which I know then begs the question why buy it at all. I just don't have an answer."

"But you had to have gotten a feel for the man," I said.

"He was a bore," Gertie said. "Some of my curtains were Mother's and I'm afraid to wash them at this point, so I have them dry-cleaned once a year at least. You know me—I'm not going to stand in front of someone and not try to chat them up, but Miles wasn't having any. He'd nod and go about ringing up the ticket and then tell me when they'd be ready for pickup. I swear, I could have been telling him where Jimmy Hoffa was, and he wouldn't have so much as blinked."

"I ran into him a couple times in the General Store, but he was never interested in conversation," Ida Belle said. "He'd say hello, get his stuff, and leave. Walter said he never had anything to say to him either."

I blew out a breath. "Good Lord, if the man wouldn't even talk to Walter, then there's no hope that he was talking to anyone else in this town."

Ida Belle nodded. "I'm pretty sure more confessions go on in that store than in the Catholic church."

"Well, this is all disappointing," I said.

My phone signaled a text and I checked the message.

"They're pulling through downtown," I said. "We're up."

We all hurried outside and were standing in the driveway

when Emmaline pulled in. Ally slowly got out of the car, and I figured she probably had a good headache going. She stared at all of us and smiled.

"What? No band?" she asked.

We all laughed and I waved her inside. Emmaline motioned to me and I walked over as Ida Belle and Gertie got Ally into the house.

"What did the doctor say?" I asked.

"Take it easy for a couple days and contact him if the headache gets worse," Emmaline said. "Nothing but regular Tylenol, so that's a relief."

Emmaline's concern was obvious and since she'd recently spent time in the hospital with a concussion, she knew how serious blows to the head could be. Even months later, she still had some gaps in her short-term memory.

"I'm going to leave her to you and head home," Emmaline said. "My hovering will just make her more uncomfortable. And she's already going to have to deal with all the police stuff tomorrow, and I'm sure that's on her mind."

I nodded. "We'll see that she gets some rest. And trust me, nothing will happen on my watch."

Emmaline gave me a hug and kissed my cheek. "You know, I couldn't have picked a better woman for Carter if I'd built you myself."

I felt a flush creep up my neck. "You're pretty awesome too."

Emmaline smiled and hopped in her car. "Call me if you need anything. Or if Carter gets out of line. That's your best friend in there, and I expect him to refrain from being pissy about certain things."

'Certain things' being me all up in his investigation.

I waved as she pulled out, and then I headed inside. I really had won the lottery here in Sinful. Great home, great friends, great guy with a great mother. It was almost scary how well everything had worked out.

Except for the dead guy.

Which kept happening.

CHAPTER SEVEN

GERTIE AND IDA BELLE HAD ALLY ENSCONCED IN MY NEW recliner with a glass of ginger ale and some cookies. She smiled at me as I walked in.

"Did you get the medical scoop from Emmaline?" she asked.

I nodded. "She's very relieved that you're all right."

"She's so sweet," Ally said. "And having just had her own issues with a head injury, I'm sure she was even more worried than she would have been otherwise. Oh well, at least there's not a dead guy attached to mine."

Ida Belle, Gertie, and I looked at one another.

"What?" Ally asked, looking slightly nervous. "Is someone dead?"

There was no point in keeping it from her. She was going to hear it tomorrow when Carter questioned her about the attack, and since it happened in the store she'd bought from Miles, I can't imagine that his questions wouldn't include everything she knew about Miles.

"We sorta found a body today while we were hunting," I said.

"Why does that keep happening to you?" Ally asked. "Who was it?"

"Miles Broussard," I said.

Ally's eyes widened and her hand flew over her mouth. "But he retired. He moved to Florida."

"Apparently not," I said.

"How did he...I mean, was he..."

"Murdered? Yes. He was shot."

"Oh my God!" she said. "I can't believe it. We were just at the title company signing papers and he didn't look nervous or anything, so I can't imagine that he knew someone was going to kill him—Lord, what am I thinking? Of course he didn't know."

Ida Belle patted her arm. "It's all a bit distressing, but it didn't have anything to do with you."

"But someone attacked me in his old business," Ally said. "Do you think they were looking for Miles? But no, he was already dead when I was attacked. That wouldn't make sense."

"We're not sure what happened," I said. "But I want you to be prepared to be questioned tomorrow by the police because Carter is not going to take this as coincidence."

Ally looked worried. "That's why you insisted I stay here, isn't it?"

"No one should be alone with a recent head injury," I said. "But yes, until we figure out what's going on, I'd feel much better if I stayed here. And if you're going to be at the shop after the other retailers have closed for the day, one of us would like to be with you."

"Oh my God," Ally said. "Why is this happening? Especially now? Everything I've been working for was finally going to be real."

Gertie took her hand and squeezed it. "And it still will be.

This mess has nothing to do with you except for being in the wrong place at the wrong time."

She bit her lower lip. "Are you sure?"

I nodded. "If this was directed at you, we'd be dealing with more than a knock on the head. Whoever was in the shop just wanted to immobilize you long enough to get away."

"But why was he there in the first place?" Ally said.

"That's what I'd love to figure out," I said. "It might be that someone thought they'd find something to steal. You've been meeting with the contractor, so someone might have assumed there would be materials or tools in the building."

Ally cocked her head and stared at me. "You don't think for a minute that a random burglary happened after you found Miles murdered. Look, I appreciate you trying not to worry me, and I'm not a detective or anything, but those dots seem pretty connected to me."

"Maybe," I hedged.

She raised one eyebrow.

"Okay, probably," I said. "But I don't think it's going to be all that easy to determine how they're connected because apparently no one knew Miles very well."

She frowned. "That's true enough. I had a couple of Mama's older linens that I dry-cleaned because I wanted to preserve them for longer, but that's the only time I've ever interacted with Miles other than the day we closed on the property. And even that was just a bunch of nodding and signing."

"What was he like that day?" I asked.

"Normal," Ally said. "He actually smiled when we were done and wished me success with my venture. I got the impression that he was ready to sit on a beach with a beer. He even said that this was his last outstanding piece of business in Sinful as he'd been renting his house. Said he already had his car packed, and he was leaving early the next morning for Florida."

"And you closed two days ago?" I asked.

She nodded.

"What about pricing?" Ida Belle asked. "If you don't want to tell your personal finances, then forget I asked."

"I don't mind," Ally said. "I paid roughly twenty percent below appraisal, but the agent said that there wasn't a lot of interest in the space. Apparently, it had been on some commercial real estate loop online a couple weeks before the listing hit locally and they hadn't had any bites."

"Do you think he lost money?" I asked Ida Belle.

She shrugged. "Without knowing what he paid for it, it's hard to say. But real estate values downtown have been fairly stagnant for a while now, so I don't imagine there was much appreciation in the five years he owned it."

Gertie nodded. "And there's only so many businesses that can make a profit in a town this size and without any tourism to speak of. The oil field work has been flat for years, so no new influx of those workers. And honestly, they wouldn't help a dry cleaner's business any. A bar would be a different story."

"Okay, then we'll get the details on that end of things just to put it all into perspective," I said. "As soon as Carter allows you back in your building, I want to go over the entire place."

"Wouldn't the forensics team be doing that now?" Ally asked.

"Probably," I said. "But they are looking for hard evidence. We tend to look at the big picture, and I want to get a feel for the space as well as the man."

"That makes sense," Ally said. "And you're really good at this PI thing."

"Can you tell us what happened tonight?" I asked.

She nodded. "I closed up the building and went home

around 6:00 p.m. and was working on layout and design because I want to order some of the furniture online. But there's a space in the front that I wasn't sure of the size because of the placement of the door. I had the dimensions on the plan but sometimes you have to see something to know whether the size and placement of things will disrupt flow."

"Walter talks about that all the time with his displays," Ida Belle said. "I honestly didn't realize so much thought had to go into stacking cereal boxes for a sale."

"The General Store is always structured well," Ally said. "I might ask Walter's opinion before I order everything."

"I'm sure he'd be delighted to help," Ida Belle said.

"So anyway," Ally said, "I guess I got excited or antsy or whatever and decided to go back to the building and look at the area I was concerned about and maybe take some pictures so I could reference them later. I don't know why I didn't just wait until this morning."

"Because you were excited," Gertie said. "It's perfectly understandable. You've been waiting for this for a long time."

"Apparently, I should have waited a little longer," she said.

"What time did you go back?" I asked.

"About eleven," she said. "I parked on Main Street, right in front of the building."

"Did you see any other cars?" I asked.

She shook her head. "I didn't even hear another car. It was completely dead downtown. Most of the homes behind Main Street already had their lights off as well. And saying that makes me realize just how foolish I was."

"This is Sinful," Gertie said. "We don't expect these kinds of things to happen here, but I suppose it wouldn't hurt us all to start being more careful."

"That's true," Ally said. "Anyway, I let myself in and turned on the lights in the front of the building. I took a couple pictures of the area I was concerned with, and then figured that while I was there, I'd get some pictures of the exposed brick on the back wall so that I can pick a good stain for the cabinets. I walked through the entry and had turned to the side to find the light switch when something hit me across the back of the head and I went down."

Gertie shook her head. "I can't imagine how scary that must have been."

"I completely panicked," Ally said. "I was afraid...well, you know, woman fears. Then I heard him running away and the back door slammed. My head was already pounding, but I'd dropped my phone and couldn't find it because my vision was blurry and the light from the front only carried into a narrow piece of the back room."

I tightened my fists as she described what had happened. If I got just five seconds alone with that guy...

"I managed to stand up and leaned against the wall to keep from falling," Ally continued. "I was so dizzy. I finally found the light switch and located my phone, then I inched down the wall and sat back down on the floor. I wanted to leave but my vision was so blurry I knew I couldn't drive, and I figured sitting outside in my car wasn't going to be any safer than sitting in there. I managed to call 911 and Carter was there in a matter of minutes even though it felt like forever."

My stomach clenched as I processed what Ally was telling me. Ally was the kindest, nicest, best person I'd ever known. I hated that something like this had happened to her, and even worse, that it had happened now and on the site where her dreams were supposed to be realized.

"I'm so sorry that happened to you," I said. "But we're really glad you're okay. Did you get any idea as to the size of the intruder?"

"Not at all," she said and yawned. "It was so dark and he was out of there so fast."

"You should get some rest," I said. "That's the best thing for a head injury."

"I'll take you up," Gertie said. "Fortune already made up your bedroom and has something for you to sleep in. Tomorrow we can pack up some things from your house."

Ally smiled. "I really appreciate this. Logically, I know it doesn't seem like someone is after me, but I don't think I would have gotten much sleep at home. Knowing that the best sharpshooters in Sinful are watching over me is better than a sleeping pill."

Gertie and Ally headed upstairs, and Ida Belle and I went back into the kitchen where our voices wouldn't drift up to them.

"I don't like it," Ida Belle said. "And I don't believe for a minute that someone was in that building for a random robbery. Contractors haul their tools in and out these days because of theft, and anyone who's been around for more than a minute knows that."

"I don't like it either," I said. "But what were they looking for? Miles was already dead."

"Unless there's more than one person looking for Miles," Ida Belle said. "The more likely explanation is the intruder is looking for something that Miles had and he wants."

I sighed. "That was my first thought, especially given those hundreds we found in the bag with him."

"I had an idea about that," Ida Belle said. "I know someone down at the bank. I want her to run those serial numbers and see if anything pops."

"You're thinking stolen, not counterfeited?"

She shrugged. "I don't know. Neither is all that easy to pull off these days."

I nodded. "We'll get Ally situated first thing and then we'll start digging into the money and Miles. And I figure we should talk to the Realtor that sold the dry cleaner's. Please tell me it's not my friend Cara Holiday."

Cara was a local girl who'd tried to move in on Carter when he returned to Sinful. She wasn't happy that I'd gotten the girlfriend slot and mostly avoided me like the plague.

"No," Ida Belle said. "She only does residential. My guess is that it was Dirk Richard, but we can confirm with Ally."

"Is he local?"

"Not anymore. He grew up here but moved to NOLA to pursue his real estate interests. There's not much call for commercial sales in Sinful but when there is one, people call Dirk because he knows the town and can pitch it better than someone who's never been here."

"So we have a plan."

Ida Belle nodded. "Carter's not going to be happy about it."

"Carter's going to have to get over it."

———

WHEN ALLY WAS SETTLED and the kitchen was back in order, Ida Belle, Gertie, and I trudged upstairs to try to get some rest ourselves. It was closer to morning than night, but we had a lot to do that day and any sleep was better than none. I had finally dozed off when someone shook my arm. Startled, I reached for my gun but it wasn't there. Then I looked up and saw Ida Belle standing next to the bed, holding my weapon.

"There's been enough shooting already these past few days," she said, and handed me my gun. "There's someone outside in a car, watching the house."

CHAPTER EIGHT

I BOLTED OUT OF BED AND PULLED ON SHORTS BEFORE heading to the guest bedroom she and Gertie were staying in. Gertie was snoring loud enough to wake the dead, so it was no surprise that Ida Belle had been looking out the window instead of sleeping.

She lifted one of the blinds. "Right there in that old Accord two doors down. It was there when we came to bed. I always check out the windows."

"I do too."

"I figured maybe he was visiting someone, and it was a late night getting home because he was in the driver's seat then. But when I couldn't sleep, I started checking every five minutes or so. It's been thirty minutes now, and he hasn't moved so much as an inch. He's chain-smoking, though. I can see the cigarette when he lights up."

"So he's in for the duration," I said. "But why?"

"Anything I come up with isn't good."

"Yeah, me either. Guess we better go find out what he's up to."

"You want me to wake Gertie up?"

"No. I think the two of us can handle one dude in an old Honda. And honestly, I'm too exhausted to launch another recovery from Gertie helping."

"Isn't that the truth."

We headed downstairs and out the back door. We skirted my neighbors' backyards, and I said a quick prayer of thanks that Ronald wasn't outside doing something strange. The last thing I needed was him in the mix. He had even worse outcomes than Gertie.

At the end of the second house, we slipped down the side, then stopped at the front edge and peered around the hedges. We'd come out just a bit in front of the car, and I could still see his shadow and the lit cigarette.

"We really need better streetlights in this town," Ida Belle said.

"Then people would see us when we're up to stuff."

"Retract that idea. So how do you want to handle this?"

"You sneak up from the back. I'm going to go to the other end of the house and cover the front."

"Are you going to shoot out his tires if he tries to take off?"

"No. Well, probably not. I guess we'll see. But I'm hoping that you can get close enough to yank the passenger door open. I'm going to make my way down those azalea bushes to that tree near the sidewalk, so it won't take me any time to launch after you get the door."

"Sounds like a plan. I'll give you a minute to get into position, then make my move."

I headed to the other side of the house and slipped down the side, sidling close to the azalea bushes as I entered the front yard. I was on the opposite side of the bushes from the car, and they extended all the way to the tree. But given how they'd thinned out in the fall, if chain-smoking lurker was watching closely, he would see movement because there wasn't even a tiny breeze. The night air was completely still and humid, and I could practically feel the rain that was headed our way. Despite it being November and my wearing shorts and a tank, sweat was already rolling down my forehead.

I took position behind the tree and peered through the bush. I saw Ida Belle slip from behind the house and hurry to a huge rosebush in the middle of the yard. The intruder must not have seen her because he made no move to leave. Ida Belle then crouched low and started her stealthy slide over to the car. She had just reached the taillamps when Ronald's front porch light flicked on, and I heard the door open.

"What are you doing in my bushes?" he yelled, and a second later I heard the pump of a shotgun.

Good. God.

The car fired up and I bolted from behind the tree toward the street. The driver turned on the headlights, which momentarily blinded me, and I could hear the engine race as he floored it.

"Move!" Ida Belle yelled.

I had time to dive out of the way of the car but that would leave me with no prize. So instead, I did what any logical person would do. Or maybe a couple of logical people. With a death wish.

I jumped on the hood of the car.

The terrified driver screamed when I hit the hood, and I grabbed the back of it to steady myself and pointed the gun straight at him. He probably could have done a quick turn and rolled me off the car, but I guess looking down the barrel of a gun was enough to scare him into braking. He slammed on the brakes and I rolled off the hood and popped up, still covering him with my weapon.

"Holy crap, that was impressive," Ronald said as he ran up

behind me. "Do you want me to roust him? I have handcuffs. They're the furry kind but I brought them with me just in case."

"Just in case he was someone you wanted to date?" Ida Belle asked.

"I don't date men who drive old Hondas." He shone a flashlight inside the car. "Especially with cloth interior. Good God the smell."

Ida Belle walked around to the driver's side of the car and opened the door. The interior lit up and I saw a young man, looking scared half to death, holding his hands in the air. He looked vaguely familiar, but I couldn't place him.

Early twenties. Five foot ten. A hundred twenty pounds soaking wet and from the look of fear on his face, part of him might be. Zero threat to anyone, even Ronald.

"Timmy Benoit!" Ida Belle yelled. "Are you trying to get yourself shot?"

"No, ma'am," the boy said.

"Then what the heck are you doing watching Ms. Redding's house?"

His eyes widened and he gulped. "I didn't know this was Ms. Redding's. I was just supposed to watch Ally, and this is where she came."

"Why in the world were you watching Ally?" Ida Belle asked.

"'Cause Scooter asked me to," Timmy said. "And I owed him over this thing with a six-pack and a cute brunette so I couldn't exactly say no."

I looked at Ida Belle, and she shrugged, clearly as lost as I was.

"Let's back things up," she said. "Why would Scooter ask you to watch Ally?"

"He said someone broke into that building she bought on Main Street and hurt her. Said she was at the hospital with Mrs. LeBlanc, and he asked me to wait downtown for them to pass and follow them and keep watch in case the guy came back."

"And why would Scooter ask you to do that?" Ida Belle asked.

Timmy stared down at the floorboard. "I think he's a little sweet on Ally. She's way out of his league, of course, but he got worked up when he heard she was hurt."

"Then why didn't he do this himself?" I asked.

"His bloodhound's about to have pups, and he didn't want to be away from her," Timmy said.

"This is better than daytime TV," Ronald said. "But I'm going to excuse myself. I did a mud mask last night and I can practically feel my pores opening in this humidity."

I stared at Timmy and shook my head. "Out of curiosity, what exactly were you supposed to do if her attacker came back? Do you have a weapon?"

"No, ma'am. I was just supposed to call the police."

"Well, at least there's that," I said. "Why don't you go home before you get yourself killed? I'm pretty sure Ally will be safe with me."

"Yes, ma'am," he said. "I'm really sorry about the trouble."

"No worries," I said. "Your intentions were good, but you and Scooter really need to work on execution."

I could tell he didn't understand what I meant, but it didn't matter.

Ida Belle closed his door and he drove off. We headed back to my house, and when we reached the sidewalk, Gertie came running outside wearing the T-shirt she was sleeping in, sans pants or glasses, and waving her Desert Eagle. Well, sort of waving it. She was clutching it with two hands and still couldn't get it steadied.

"Stop or I'll shoot!" she yelled.

"Put that down before it tips you off the front porch," Ida Belle said.

"Or even worse, she fires it," I said.

"Oh, it's you," Gertie said and dropped her arms.

Unfortunately, dropping her arms just caused a momentum swing and the next thing we knew, she pitched off the porch and into my hedges. Ida Belle and I both hit the ground. When there was no shot fired, we slowly rose and went over to the bushes.

"Give me a hand here," Gertie said. "I've got a branch up my butt and I sleep commando. This is a situation."

Ida Belle stared in dismay. "You're sharing a bed with me. I expect you to have proper undergarments."

"If you had your way, I'd be sleeping in a full body suit," Gertie said.

"Definitely a mask," I said. "With the snoring and all."

Ida Belle nodded.

"The stick?" Gertie said. "My butt?"

We reached down and each grabbed one of her arms and hauled her out of the bushes.

"Thank God," Gertie said as she scratched her rear. "Holly is no joke on bare skin, and I'm sort of allergic."

I cringed, and Ida Belle retrieved Gertie's gun from the bushes but didn't offer it to her.

"What the heck are you doing running out here with this hand cannon?" Ida Belle asked.

"It was the first piece of metal I felt in my duffel bag," Gertie said.

Ida Belle shook her head. "You have got to stop carrying

that thing. You can't shoot it at anyone because there wouldn't be anything left to identify."

I nodded. "And if you shoot it in town, you'll probably destroy a house. Let's get this show back inside before we wake Ally up."

"Thank God she had those pain meds," Ida Belle said.

"Wouldn't mind a couple myself," Gertie said. "But I'd settle for antibiotic cream and an antihistamine."

"I'd settle for coffee and cookies," Ida Belle said.

I glanced at my watch—5:00 a.m.

Might as well.

———

ALLY WANDERED into the kitchen a little after 7:00 a.m., where Gertie was cooking eggs and bacon. We'd already gone through the cookies and since none of us was interested in trying to go back to sleep, we figured we might as well make some notes and get our day started. I'd also done a load of laundry and now had clean clothes again.

"I thought I smelled bacon," Ally said.

"How are you feeling?" Gertie asked and poured her a cup of coffee.

"All right," Ally said. "The headache is gone and my scalp doesn't hurt unless I poke at it."

"That's good," I said. "Did you sleep decently?"

She nodded. "Probably the drugs, which I'm grateful for. I can't imagine how bad that headache would have been without them." She looked around at us. "But you guys don't look like you slept at all."

"Some of us didn't," Ida Belle said.

"And some of us slept a couple minutes," I said.

"Oh no," Ally said. "I hope it wasn't because of me."

"Nope," I said. "Well-intentioned idiots were to blame for this one."

Ally looked confused and Ida Belle and I recounted our events from the night before. When we were done, Ally was staring at us, her expression wavering between somewhat horrified and amused.

"I'm not sure whether to laugh or be worried," she said finally.

"Yeah, that's pretty much where my thought process was," I said. "Did you know Scooter had a crush on you?"

"No," she said. "He's always nice to me when I see him around town but he's nice to everyone. And he does look down a lot when he's talking, but he's shy. I never thought anything of it. Good Lord, I really don't need more on my plate right now, and he could have gotten Timmy killed. Not by you guys, of course. I know you don't just go shooting, but what if he'd taken off in the car and crashed?"

"Certainly a possibility," Ida Belle said. "So I take it you're not interested in pursuing a romantic relationship with Scooter?"

Ally shook her head. "Like I said, he's nice but I just consider him a friend. I could never feel that way about him, which sort of makes me feel bad, but what can you do?"

Ida Belle patted her hand. "Don't you worry about that. You don't owe someone a relationship just because they have feelings for you. When the right man comes along, you'll know it."

Gertie served us all bacon, eggs, and biscuits and slipped into her seat.

"Ida Belle is right," she said. "And Scooter will get over this thing he has for you and move on to someone else."

"Probably sooner than later after last night," I said. "I'm going to text Carter that you're awake if that's okay."

"Of course," Ally said. "I know I'll need to give my statement and all. He wouldn't let me do it last night. Just made me sit quietly until the paramedics came and called Emmaline to follow them to the hospital."

"Your health comes first," Ida Belle said. "And you're not likely to forget anything overnight."

My phone dinged and I checked the display.

"He wants me to bring you to the sheriff's department in an hour or so if that's okay," I said. "Should be plenty of time to finish up breakfast, and I can take you home first for a shower and a change. We'll go back after you give your statement and put together some things for you to bring here."

"That would be great," Ally said. "But you don't have to chauffeur me around. I'm sure my house is fine, and I can drive myself to the sheriff's department."

"But if Fortune doesn't take you, then she misses an opportunity to pump Carter for information," Gertie said.

"Oh!" Ally said. "I get it. Then I will gladly accept your personal taxi offer."

An hour and a half later, I pulled up in front of the sheriff's department. It was still early and also Sunday, so there weren't many people milling around yet, but I still saw the curious stares of some of the early café customers and church employees as we climbed out of my Jeep.

"Looks like the rumor mill is already flapping," I said.

"I don't know how these things get around so quickly," Ally said. "No one was downtown at the time. The paramedics aren't from Sinful. And the hospital people aren't supposed to talk."

"And yet, Scooter knew last night because he sent a bodyguard. Of sorts."

She frowned. "Yeah, I'd like to find out how that happened…"

"But you don't want to talk to Scooter. Don't worry. I'll handle it."

"Don't be mean to him."

"Why would I? In his own ineffective way, he was trying to help. I just need him to stand down before he gets someone hurt. Although I figure after his buddy reported in, his days of playing superhero are probably over."

Ally grinned as we headed inside. "Especially when you're already on the job."

"It's not like I need more redundancy. I already have Ida Belle and Gertie."

"You're not supposed to speak those names in these hallowed halls." Carter's voice sounded from the hallway and then he rounded the corner into the lobby area.

"If my walking in here doesn't bring the walls down, I seriously doubt speaking names will," I said.

"I have to go with Ms. Redding on this one," Gavin, the daytime dispatcher, said. "After all, Celia's in church every Sunday, and it hasn't exploded."

Carter shook his head. "Are you ready?" he asked Ally.

She nodded.

"Call me when you're done," I said.

Carter raised one eyebrow. "You're not going to try to sit in on the interview?"

"Why? I heard it all last night. Is the building still a crime scene?"

"No," he said.

Ally fished keys out of her purse and handed them to me. "Knock yourself out. Well, not for real…oh, you know what I mean."

"Fortune—" Carter started to speak but I already knew what was coming.

"Later!" I said and hurried out the door. I'd hear his standard speech later. It wasn't as if anything new was forthcoming on that conversation.

I pulled out my cell phone and sent a text to Ida Belle.

We're up.

CHAPTER NINE

I UNLOCKED THE FRONT DOOR AND HEADED INTO ALLY'S new bakery space. Nothing had changed since we'd stood here a couple days before, but everything felt different. Now this was a crime scene and we had to figure out why.

"I just don't take this as a burglary," Ida Belle said. "Anyone in town would have known that nothing had been delivered yet for the remodeling and with contractors not leaving tools on-site, what would there be to steal?"

Gertie nodded. "And it's not like anyone from out of town would even know about it, so we're back to a specific reason they were in this space. And that all goes back to Miles as far as I'm concerned."

"Given how his 'retirement' panned out, I'm inclined to agree," Ida Belle said.

"So what was the intruder doing here?" I asked. "He wasn't here for an opportunistic robbery, and Miles was already dead. The place has been cleared out except for the random old cabinets and such."

"He was in the back," Gertie said.

"But he might have hidden there when Ally came inside," Ida Belle said.

I frowned. "Which leads me to another thought—why didn't he just run out the back door when Ally first came in? Even if he was already in the back area, he would have heard her opening the door. Why stick around and risk being seen? I don't like the implications of that decision."

"Me either," Ida Belle said. "That's someone who's either desperate or has no problem killing someone."

"But he didn't kill her," Gertie said, "and he could have. If we assume it's the same person who killed Miles, we know he has a gun."

"It's probably not the smartest idea to go firing a weapon across the street from the sheriff's department," Ida Belle said.

"There is that," Gertie agreed. "But still, once she was down, he didn't have to stop there. Ally's a small woman. It wouldn't take a weapon or a big guy to take her out, especially as she was already stunned."

"I agree," I said. "Obviously, his goal wasn't to kill her or we'd be having an entirely different conversation. But since he didn't flee when he had the opportunity, we have to assume that he was gambling that she'd leave without seeing him and if she didn't, he had no trouble making sure she couldn't identify him. None of that sits well with me."

Ida Belle nodded. "So let's play this out—he sees Ally drive up, heads to the back of the building, and ducks down behind the cabinets on the side of the room opposite the light switch, hoping she'll get whatever she needs and leave quickly without discovering his hiding place."

"But then she comes into the back area," I continued. "The cabinets run all the way to the back wall so he can't leave without either jumping over them or exiting through the opening at the front of the room. Either leaves him completely exposed if he tries to make a run for it and she finds that light switch."

"So he conks her on the head and gets away," Gertie finished.

"I think that plays out very well," I said. "But the big question is, what did he think was here that's worth taking that risk?"

"Given those hundreds in that dry cleaning bag, I have my ideas," Ida Belle said.

I nodded. "Then let's get to looking."

Thirty minutes later, we'd covered every square inch of the building and hadn't found a single thing. We'd even tapped on walls and poked at the ceiling. Finally, we gave up and sat on a folding table in the back room.

"I got nothing," I said. "If something was hidden in the cabinets, we would have found it. And those walls show no sign of tampering. The paint on the drywall ones is faded except where things were hanging. The wallpaper wall has old-style wallpaper with stains and tears. The brick wall matches the outside, so it's original to the building, and the mortar is aged. If any of those had been patched, it would show."

Ida Belle nodded. "And the flooring is ceramic tile over cement. Let's face it—there's nothing here."

"Which is the same conclusion the intruder would have come to if they'd had a chance to finish the job," I said.

"Since Ally interrupted him, doesn't that mean he'll be back?" Gertie asked.

"It would be risky as heck, but I can't say that he wouldn't try it," I said. "Desperation does odd things to people."

"Which is why Ally won't be here at night alone," Ida Belle said.

"And why a security system will be installed today," I said.

"Can a security company get it done that quickly?" Gertie asked.

"Probably not," I said. "But Mannie can. I called him right after I rang you guys."

"Perfect," Gertie said. "Mannie will get Ally fixed right up. What did he say about our latest find?"

"'No surprise there' were his exact words," I said. "I think we have a reputation."

"You're just now realizing that?" Ida Belle asked.

"Anyway, I explained our concern, given what happened to Ally, and he said he'd be over here in a couple hours with everything the place needed," I said.

"Hello?"

We looked through the opening and saw Scooter standing just inside the front door. He caught sight of us and waved.

"I thought I saw you guys come in here," he said as he approached. "How is Ally?"

"She's fine and giving her statement to Carter as we speak," I said.

His relief was apparent. "That's great. Really great."

He looked down at the floor and shuffled a bit. "I'm really sorry about what happened last night with Timmy."

"That situation could have gone really badly," I said.

"If I'd known Ally was at your house, I would have never sent him. I figured she'd go home and Emmaline would stay with her. Timmy didn't know whose house it was."

"Do you really think that Carter would have let Ally go anywhere that she wasn't covered?" I asked.

He flushed a bit. "No. Carter's really good like that. I guess I just panicked. It was stupid, I know."

"How did you find out about it in the first place?" I asked.

He pointed to the back door. "I live with my dad just behind this building. He has heart problems and don't get around too well. I moved back in a couple months ago to help him with stuff until the doctors can get him on better footing."

"I'm sorry to hear that," I said.

"Thanks," Scooter said. "Anyway, I was up with my hound, waiting on the puppies, and I heard someone run down the side of the house. It's a strange time and place for someone to be, so I put on some shoes, grabbed my gun, and went outside to look. There was no sign of anyone behind the house, but when I walked to the front, I saw the back door on Ally's building was open. Then a light clicked on, and I went over to make sure everything was all right."

"And Carter was already there," I said.

"Yes, ma'am. Ally was so pale, and I could tell she was in pain. The paramedics got here fast and left, and Emmaline wasn't far behind them. Carter said Ally would be fine and just needed to be checked out. Emmaline would bring her home after that."

"And you figured she needed a bodyguard," I said.

He gave me a sheepish nod. "It seemed like a good idea at the time, although I can see now I was way off the mark on that one."

"It's thoughtful of you to want to help," I said, "but in the future, leave that to the professionals. People get hurt when they try to do things they're not really equipped to do."

"Trust me, I won't be stepping out of my box again," Scooter said. "And I won't be asking anyone else to do it either."

"Good," Gertie said. "Now, for the more important discussion, did your dog have the puppies?"

Scooter grinned. "Yes, ma'am. Ten of 'em, and all healthy as a horse. She's a prizewinning hunter and so is the daddy. I already got people calling about 'em."

"Put me on that list," Gertie said.

"No way," Ida Belle said. "You do *not* need a puppy. You can barely handle that bird, and you have an alligator who follows you around for food."

Gertie frowned. "I hadn't thought about that."

Ida Belle turned to Scooter. "Put *me* on the list."

I stared.

"What?" Ida Belle said. "After I lost my last hound, I haven't been ready to get another one."

"That hound passed over a decade ago," Gertie pointed out.

"I take a long time to make up my mind on things that require years of commitment," Ida Belle said.

Scooter nodded. "Walter is a sure indication of that one. I mean, not that it's any of my business. I'm happy to put you on the list. I'll let you have second pick. I'm keeping one for myself. Well, I got a brake job waiting over at the shop. Thanks for looking after Ally and again, I'm sorry for the mess I created."

As he headed out, my phone signaled an incoming text. It was Carter.

You got a minute?

I replied and sighed.

"I've been summoned to the sheriff's department," I said. "I'm sure it's for my regularly scheduled speech about not interfering with a police investigation."

"Just nod and smile," Gertie said. "That's what I do when I have no intention of doing what someone asks."

"Not today, you don't," I said. "It's Sunday."

Gertie had a long-standing personal rule against lying on Sunday. Which meant if we were up to our necks in police business, she had to avoid Carter.

"Crap," she said. "I forgot completely. I've got my days all messed up since we came back from the camp early."

"Well, the safest thing is for you and Ida Belle to head back to my house," I said. "I'll talk to Carter and then see what Ally plans on doing. Hopefully, she's going to rest today, and we can pick her up some things and get her settled at my house."

"Then we can do some investigating, right?" Gertie asked.

"Sure," I said. "If we can figure out something to investigate. It *is* Sunday and our options were already slim."

Gertie sighed. "We never get to have any fun."

"You bagged four turkeys and found a body yesterday," Ida Belle said. "Don't be greedy."

"Two turkeys," Gertie corrected. "One was playing dead, and I exchanged another one for Miles, which doesn't seem equitable."

I grinned.

————

ALLY WAS WAITING in the lobby of the sheriff's department when I walked in. She looked tired and I figured the interview had probably stressed her a little. After the attack, head injury, and only a few hours' sleep, she probably felt as if she'd already put in a full day.

"Let me go get my 'stay out of police business' directive from Carter," I said to her. "Then we'll stop by your house to pick up some things and you can spend the rest of the day in my good recliner."

She gave me a grateful smile. "I was all set to work on bakery stuff today, but I don't have the energy to argue. Your recliner sounds great. And I might have made a batch of chocolate peanut butter cookies yesterday before I decided to entice an intruder into clocking me. I bet they'd go well in your kitchen."

"They'll go better in my stomach," I said.

I headed to Carter's office and as the door was open, I walked inside. I closed the door behind me, because for whatever reason, Carter still thought that prevented people in the hallway from hearing him talk, and then plopped into one of the chairs in front of his desk.

"So?" I asked. "You want to get the speech out of the way so I can get Ally situated at my house?"

He held his hands in the air. "No speech. There's no point. Whatever was going on with Miles, Ally got hurt in the middle of it and you're not going to rest until you have answers and know for certain that she's safe. I'm not about to try to talk you out of it. I'd just like to ask that if you get something, please let me know. I want to be sure she's safe as well. And I think it's a great idea for her to stay at your house until this is all settled."

"You don't think there's any chance she was the one targeted, do you?"

"No. But I also figure that's not a risk either of us is interested in running. What if this is the one time our instincts are wrong?"

"I'm with you on that one. So why did you want to talk to me?"

He smiled. "I have to have a reason to want to talk to my girlfriend?"

"When you just caught a murder investigation, yeah."

"Okay, so I wanted to know about this thing with Scooter and Timmy last night. Ally mentioned it but told me to ask you about the details. I got the impression she slipped up telling me."

"It's no secret, so she didn't slip on anything."

I told him about Scooter's suspected crush, the imminent arrival of the hound dog's puppies, Timmy's lack of knowledge on residential housing occupancy, and how Timmy would probably never sit in a parked car at night again, much less do favors for Scooter.

His expression when I finished was part amusement and part dismay.

"Does Scooter realize how badly that could have gone?" he asked.

"I think I've made that clear, although Timmy was never in any danger from me or Ida Belle, and Gertie was still sleeping."

"It's not the two of you I'm afraid of, although the point about Gertie sleeping is a definite plus. It's the part where Ronald came out with a shotgun."

"Yeah, that was a little iffy."

I wasn't about to mention how Gertie came out with her Desert Eagle and fell off the porch. That one would send him straight for the bottle, and it was a little too early for that.

"You know he's got a sort of crush on you, right?" Carter asked.

"Ronald? I think he's into men, although I can't be certain about anything concerning him."

"I don't mean that kind of crush. It's more of a hero-worship thing. And when Ronald is into something, what does he do?"

I stared at him, confused by the question, then I thought about it and sucked in a breath.

"He imitates them," I said. "Hence all the costumes and role-playing in the backyard."

Carter nodded. "I don't want you to be the next role he decides to play."

"Crap. I hadn't even thought about that. I'll have a chat with him about the gun thing. If he really worships me then he'll listen, right?"

"We can only hope."

"Any word on the autopsy? Or is this information highway only one way?"

"You know it's one way and has to be. But there's nothing that came up in the autopsy that you hadn't already seen."

"Except time of death."

"Twenty-four to thirty-six hours is the best that he can do. Between the cold water and not knowing where he was killed, there's too many variables."

"I figured. Well, we just went over the building—I know your guys already did that, but they were looking for evidence."

"And what were you looking for?"

"Something left behind?"

He nodded. "You're thinking Miles had something and the intruder was looking to see if it was in the building."

I shrugged. "Until I have a better thought, yeah."

"You realize the implications there, right?"

"Sure. Either Miles didn't tell them where it was hidden before they killed him or claimed he didn't have it anymore. Or one person killed Miles and another broke into the building, which means we've got two crazies running around Sinful. I'm not a fan of option two."

"Neither am I."

"Well, the good news is that Mannie will be here today to install a state-of-the-art security system on the building, so anyone trying to get in after today will wake up the whole downtown and will be caught on camera."

Carter frowned but knew better than to say anything. His feelings on Mannie and the Heberts were complicated— mostly because they'd done good things for me, him, and others, but still operated on the wrong side of the law in a lot of other ways.

"Boss, sorry to interrupt, but we have a situation." Gavin's voice sounded on the intercom.

"What's wrong?" Carter asked.

"Cara Holiday is on the line and said when she went to set up that house Miles Broussard had been renting for a showing this morning, it had been vandalized."

Carter and I stared at each other.

"Sir?" Gavin said.

"Yeah," Carter said. "Tell her I'm on my way."

"I guess the hidden valuables option is looking better and better," I said.

Carter nodded. "But what the heck was Miles hiding?"

"Something worth murdering over."

CHAPTER TEN

I DIDN'T TELL ALLY ABOUT THE BREAK-IN AT MILES'S HOUSE. It would only worry her even more. But as soon as I got an opportunity, I'd fill Ida Belle and Gertie in. First, I drove to Ally's house and she put together toiletries and a few changes of clothes, then grabbed her notes and architectural plans for the bakery. I made sure we didn't forget the cookies.

We got her comfortable in the recliner and Gertie made her chocolate milk. Thirty minutes later, she was fast asleep and we headed to the kitchen so I could fill them in on the autopsy results and the break-in.

"I can't help but think that someone has this all backward," Ida Belle said. "If Miles had something of value in the building, he would have removed it before he sold. If he had something of value in his home, same thing, he would have removed it before he moved. He sold off a ton of stuff, and since there was no mention of a moving truck, I assume all that he kept was what was loaded in his car, which must be missing, right?"

"Carter hasn't indicated that it's been found," I said. "We have to assume the killer disposed of it to make it look like

Miles left town and was figuring the body would be consumed by water wildlife and never found."

Gertie nodded. "And since Miles didn't have anyone in town who would be looking for him, no one would be the wiser. But that also means the goods weren't in the car, or they wouldn't have vandalized the rental home or returned to the dry cleaner building."

I nodded. "You wouldn't load something valuable in your car and leave it in your drive overnight. You'd keep it in its hidey-hole until you were ready to leave with it. So if the goods weren't in the car, then it's more likely they were in the house."

"That would put time of death prior to Miles leaving town," Ida Belle said. "But we don't know that for sure because of the state of the body."

"We don't," I agreed. "And for all we know, Miles could have stashed the goods in Florida already or maybe in New Orleans to pick up on the way. The only thing we can assume is that he either didn't tell the killer where the goods are and that's why he's still looking, or he *did* tell the killer, who is off with the prize, and there's a second person who's arrived and is looking for the same thing."

"If a second person is in the mix, he might be looking for information on where Miles went to try to track him there," Ida Belle said. "All Miles ever said was Florida, and that's a lot of ground to cover. They probably went through the trash and anywhere else they could find paperwork."

"Well, that's good," Gertie said. "Maybe he's off to Florida, and we don't have to worry about Ally anymore."

"It's good if a murderer gets away?" I asked. "Or two potential murderers?"

"Yeah, scratch that," Gertie said.

"Who owned the house Miles was renting?" I asked.

"The owner had a job transfer back decades ago and kept

it, figuring to come back for retirement," Ida Belle said. "But he ended up staying gone so long he passed away. Since then, it's been tied up in an estate fight. The law firm handling the estate keeps it rented to minimize the cost to the estate for maintaining it. The heirs are busy suing each other for everything. They'll probably all die before it's settled."

A thought occurred to me. "Who rented it before Miles did?"

Ida Belle's eyes widened. "Jasper Cummings, the previous owner of the dry cleaner's. He joked that it was sort of a package deal."

"So maybe it wasn't Miles who was hiding something," Gertie said.

I frowned. "But if Jasper had hidden something, why is someone just now looking for it? And why kill Miles if he wasn't involved? Why not just wait for him to leave and search the building and his house?"

"All good questions," Ida Belle said.

I sighed. "I'm running myself around in circles. The problem is, we don't have enough to go on."

"Then we should look into everything," Gertie said.

Ida Belle nodded. "This is one of those rare times when I'm going to agree with Gertie's investigation plan. The wider we cast the net, the more likely we are to haul something in."

"Okay," I agreed. "So what can you tell me about Jasper?"

Ida Belle and Gertie looked at each other and frowned.

"Boy, our net is looking limp," Ida Belle said. "Jasper was pretty much like Miles."

"Didn't participate in town things and spent his time off in NOLA?" I asked.

"And Mexico," Gertie said. "That's where he moved after he retired. I think he was looking for a retirement place there from the moment he arrived in Sinful. I guess he just had to build the cash up first."

Ida Belle nodded. "When he bought the dry cleaner's, it was probably still making decent money. Women still had a lot of dry-clean-only clothes for church, curtains and the like were almost always dry-clean, and men still wore suits to things."

"So Jasper wasn't from Sinful either," I said.

"No. Showed up when he bought the dry cleaner's," Gertie said. "Owned it about ten years before selling to Miles."

"And you're *sure* Jasper moved to Mexico?" I asked.

Ida Belle sighed. "You mean like Miles moved to Florida? I don't know for certain that he moved. I just know he packed up what he planned on taking, sold everything else, and drove out of here one day."

"Is there anyone who would know how to get hold of him?" I asked.

"Dinah Benoit might," Gertie said.

"Any relation to Timmy?" I asked.

Gertie shook her head. "No relation. But Dinah was the second owner of the dry cleaner's. She moved to Sinful with her husband when she was only eighteen and got a job there. That was not long after we returned from Vietnam. Did such a good job that when the owner retired, he offered her an option to buy the place and pay him out."

"So Dinah owned the place for a long time," I said.

"Twenty-five years or thereabouts," Ida Belle said. "She was good at it, too. Did some seamstress work as well, and you couldn't tell the difference between her work and the original."

Gertie nodded. "She repaired some of my mother's embroidered pillows. I thought I was going to lose them but she worked a miracle."

"And she's still in Sinful?" I asked.

"Still in the same house her husband moved her to after

they married. It's just up the highway. The place was practically falling down when they bought it, but with time and money, they made it nice. A lot of those old farmhouses have good bones."

"Still married to that husband?" I asked

"He died fairly young," Ida Belle said. "Midthirties, I think. Same year she bought the business. A lot of people never thought she'd be able to pull it off. All by herself with a young boy to raise and a business to run, but she made it work."

"Did she know Jasper before she sold him the business?" I asked.

"I think so," Ida Belle said. "I believe I heard she met him at some convention in NOLA. But after she sold, she stayed on and helped get him adjusted and still did the seamstress work."

Gertie nodded. "My guess is she didn't really want to retire so much as she needed to. She has back issues and from what I hear, they keep getting worse. Got to where she couldn't stand or walk for very long without needing to sit. I think her last year owning the dry cleaner's, she only did the sewing mostly. She had someone else doing the dry-cleaning, although she helped work the counter."

"What about her son?" I asked. "He didn't help?"

"He went into the military right after high school and it looked like he was going to make a career out of it, but he sustained a knee injury and was discharged when he was twenty-eight," Ida Belle said. "He worked local for a couple years in the oil field, then went to Alaska to work the pipeline after that. He ended up getting killed in some work-related accident about six years later. Right after Dinah sold the business to Jasper. He was an only child and she took it hard."

"Jasper did look out for her some while he was here," Gertie said. "Especially when she stopped working at the dry cleaner's altogether. He picked up her groceries at the General Store and took them to her and helped fix things around her house from time to time."

"So maybe Dinah stayed in touch with Jasper after he left," I said. "At least long enough to know if he went to Mexico. I'm certain I've never met her. I don't even think I've heard her name."

"She's kind of a recluse at this point," Gertie said. "I saw her at the eye doctor last time I was there, but that's been a while."

"Like a decade," Ida Belle said.

"It hasn't been that long," Gertie argued. "I don't think so anyway. Okay, maybe. Anyway, she was using a walker then, so I'm guessing she leaves her house as little as possible. I didn't get a chance to talk to her because she was headed in with the lab assistant when I arrived. But she was always rather introverted, so she's probably happier just keeping to herself and not having to navigate around all this old architecture with a bad back."

"Do you think she'll talk to us?" I asked.

They both shrugged.

"Doesn't hurt to drive out there and ask," Gertie said. "We could bring food. Everyone loves not having to cook their own dinner."

"I'm kinda surprised that you guys aren't friends," I said. "Her husband died young enough for her to easily make the Sinful Ladies cut, and she sounds like the kind of woman you like—hard worker, businesswoman."

"We invited her to join the Sinful Ladies," Gertie said. "But she said it really wasn't her thing. That being around a lot of people made her anxious, so she'd just stick to her house and take in her church service on television."

"For a town full of busybodies, Sinful has a lot of recluses," I said.

"Mostly because of the busybodies," Ida Belle said.

"So maybe after Mannie gets started with the security system we can take a drive out there," I said. "I assume visiting on a Sunday is allowed by Sinful senior rules."

"Sunday is the day a lot of people did their visiting," Gertie said. "It was the only day most people had off, so they spent it with family and looked in on relatives and friends. With Dinah being a hermit, any day is probably a good one, but I can't see her caring about it being a Sunday. We just need to go after noon since she watches church on television."

"It's almost eleven," I said. "By the time Mannie gets here and we get him going, that should work perfectly."

My cell phone signaled an incoming text.

"Speak of the devil," I said. "Let's wake Ally up. Mannie will be there in thirty minutes."

———

ALLY LOOKED a little nervous as she pushed the door open to her new space and walked inside. It made me angry that the attack had put a damper on opening her bakery. This had been her dream for a long time, and she shouldn't have to spend one second of her time fearful or worried. And if it was the last thing I did, I was going to make sure she didn't have to worry going forward.

Mannie pulled in just minutes after we did and headed inside, greeting everyone with a smile.

"You remember Ally?" I asked him.

"Yes," he said and extended his hand. "It's a pleasure to see you again, although I'm very sorry for the circumstances. How are you feeling?"

"Thank you for doing all this for me," Ally said. "I'm feeling good. My headache's almost gone."

"I'm glad you weren't seriously injured," he said. "Now, let's make sure no one can ever get into your property again without alerting the entire downtown area. I don't want you to worry about a thing. Between myself and these ladies, you're in good hands."

Ally blushed just a bit and nodded. I glanced over at Gertie, who was studying the two of them, and already knew what she was making of the situation. I had to admit, I was no romance expert, but beneath Mannie's professionalism and Ally's exceptional manners, the attraction was there.

Interesting.

"Let me tell you guys what I have in mind," Mannie said. "Then you can bring up any issues with that plan."

We all nodded.

Mannie started with the front of the building and worked his way through it and to the back, giving a detailed explanation of the sensors on doors and windows and the camera system that would be installed inside and out.

"Are you changing anything on the outside of the structure?" he asked when he was done.

Ally shook her head. "Just the signage. Sinful rules don't really allow for anything else. I even have to get permission to change the color on the awning."

"What about the inside?" he asked.

"Pretty much everything will change except for the actual structure," she said. "The brick wall in the back is all that will remain the same. Everything else will be painted. Those outdated ceiling tiles will come down and be replaced with a more modern look. All the built-ins will come out. The floor replaced. Then all of my stuff has to be installed."

Mannie nodded.

"That means you can't put any cameras inside, right?" Ally asked.

"I still can," he said. "I'll just put portables in here during the construction. There's even stands they can go on so that you don't have to figure out a surface to sit them on. That way, they can be moved around depending on what area is being worked on. It's something you'll have to check every night though. I wouldn't rely on the contractors getting them placed properly."

Ida Belle snorted. "Heck, you're lucky if you can rely on contractors to just show up and do the job they're being paid to do."

"Isn't that the truth," I said. "I've had a window glass fogged up and called two months ago about having it replaced. I can't even get the guy out there to measure it. Says he's backed up because of the hurricane, which was ages ago."

"Ha!" Gertie said. "The glass guy is backed up because he doesn't want to set his beer down at the Swamp Bar. When he runs out of drinking money, then he'll be shoving glass in windows 24-7."

Ally gave Gertie a nervous look. "I hope the guys working on my bakery aren't on a bender at the Swamp Bar. They promised me since the bulk was cosmetic, they could have me open in a month."

Gertie patted her arm. "Don't worry, dear. That's why you hired a company. Then the general contractor is responsible for running herd over all the subs. You only have to ride herd over the general contractor."

"True," Ally said. "But I got the impression he would have liked a cash-only-no-invoices sort of deal, which obviously, I'm having no part of."

I nodded. "You don't need the kind of trouble that could

bring, and besides which, you need those invoices for your business accounting."

"If you run into any delays that you don't think are reasonable, let me know," Mannie said. "Most contractors owe the Heberts in one form or another. It would only take a phone call to get things moving again."

Ally brightened. "That's so nice of you to offer. I hope I don't need it, but I won't hesitate to use the favor. This bakery is going to happen. On time and correctly."

"Darn right it is," I said, happy that Ally seemed to have gotten some of her spirit back.

"I've got to grab some different brackets for the outside brick," Mannie said. "I'd like something sturdier than what the cameras come with. I'll be back in about an hour if that's all right."

"That's fine," Ally said. "I was going to take some measurements anyway, so I'll still be here."

"Just in case you decide to leave, can I get your phone number?" Mannie asked. "That way you don't have to wait if something comes up. I can just call you when I'm on my way back."

I saw a tiny blush on Ally's neck as she gave Mannie her phone number. He punched it in and dialed. "Now you have mine."

He gave us all one of his brilliant smiles, then headed out. We all watched as he left and Gertie shook her head and sighed.

"That man is the only thing that makes me really hate aging," she said.

"We know," Ida Belle said. "If you were thirty—cough —*fifty* years younger."

We all laughed.

"He's definitely an alpha male," I said.

"Says the woman who already has one," Gertie said.

"Being in a relationship doesn't make you blind," I said.

Everyone laughed again, but I noticed the blush that Ally had developed earlier had never gone away.

I heard the church bells ring and glanced at my watch. Noon.

I was a tiny bit disappointed that I wasn't going to make the banana pudding run this morning—even more disappointed that I wouldn't get banana pudding—but it was all for a good cause. Celia could have her one Sunday a year. It wasn't as if it was a big victory when no one else was racing you.

We were still standing in the back of the building when we heard screaming.

"None of the Sinful Ladies are racing today, are they?" I asked.

Ida Belle frowned and shook her head. We all hurried out of the building and the reason behind the screaming was crystal clear.

Godzilla.

CHAPTER ELEVEN

GERTIE'S GIANT LIZARD FRIEND MUST HAVE DECIDED THAT he was in the mood for an easy meal, and the breeze was carrying the smells from the café right down to the bayou. Now he stood in the middle of Main Street swinging his head from one side to another, keeping both Catholics and Baptists frozen in silence on the sidewalk.

Except Celia, of course, who was screaming. Her mouth always seemed to work.

"I don't have a casserole," Gertie said.

Francine had come up behind her when the café emptied, looking for the source of the screams.

"I'll get something," she said and hurried off.

Deputy Breaux came out of the sheriff's department, took one glance at Godzilla, and then looked over at us, clearly panicked. I couldn't blame him. This was exactly the situation Carter had warned Gertie about. Repeatedly. The gator was too comfortable with people and liked the easy food payout that he could get from them.

Godzilla lifted his head and turned it from side to side, probably trying to decipher where the food was. Then he turned around to face the churchgoers and 'frozen' became a thing of the past. They scattered in all directions, dropping purses and Bibles as they fled.

"It looks like Christ returned," I said, pointing to the discarded items.

"And he left Celia," Gertie said. "Highly appropriate."

Celia was the only one who hadn't had the sense to run, but then, that didn't surprise me. She probably thought she could yell the alligator back into the water because that's what she wanted.

"You need to slowly back away," I said.

"Don't tell me what to do," Celia said. "If it weren't for that crazy woman feeding him, that gator would be in the bayou where he belongs."

And that's when Godzilla launched.

Celia's eyes widened, then she spun around and started running, which only spurred the gator into running after her. The only positive about the entire situation was that Celia had on tennis shoes. Not that they appeared to be helping. Her gait was awkward with a slight limp on one side. It wasn't as though she was a speed runner to begin with, but now things were even worse.

I glanced over at Deputy Breaux because I had no idea what to do, and technically, he had the authority. But based on his expression, he was fresh out of ideas as well. We couldn't shoot the gator because we'd risk hitting Celia or the rest of the crowd of people who had fled to the far end of the street. And if we didn't kill him with one shot, it was likely to make him mad rather than retreat.

Celia was almost to a parked car that her cousin Dorothy was standing on top of. If she could make it to the car, she could jump up with Dorothy and then we could figure out how to deal with the gator.

"Throw your purse!" Dorothy yelled. "It's the banana nut bread."

I groaned. If Celia was carting around a loaf of bread in her purse, no wonder Godzilla was chasing her. Heck, I might chase her for a loaf of banana nut bread. But instead of throwing her purse or jumping up on the car, Celia went running right past.

"She's trying to commit suicide," Ida Belle said.

Francine ran up with an apple pie and thrust it at Gertie. "I don't think he'll follow me."

"We have a bigger problem," I said.

Celia, apparently deciding God was going to save her, went running into the Catholic church. Godzilla was right behind her. The screams that erupted from inside the church put every horror movie ever made to shame. People came running out the front door and others climbed out windows on the side. It looked as if cops had burst into a crack house except everyone was dressed better.

I took off running a split second after Deputy Breaux and could hear the others coming behind us. If that gator got hold of anyone, Gertie would be blamed for the entire mess. I beat Deputy Breaux to the church and ran inside, then slid to a stop. Deputy Breaux drew up short beside me and blew out a breath.

"What a shocker," Gertie said as she came up beside us. "Celia's on the cross again."

Except this time, it wasn't figuratively. Celia had literally climbed up the huge cross at the front of the church and was draped over one side of it. She looked like a giant sloth perched on a branch. Father Michael and Sister Mary Catherine were both off to the side, sitting on top of the piano and drinking Communion wine.

"Peace be with you," Father Michael said and held up the wine decanter.

"And also with you," Sister Mary Catherine said and took the decanter from the priest.

"Why don't you both shut up!" Celia yelled.

"It's not very Christian to yell at a priest and a nun," Gertie said.

"You shut up too!" Celia yelled. "And get that demon creature away from me."

"Twenty bucks says that cross doesn't hold," Ida Belle said.

"You're on," Gertie said.

Deputy Breaux nodded. "I'd like to get in on that one as well."

"Why aren't you doing something?" Celia yelled. "I pay your salary, Breaux!"

I leaned over and whispered to Gertie, "Where's the pie?"

"I put it in a pew," Gertie said. "I'm not wasting a perfectly good pie on that woman when she's carrying around bread in her purse. She should have cleared the street when everyone else did and we wouldn't be here now."

"Throw me your purse," I said to Celia.

"I'm not giving you my purse," Celia said.

"Why not?" I asked. "You think you have something worth stealing, while I'm standing in a church, and in front of a cop, a priest, and a nun? I don't have that kind of karma credit to cash in."

"That sounds like the beginning of a good joke," Ida Belle said. "Except for the part where Celia's in it."

"You've got food in your purse, you idiot," Gertie said. "That's why Godzilla is chasing you."

Celia's eyes widened and she looked at the purse that was looped through one arm. Both arms were wrapped around the cross, and that was the only reason she was still airborne.

"I can't get the bread out," Celia said.

"Just toss the whole shooting match down," Deputy Breaux said.

"This is my favorite handbag," Celia said.

"It looks like old drapes," Gertie said. "Probably smells like them too, with you carrying food around in it."

Ida Belle and I both stared at Gertie.

"What?" she asked. "My purses are always leather. Doesn't hold smell like old drapes."

"More likely they don't last long enough to acquire smell," Ida Belle said.

"You can either toss your purse," I said, "or we'll all wait until you fall off that cross and he'll get it then. Your choice, but it doesn't look overly comfortable up there."

"Shoot him!" Celia demanded.

"We're not shooting that gator," Deputy Breaux said, "and definitely not in the church. There's just something wrong with that."

"But you'll let him eat me in the church?" Celia asked.

"He doesn't want to eat you," I said. "He wants that bread in your purse, so toss it over and let him have breakfast, then we can all get back to our own lives instead of having to dwell in your messy one."

"I'm suing for this," Celia said. "I'm suing the sheriff's department for not shooting that monster and Gertie for causing him to be here in the first place."

"If you don't throw that purse, you're not going to be able to sue," I said. "Because I give you another ten seconds before those arms with zero muscle supporting that body with all that extra fat give out."

Turns out, ten seconds was really generous.

Celia glared at me and the strain on her face must have been enough to signal to her arms to give up the ghost. She spun around on the cross post until she was hanging off the bottom of it—definitely looking like a sloth—and then she dropped onto the hardwood floor.

Godzilla charged and Celia struggled to get up, but she wasn't going to make it before Godzilla got to her. I pulled out my weapon and noticed Ida Belle had done the same. I didn't want to shoot the gator, but I couldn't let him attack someone. Not even Celia.

He inched up the stairs at the front and stopped to sniff. Celia had managed to sit up but found herself staring directly at Godzilla, who was perched not five feet in front of her. If he charged, it was over. I was fast enough to get away in that situation, but Celia couldn't have done it even with a twenty-second head start. I was officially out of options.

I leveled my pistol at the back of the gator's head but before I could squeeze off a shot, Ida Belle fired twice. I cringed for a split second, then the bullets hit each end of a cord holding a banner hanging over the ambo—pulpit for us Baptists—and the banner dropped. I knew she'd meant for the banner to drop over the gator and confuse him long enough for Celia to get away, and the plan was genius, except that the banner got caught in a draft on the way down and flew a bit to the side.

Directly on top of a standing candelabra.

And the candles were still lit.

The weight of the banner was too much for the candelabra and it tipped over as the banner went up in flames. It crashed in between Celia and Godzilla, right at the bottom of the cross. If that cross started burning, it was going to be the worst look ever for a church. I sprinted to the back of the church and grabbed the bowl of holy water, then ran to the front and doused the banner, getting Celia in the process.

Godzilla, apparently deciding it was all too much for him,

grabbed the purse and hauled butt up the aisle and out of the church. Ida Belle, Gertie, and Deputy Breaux jumped onto the pews as he passed, swinging the purse in his mouth. Father Michael and Sister Mary Catherine cheered and drank another round. Celia just sat there sputtering.

"Got it!" Deputy Breaux gave us an exuberant look and waved his phone.

Gertie shook her head. "You know we're going to hell for this."

"You were already going to hell for defrocking Sister Mary Catherine during that parachuting mishap," I said as we made our way out of the church.

"That was a fluke," Gertie said.

Ida Belle and I both grinned.

A crowd of people were still huddled together at the other end of the street, and I scanned the area for Godzilla. There was a big splash right across from us, and I saw Godzilla swimming away from the bank, the purse still clutched in his mouth.

Carter, who must have still been working Miles's rental house with the forensics team, pulled up beside us, took one look at the gator with the purse in his mouth, another at the crowd at the end of the street, and held up a hand.

"I don't even want to know," he said.

Celia chose that moment to burst out of the church and point at Godzilla. "I need to report an identity theft!"

"And I'm out of here," Carter said, and drove straight past the sheriff's department and out of downtown.

"Looks like you're up," I said to Deputy Breaux.

Deputy Breaux stared at Carter's rapidly disappearing truck in dismay. "Where's he going?" he asked.

"Probably to the East Coast to find another job," Gertie said.

"I want to press charges against that alligator and his owner," Celia said, holy water dripping from her hair onto the pavement. "My property and identity have been stolen."

"He's not going to run up your Visa bill," I said. "And I doubt your driver's license is going to do him any good either."

"He's probably going to deliver the whole thing to her," Celia said and pointed her finger at Gertie. "No telling what kind of havoc she can wreak."

"Neither your pudgy license photo nor your subpar credit rating interests me," Gertie said.

Celia's eyes widened and she gasped. "I do *not* have a subpar credit rating."

Gertie leaned toward Ida Belle and nodded. "See, she's admitting to the pudgy thing."

I stared in amazement as Celia stomped her feet like a petulant child and pointed her finger at Deputy Breaux.

"I want that woman arrested for collusion in the theft of my identity," Celia said.

"Ma'am, it's not a crime until she *uses* your identity," Deputy Breaux said. "And I've got to be honest when I say I don't really see the benefit."

I tried to hold in a laugh, but I couldn't help it. Apparently, when Deputy Breaux had reached his limit of absurdity, his backbone kicked in. It was rather an interesting sight, except the part where Celia was turning bloodred in the face.

She was practically shaking when she waved her arm at all of us. "You people will not have your buddies in charge here forever. And when they're gone, I'll make it my life's work to drive every one of you out of this town."

"Good luck with that," Gertie said. "We could have a popularity vote if you'd like to see who everyone wants to run out of town. I have news for you—it's not us."

Ida Belle nodded. "Maybe you should take this opportunity,

while getting a new driver's license, to change your home address. I'm thinking Alaska."

"She'd melt the ice caps," I said.

"Global warming's friend," Gertie said.

"I'm surprised she didn't turn to ash when you doused her with that holy water," Ida Belle said. "Anyway, we've got things to do. See you later, Deputy Breaux."

We walked off, leaving Celia standing there, sputtering and dripping.

"Wait!" Gertie said. "The pie!"

"I'll get it," I said. "Make sure Ally doesn't need anything and pick me up so we can go see Dinah."

I hurried back to the church and went inside, checking the back pews for the pie, but didn't see any sign of it.

"Fortune!" Father Michael called out.

I looked toward the front of the church and saw that he and Sister Mary Catherine had moved from the piano and were now standing in front of the altar.

"Instead of manna, the Lord has provided pie," Father Michael said with a smile. "Would you like a piece?"

I grinned. "Not today, Father. You guys enjoy."

CHAPTER TWELVE

I HEADED BACK OUT AS IDA BELLE PULLED UP. GERTIE GAVE me a questioning look when I jumped in the SUV, and I had to explain the loss of the pie.

"Oh well," Gertie said. "At least Celia didn't get any. I'll pay Francine for it next time we're at the café."

"You know you're going to have to do something about that alligator, right?" Ida Belle said. "He's getting lazy. If he stakes out downtown as his territory, he'll be declared a nuisance."

"He isn't already?" I asked.

"I mean by Wildlife and Fisheries," Ida Belle said. "For gators over four feet in length, it doesn't end well."

"They don't have farms or something?" I asked.

"Yes, but that's not usually where they go," Ida Belle said. "The state has nuisance hunters on a list and they pay them a small fee—really small—to get the gator out of the situation. The hunters then own the gator and can do what they want with it. Since they've usually spent more than the state payment in acquiring the gator, not even including their time, they usually sell them for the hide and meat."

"But Godzilla has helped us with bad guys," Gertie said. "He's a hero."

"What if the next guy he grabs isn't a bad guy?" Ida Belle asked. "You act like that gator has some sort of way to discern people, but he doesn't. We've just been lucky so far."

Gertie frowned. "I'm going to try to get him to relocate to my camp area. There's plenty of fish and I haven't seen a lot of gators. He could establish a territory."

"Well, you best get on it quick," Ida Belle said. "Because our little circle is the only people who know about Godzilla's hero antics. The rest just know the destruction he's causing."

Gertie sighed. "It's not that easy, you know?"

"Good Lord, woman," Ida Belle said. "You caught the darn thing with a pair of your pants. You kept him in your bathroom. You walked him on a leash. Surely you can figure out a way to get him to stay away from downtown."

"That's true," Gertie said and brightened a bit. "He is really smart. Maybe I'll have a chat with him about things."

"If you figure out how to talk to that gator, maybe you could try with that bear," I said. "She keeps popping up and desperately needs an anger management class. Plus, she's got kids. We'll have a whole clan of pissed-off bears soon."

We'd had a couple run-ins with a mama bear lately and I was really hoping to avoid any more in the future. Gators were bad enough, but at least I could ditch them on land as long as there was a way to get elevated. Bears, on the other hand, could follow you right up a tree or bust out a door.

"The bear needs Celia's license," Gertie said. "It's a much better fit."

Ida Belle turned off the highway and onto a dirt road, which was common for property outside the downtown area. We bumped along for about a mile, then she turned into a well-kept drive and pulled up in front of a pretty white farmhouse with yellow shutters and flowers of all colors blooming around the front porch. Giant planters carried the color onto the porch, where a rocking chair sat with a small table next to it.

"This is pretty," I said.

Gertie nodded. "I guess when you rarely leave your house, you make sure it's as nice as it can be."

We walked up the steps and knocked on the door. I heard some shuffling inside, and after a while, the door swung open.

Seventies. Five foot five. A hundred twenty-five pounds. No threat unless she could hit us with the cane she was using.

She stared at us for a moment, her expression blank, then she narrowed her eyes.

"Gertie Hebert?" she asked. "Is that you?"

"Yes," Gertie said. "It's good to see you, Dinah. Do you remember my friend Ida Belle? And this is our friend Fortune. We'd like to visit with you for a bit if you have the time."

She hesitated for just a moment—probably the hermit thing—but then Southern manners kicked in and she backed up and waved us in.

"I made some tea this morning if anyone would like a glass," she said as we stepped inside. "Afraid I don't drink much else but that and coffee."

"We're fine, but thank you," Gertie said.

She motioned us to the living room, which looked a lot like the porch. I counted at least twenty pots of plants and flowers before I gave up. The wall of windows on the side of the house provided excellent light for them, and although it looked a little crowded, I had to admit it was also pretty. But I didn't even want to know how much time taking care of all of that took.

"I don't get company much," Dinah said as she sat in her recliner. "Not at all is probably more appropriate. Deliverymen and repairmen are usually the only ones standing on my porch. Well, and that durn pastor. He keeps trying to visit, and I keep sending him on his way. Get my church on television and don't need no one sitting in my living room praying for me."

"He's just checking in on his flock," Gertie said. "Sort of a professional liability."

Dinah snorted. "'Cept I'm Catholic. Or was. At least that's what my parents said, although they didn't spend too much time behind those church doors either. Anyway, at least that Father Michael doesn't show up wanting to talk and pray, but then I suppose he'd have to put down the bottle long enough to drive out here."

I blinked and stared. Dinah noticed my expression and grinned.

"That delivery guy of mine keeps me in the know," she said. "I'm usually a week or so behind on things, but I don't miss much."

"When was the last time you got a delivery?" Ida Belle asked.

"Early last week," Dinah said. "Should have another coming tomorrow or Tuesday. I like fresh produce and since I can't garden anymore, I had to start ordering more often."

"Your flowers and plants are lovely though," Gertie said.

She nodded. "I can't spend time on them like I used to, but if I do a little bit each day, I can keep them maintained. Thought about putting in a small vegetable garden at one end of the porch. Just in the beds, mind you. I'm not about tilling a patch of ground these days."

"You could do one of those raised gardens on one end of the porch," Gertie said. "That would save you the bending over part."

"That might be an idea," Dinah said. "I'd hate for vegetables to spoil on the vine because I couldn't pick them, and some days are worse than others."

"I'm sorry you're still struggling with your back," Ida Belle said.

Dinah shook her head, her expression sad. "It's frustrating, that's for sure. Worked my whole life just about in that dry cleaner's and at home, raising my son and catering to that bully of a husband of mine. Then my husband does me the pleasure of dying and my boy's approaching capable and my back starts giving me problems. Just when I thought I was going to start living life."

Thank goodness I'd spent years training to keep my expression blank, because the comment about being pleased that her husband died had come out of nowhere. But given her age and the small-town thing, I could only imagine the mentality about a woman's place back then. Still, I imagined more women of that era got their pleasure from things like the dishwasher becoming mainstream rather than their husbands' dying. It said a whole lot about the man and none of it good.

"I didn't think your back started bothering you until around the time you retired," Ida Belle said.

"Yes and no," Dinah said. "I have arthritis in my spine and it's been there for years. Had a couple of bad falls when I was a young bride—the kind you don't talk about—and the doctors think that's what kicked things off. It was hardly noticeable for years. I'd be sore if I overdid, that sort of thing, and the heating pad became my friend, but I just took an aspirin and didn't think much of it."

Gertie nodded. "If you're a busy wife and mother, that pretty much describes most days."

"And that's exactly why I didn't make anything of it," Dinah said. "You know how it was—women of a particular age group didn't complain. We just ignored and kept going. Well, that ignoring is what caused all the real problems. I spent far too many years taking aspirin when I should have been seeing a specialist."

"Can you have surgery for it?" I asked.

"Already did back years ago, but I waited too long," Dinah said. "Things just kept getting worse. Doctors said I had nerve damage and that it would progress. When it got to be too much to stand at the dry cleaner's, I sold it and semiretired. Sitting's usually not too bad, so I kept up the seamstress work for a bit since I could do it here, but when Jasper decided to cut out for Mexico, I didn't feel like starting up with the next owner. Miles was nice enough, but I had a decent nest egg to retire with. I did a few specialty jobs for my good regular clients, but he knew not to let out that I was still doing some occasional work."

"I would think it would be hard to work for someone else after owning the business," Ida Belle said. "Did you know Jasper before he bought the dry cleaner's?"

"Just a bit," she said. "I met him at one of those small-business conventions in NOLA. I was looking for some new accounting software—the accounting stuff was always the bane of my existence—and ended up chatting with him for a while. He was bought out of a long-term position when the company he worked for went through a restructure and said he was looking to invest some of that money in a small business that he could work until he was ready to retire. I'd been thinking about selling anyway and had the business and the building evaluated, so it seemed prophetic. I came home and promptly fell off my porch steps when my leg gave out, and my decision was confirmed."

"Seems like good timing," Ida Belle said. "I know Jasper used to help you out with things back then. Did he stay in touch after retiring?"

"Oh, for a bit I'd get an email," Dinah said. "But you know how it is. You get off somewhere, starting a new chapter in your life, and that tends to take over. And it's not like I was family."

Dinah looked at us and frowned. "Why all the questions about Jasper?"

"Since your delivery guy hasn't been by since last week, we'll fill you in on the latest Sinful news," Ida Belle said. "Miles Broussard was found dead this weekend. He'd been murdered and dumped in the bayou."

Dinah's eyes widened and she looked from one of us to another, maybe waiting for the punch line. When none was forthcoming, she shook her head.

"Good Lord," she said. "That's something. But what does it have to do with Jasper? I don't think they knew each other all that well. Jasper said Miles was looking for a similar situation to what he had when I sold to him."

"We don't know that what happened to Miles has anything to do with Jasper," I said. "But Ally Lemarque bought the building from Miles to open a bakery, and last night she was attacked inside. Then someone broke into Miles's house as well and trashed it. The Realtor called it in this morning."

"But why?" Dinah asked.

I shrugged. "The only thing we could think is that someone was looking for something. But they attacked Ally after Miles had been killed, so we wondered if maybe Miles didn't have what they're looking for."

Gertie nodded. "And since Miles bought the building from Jasper and rented the same house Jasper was renting... "

"Oh!" Dinah said. "So, you think the real target was Jasper, or something Jasper had, I should say? That seems a bit far-fetched, doesn't it?"

"We honestly don't know," I said. "But it's one working theory. We have several."

"But why?" Dinah asked again.

"Why what?" I asked, not understanding the question context this time.

"Why do you have working theories?" Dinah asked. "Are you a cop?"

I shook my head. "No, but I am a private investigator and Ally is one of my best friends."

"I see." Dinah nodded. "Well, this all sounds like something out of a movie, but I don't know that I can help you. I didn't know Jasper very well. He didn't really talk about his private life, and I saw Miles even less than Jasper. We chatted a bit when he brought the odd seamstress job by that I agreed to do, but it was mostly about my flowers or the business or my paintings."

"I guess we were just wanting to make sure that Jasper had actually left for Mexico," Ida Belle said.

Dinah's eyes widened. "Because...oh. Well, I can only tell you what I know. I got email from him after he arrived. Had a picture of him sitting at a bar, of course. The one thing Jasper wasn't shy about was his love of beer. The bar looked mostly like a shack and there was water in the background. After that one, I got a couple more every year for two years maybe, then nothing. But he never said anything beyond how great the fishing was."

I nodded. It sounded completely normal. And yet a man was dead and my friend attacked, and I had a feeling that there was more to Jasper than anyone had seen.

"I don't suppose Jasper said where he was going in Mexico, did he?" I asked.

"If he did, I don't recall," Dinah said.

"When was the last time you saw Miles?" I asked.

"Last Thursday," she said. "He stopped by to tell me he'd sold the building and that the dry cleaner's was officially closed and he was off to Florida to retire. When he was cleaning things out, he'd found some old photos from back when I first bought the place and thought I'd like to have them. We toasted with some sweet tea to his retirement, and he finally talked me into selling him one of my paintings that he'd always wanted."

She waved a hand at the wall and I looked at the collection of seascapes.

"Very pretty," I said.

She nodded. "My great-aunt painted them. She's been gone forever. I never thought I'd part with them, but I'm not getting any younger and I have no one to leave them to. I figured if it made him that happy, then why not. I tried to give it to him, but he insisted on paying me."

She frowned. "I'm even more glad I sold it to him now. At least he had a little time to be happy about it. I hope you figure out what happened. Like I said, I didn't know him well, but he seemed like a nice enough man."

"Well, I suppose we best get out of your hair," I said.

"If you're up for the company, I'd like to visit again," Gertie said. "Maybe under more pleasant circumstances."

Dinah brightened. "I'd like that. I prefer to stick to home as it's more convenient and I never was one for crowds anyway, but it would be nice to talk to someone of the same era. Young people these days just don't know a thing."

She looked over at me. "No offense, dear. You do seem more mature than the rest of your crowd."

"Thanks," I said, and we all rose. "Can I use your bathroom before we leave?"

"Certainly," Dinah said. "It's just down that hall—first door on the left."

I headed down the hall and into the bathroom. It was far larger than what you'd usually find in an old farmhouse and I figured it must have been constructed later on, taking some square footage from a neighboring room, because this bathroom was outfitted for someone with a disability. There was a huge walk-in shower with a bench seat and grab bar. The opening was large enough for a wheelchair or walker to easily get through. Above the showerhead, there was a plant ledge with a rectangular window the length of the shower. A row of pots with ivy lined it, and the vines hanging down in the shower were a pretty touch to the white subway tile and soft green accent tiles on the wall.

I sighed. I really needed to remodel my house. I'd done a few things, but the interior was dated, and now that I'd seen this huge walk-in shower, I really wanted one. It would be nice to wash my hair without banging my elbows on the wall in the standard bathtub/shower that I had. In fact, all of the bathrooms and the kitchen could use an update. But Lord, the noise and the mess and contractors. Dealing with contractors was enough to have me banging my elbows into the wall for another decade or more.

I headed back out to the living room and told Dinah it had been nice meeting her. She narrowed her eyes at me.

"You're the CIA lady, right?" she asked. "It didn't click at first, but I remember my delivery boy telling me about you. He says you've solved quite a few mysteries in Sinful since you've been here."

"I might have poked my nose in a bit," I said.

"Well, I hope Ally is all right and that she doesn't have any more trouble," Dinah said. "I heard her mother finally passed. Such a long time to be in pain, but I think losing your memory is even worse."

"I can agree with you there," Gertie said. "Once my mind goes, I don't want to be here."

"You don't remember what you had for breakfast," Ida Belle said.

We all laughed as we headed out the door. Dinah waved as we pulled out.

"So," I said. "What's the deal with her bully husband and being glad he died?"

"There were rumors that he was a tyrant," Ida Belle said. "But people didn't talk about such things back then."

I looked at Gertie. "Not even kids? Because I figure you might have known the son from school."

Gertie nodded. "I did. He was a quiet boy. Smart and stayed out of trouble."

"Any sign of issues at home?" I asked.

She shrugged. "Who knows? Sometimes he had bruises, but no more so than any other normal boy. And I know his father had him working the shrimp boat with him sometimes on weekends."

"So Dinah's husband was a shrimper? How did he die?"

"Shrimping," Ida Belle said. "Got caught in one of those bizarre storms we get sometimes and never came back."

"Did they find the boat?" I asked.

Ida Belle shook her head. "But he ran a big commercial boat and was out in the Gulf. Sometimes that place is like the Bermuda Triangle."

"And the son died in Alaska," I said. "So I guess talking to him is out of the question. Did Dinah really not have a single friend who might have known what was going on back then?"

"You think Dinah's past has something to do with Miles's death?" Ida Belle asked.

"No," I said. "Not really, but my curiosity is piqued. I'm

sure plenty of women aren't unhappy when their husbands die, but most don't admit to it."

"This is the South," Gertie said. "The more experienced among us tend to be blunter and more honest."

"You mean the closer you get to death, the less you care about what you say," Ida Belle said.

"Then I guess you were born close to death," Gertie said. "Because you've never had a problem with honesty or blunt. Especially blunt."

Ida Belle shrugged. "Saves time."

Gertie sighed. "It offends people, so they don't want to talk to you."

"Like I said—saves time," Ida Belle said.

"So no friends?" I asked again.

"Just one," Gertie said. "Maggie Parker. But she passed years ago."

"Her daughter Sharon moved back here recently though," Ida Belle said. "She was a toddler when Dinah and her husband moved to town, so she probably saw more of Dinah over the years than anyone else except her mother."

"Did she go to school with Dinah's son?" I asked.

"Yes, but he was a couple years older," Gertie said. "And Sharon was one of those fun-loving people always surrounded by a crowd. They weren't exactly the types to hang out together."

"I think we should talk to Sharon," I said. "It can't hurt, and it's not like we have a bunch of other people to question."

"I agree," Ida Belle said. "But I have another thought. We need to get into Miles's house as soon as forensics is done. I want to see it before repairs are made. Maybe it will give us some more ideas."

"Carter will never let us in that house," Gertie said.

"He doesn't have to," Ida Belle said. "I'm going to call Cara and tell her I have a friend interested in a rental, but she wants me to check it out before she makes a trip here."

"If you can get us in that house, that would be great," I said.

"Well, it's midafternoon," Gertie said. "The house probably won't be released until late today. Sharon is out of town this weekend—I heard her telling Walter at the General Store. We need to be on guard duty for Ally once the sun sets, so that still leaves us a couple hours. I can't lie today, so we need to avoid Carter. Any ideas? Because eating and watching a movie doesn't seem to hold much appeal after all that turkey excitement and finding a body."

"I had a thought," I said. "Remember how Dinah said Jasper loved his beer? And Miles didn't head out for New Orleans every weekend."

Ida Belle sighed.

Gertie cheered. "Swamp Bar!"

CHAPTER THIRTEEN

It had been a while since we'd been to the Swamp Bar, and I wasn't really in any hurry to get back there, but it seemed like the only avenue for investigation at the moment. And it would probably be a lot more interesting than watching television. I just hoped it wasn't *far* more interesting than watching television. Things at the Swamp Bar had a way of going from sketchy as heck to questionably criminal in a matter of seconds.

But at least we'd made our peace with the bar owner, Whiskey, and were on good terms. If he couldn't answer our questions, then he might be able to direct us to someone who'd spent time chatting with Jasper or Miles over beers. And hopefully, since it was nice weather, the evening crowd would be fishing now and show up to get drunk and tell lies about fish later. The fewer people there, the less chance of an episode.

Gertie could hardly contain her excitement and bounced on the back seat the whole drive over. Despite the fact that she was usually the one wearing the 'questionably criminal' name tag when things went down, she looked for any reason to go there. Ida Belle would probably prefer the whole thing get taken out by a hurricane, but then she'd also seen Gertie have near-death experiences more times at the Swamp Bar than she had in Vietnam.

But all my hopes of a quiet chat with Whiskey were dashed when we pulled into the full parking lot.

"What in the world is going on?" Gertie asked.

"They must be doing a fish fry or something," Ida Belle said. "There's more people near the bayou than inside the bar by the looks of that crowd."

"Well, that might work in our favor," I said. "Let's go inside and see if Whiskey has some time."

We headed for the bar, but I could tell Gertie's attention was on the crowd near the dock as they appeared to be whooping it up and clashing beer cans with some frequency. It looked as though they were having a great time, and it also looked like the primary place for trouble to start. With any luck, we could get our information and get out before Gertie wandered down to get in the middle of whatever was happening.

Ida Belle had been right about most of the crowd being outside. There were a couple of people standing at the bar to get drinks, and two tables were occupied by older fisherman who were probably regulars, but otherwise, the place was quiet. Whiskey was behind the bar and gave us a big smile as we walked in.

"Ladies," he said. "This is a surprise. What can I do for my favorite detectives? I have a new wine that's popular with your crowd. It's fruity. And I've got peach cobbler if you really want to bulk up on your sweetness."

"I don't need to bulk up," I said as I slid onto a barstool. "I'm all sweetness and light."

Whiskey laughed. "Yeah, that's exactly how I would describe you."

"I'll try the wine," Gertie said. "I need all the sweetness I can get. Life knocks it right the heck out of me."

Whiskey nodded and poured her a glass. "Truer words. What about you two?"

"Why not," I said, and Ida Belle nodded.

"Won't hurt to have one," Ida Belle said.

Whiskey passed her a glass. "Designated getaway driver, right? So what might you need to run from today? Because this is not your usual hangout. In fact, I heard you were supposed to be hunting."

"How did you hear that?" I asked.

He shrugged. "One of the regulars heard Walter talking about it. We have a pool about which one of you would shoot something—the three of you are included in the 'something.' But since you're all sitting here intact, I'm assuming things went well? Or not at all?"

"We got our turkeys," Gertie said. "And we pulled a body out of the bayou."

Whiskey's eyes widened. "Miles Broussard? There's been some talk, but I wasn't sure if it was true."

"It's true," I said. "I imagine Carter will be releasing a statement as soon as he gets everything official from the ME."

"And then Ally was attacked last night in the old dry cleaner building," Ida Belle said. "She bought it to open her bakery, in case you hadn't heard."

Whiskey frowned. "I heard about the bakery and can't wait to put in my order for the bar, but I hadn't heard about the attack. Is she all right? What happened?"

I gave him a rundown and he shook his head.

"That really upsets me for her," he said. "I know you three would be comfortable and safe walking through the Middle

129

East wrapped in an American flag, but others lack your skill set. I'm glad she's all right, but I hate hearing that something might have taken a bit of the shine off her opening the bakery."

I raised an eyebrow and stared at him.

"What?" he asked, catching my look. "I can empathize with the excitement of starting a new venture. My dreams extend beyond serving up beer to drunk fishermen every day."

"You never cease to surprise me," I said.

He smiled. "So what can I really do for you? Because I know you're not here for the drinks or the boat race."

"Boat race?" Gertie perked up.

"No way," Ida Belle said.

"Well, you know how we have this problem with sticking our nose into police business..."

He nodded. "I know and have used it to my advantage, so I'm perfectly okay with it."

"Well, given that Ally is my friend, we're poking. But the thing is, it's all sort of confusing. We don't know that the attack on her is related to Miles being killed, but it's suspicious timing. Add to that the house he was renting was broken into, and we have a bunch of things that seem connected but we don't know why."

"You're right," he agreed. "That seems a bit much for coincidence. But how can I help? I didn't know Miles at all. Probably the most I ever said to him was hello and that was only walking in or out of the General Store. He certainly wasn't a Swamp Bar regular. In fact, I don't recall ever seeing him in here. My understanding was he preferred to do his days-off business in New Orleans if he left his house."

"Yeah, Miles is definitely a mystery," I said. "But I thought I might take it back a generation—a dry cleaner's generation, anyway. Did you know Jasper Cummings?"

Whiskey blinked, and I could tell he was trying to connect Jasper with everything that was going on now and coming up short. Finally, he nodded.

"Jasper was definitely a regular," he said. "That man could drink alcoholics under the table and still walk out of here like he'd been sipping on bottled water the entire night. It was sort of impressive as far as those things go."

I frowned. People who could hold their liquor didn't tend to be as loose-lipped as those who couldn't.

"Then I guess he never got drunk and revealed any cool secrets," I said.

"Like what?" Whiskey asked. "I don't think he knew Miles much before selling to him, and if he had an opinion on the man, I'm guessing it was that he was a bit of a sucker for buying a dry cleaner's in a small blue-collar town when most everything is wash-and-wear these days."

"Yeah, we wondered about that 'investment' as well," I said. "Doesn't seem like good timing, but then not everyone is good at business."

"That's true enough," Whiskey said. "You wouldn't believe the stupid ideas I hear at this bar. And people invest in the dumbest things. I try to talk sense into them because I can smell a scam running a mile away, but the get-rich-quick lure is too much for some of them."

"So you don't know anything interesting or out of the ordinary about Jasper?" I asked.

"I really can't think of anything," he said. "Like I said, he didn't really get drunk. Not like the rest of them. I know he was headed to Mexico after selling the business. Said he already had the perfect spot picked out and a favorite bar. Said he might even see if he could talk them into letting him in on the business. I told him he'd drink all the profits."

"A guy who can outdrink alcoholics doesn't sound like the best person to own a bar," Gertie agreed.

Whiskey nodded. "Rule number one of bar ownership—don't drink where you eat. Too many people think this is their ticket to partying like frat boys every night. That's the quickest way to run your bar in the ground and send your profits out the door. I do my drinking at home, where it belongs."

"Is there anyone that Jasper might have talked to in more detail?" I asked. "Any regular that he spent more time with?"

Whiskey considered this for a moment, then nodded. "Maybe. He used to sit with Corndog a lot. And I think they might have gone fishing a time or two."

"Corndog?" I asked.

Gertie nodded. "He won a corn dog eating contest when he was eight years old. Beat out every adult there, even Chub Henry, and that man was five hundred pounds if he was an ounce."

"Sounds like 'Chub' was a bit of a hedge," I said.

"More than a bit," Ida Belle said. "I don't suppose you've seen Corndog around lately?"

"Sure," Whiskey said. "He's out at the dock waiting for the bass boat race to start."

"What's this bass boat race?" Gertie said with entirely too much interest.

"Forget it," Ida Belle said. "You don't even have a boat to race."

"You could lend me yours," Gertie said.

Ida Belle gave her a derisive look. "I'd lend you Walter first, and may I remind you that I'm subject to all your sexy-time talk and still making that statement."

Whiskey started chuckling, and I couldn't help but grin.

"You know better, Ms. Hebert," Whiskey said. "Boats are

more sacred than the cross around here. But you can get in on the betting if you're interested."

"We'd better pass, but I think we'll see if we can find Corndog," I said. "Thanks for your help."

"Thanks for not tearing up my bar or causing a fight," Whiskey said.

"We haven't left yet," I said.

He snorted as we headed out and cut across the parking lot for the crowd gathered at the dock. Ida Belle and Gertie scanned the people and I waited, as I had zero idea what Corndog looked like, and finally, Ida Belle pointed.

"Over there," she said. "By the guy wearing the beer funnel hat."

"The guy with the hair shirt or the one with toothpick arms?" I asked.

"Toothpick arms," Gertie said.

Midthirties. Six feet tall. A hundred forty pounds maybe. This guy might be the reason some people were referred to as a beanpole. Zero threat to most anyone with that lack of muscle content.

We started that direction, and when we got up behind them, Ida Belle tapped Corndog on the shoulder and he turned around. His eyes looked clear, which was good. At least he wasn't so drunk we couldn't question him. He squinted at Ida Belle for a moment, then looked at Gertie, and finally came to rest on me. But his expression was nothing but confusion.

"It's Gertie Hebert," Gertie said. "And you remember Ida Belle—she's married to Walter now."

"Oh yeah," he said, nodding. "I knew you looked familiar, but it's been a while since I've seen you."

"Maybe because you're spending too much time at the Swamp Bar?" Gertie suggested.

He flushed a bit. "You're probably right about that one. My

mama keeps complaining, especially when I don't do family lunch on Sundays."

"Then why aren't you there now?" Ida Belle asked.

"No one really complains but Mama," he said. "The rest of 'em like to get seconds and if I'm there, I tend to clean off the table the first round."

"Has anyone thought about cooking more food?" I asked.

"Doesn't matter," he said. "I got a hollow leg. If you put food in front of me, I can eat until there's not any left. Can't gain a pound though. Most of the women I know hate me for that."

"I might have to join the club," Gertie said. "I started working out, but the pounds aren't coming off."

"Because you're always carrying snacks around in your bra," Ida Belle said.

Corndog looked confused and I had no desire to explain Gertie's bra stuff, so I turned the conversation back around to our original purpose.

"I'm Fortune," I said. "I moved here last year—the former CIA agent? You might have heard about me."

His eyes widened. "Yes, ma'am. I heard all kinds of stories about you. Mostly the James Bond kind of stuff. I hope I didn't do anything to get on your bad side."

"Nothing like that," I said. "I'm a private investigator now and looking into some old stuff that might have to do with Jasper Cummings. I understand the two of you were friends."

"Jasper?" he said. "Wow, I haven't heard that name in a long time. I wouldn't say as we were friends so much as we usually talked it up at the bar when we were there. But I never went to his house or anything."

"That's okay," I said. "Have you heard from Jasper since he retired?"

"Not in a long time, but he sent some emails after he got to Mexico. I got maybe a couple with some pictures of a bar, then nothing else. But I didn't think anything of it. Like I said, we weren't particular friends or anything. Why? Did something happen to him?"

"Not that I know of," I said. "I was just hoping to locate him, and no one seems to have maintained contact. I thought maybe Dinah Benoit would know, but she only got a couple emails, same as you. And he never told her where he was going. Did he ever tell you?"

"Shoot yeah. He darned near didn't talk about anything else right before he left. Said he was done doing other people's bidding and he was going to enjoy the fruits of his labor in a glass on a beach and do his best to die right there in the sunlight."

"It's not the worst plan," Gertie said.

Corndog nodded. "I have to admit, it made me wish I was a little older and a lot richer. I could stand that lifestyle now."

"Drinking all those labor fruits might lead to that death part a little earlier than expected," I said.

He shrugged. "Just as well. I ain't got the rich part down at all."

"So do you remember the name of the city?"

"Not exactly. It was something like Bar of Pots. I remember thinking it made sense for him to move somewhere that 'bar' was in the name. But that's not exactly it. I don't speak any Spanish."

I looked over at Ida Belle and Gertie, who both shook their heads. Apparently, none of us were familiar with the Bar of Pots location.

"Any idea what side—Gulf or Pacific?"

"Pacific side, definitely," he said. "He said he was tired of looking at the Gulf but the place wasn't some big tourist town. He said it was small and what they called 'undiscovered.'"

"Kinda like Sinful," I said.

He shrugged. "Yeah, except for the Gulf ain't so pretty here and I don't want to see most of the town in bikinis."

Ida Belle mumbled her agreement.

"Did he mention a bigger city?" I asked. "Maybe somewhere that he flew into or purchased bigger-ticket items like appliances or furniture?"

"He did say that if he wanted more nightlife, he was a couple hours from Acapulco."

"That helps," I said. "I don't suppose you still have the emails, do you?"

"Nah. All my stuff is set to automatically delete. Not sure how I turned that on but it doesn't matter. If I forgot about it for thirty days then it probably isn't important."

"Didn't you spend some time in jail recently for unpaid traffic tickets?" Ida Belle asked.

"Oh yeah." He nodded. "Maybe I ought to figure that out. Well, that and check my email more regular like."

"Seems like a good idea," I said. "So did Jasper talk about the business at all? Or what he did before he came to Sinful?" I asked.

He thought on this a bit, then shook his head. "I can't recall him saying anything about what he did before buying the dry cleaner's. And he didn't talk much about that either, but how much is there to say? People brought in dirty clothes and he cleaned them. I do that myself every week in my laundry room but can't see that I need to talk about it."

I couldn't disagree, but I wished Corndog had been a better listener because my guess was he'd probably heard more than he thought. He just didn't remember. I handed him my card. "On the off chance that you think of anything else or actually hear from Jasper, please give me a call."

He gave me a look up and down and smiled.

"*Only* call about Jasper," I said.

He sighed. "Yeah, all right. I guess someone who looks like you is already taken."

I stared. "I've been dating Carter LeBlanc for over a year now."

Ida Belle shook her head. "You might want to think about laying off the booze like your mama is requesting if you're that out of touch with Sinful news."

He studied the beer in his hand and frowned. "Maybe tomorrow?"

"Whatever works," I said. "Let's get out of here."

"Can't we at least watch the boat race?" Gertie begged. "It's about to start and I can't get into any trouble standing on the dock watching."

I couldn't shake the notion that somehow, it was a bad idea, even standing the dock. But I also couldn't argue that we had anything more relevant to do, when in fact, we had absolutely nothing else to do but check in on the security work when Mannie was done and make sure someone had eyes on Ally after dark.

"I suppose it couldn't hurt," I said.

Famous last words.

We stepped toward the dock, and Ida Belle and I hung back on the bank as Gertie weaved her way through the crowd to get onto the dock in front of the boats.

"You should see the engine on this one!" she yelled at Ida Belle. "It's been modified. The guy says it's faster than a Corvette."

Ida Belle shook her head. "I know that guy, and he's conveniently leaving out the Corvette model. I love the cars but that bear we keep running into is faster than some of them."

"If I ever decide to buy a fast car, you know I'm coming to you first," I said.

"Goes without saying."

"Look at this life vest!" Gertie yelled. "It's like being in a racing harness. No way you're coming out of this thing."

We looked over and saw Gertie in a bright blue vest with pristine white straps on it. It looked as though she was ready to get into a fighter jet.

"Why would someone need that in a fishing boat?" I asked. "I mean, besides Gertie."

"Drunk fishing," Ida Belle said.

"Ah." I nodded, then yelled, "We'll find you one this week."

Gertie gave us a thumbs-up and then Whiskey stepped up to the edge of the dock and whistled to get everyone's attention.

"The first two boats are ready to go," he announced. "They'll both start here at the dock, head down to the corner and make a turn around the sunken cypress tree, then back to the dock. First one to pass the first piling is the winner. This is a single elimination tournament, so no do-overs, and no complaining. Boaters, start your engines, and when I fire my pistol, you take off."

"This is the best place!" Gertie yelled. "I'll totally get roosted."

Ida Belle sighed. "I'm glad I ordered those seat covers in bulk."

"Probably should just have the whole back seat redone in plastic, maybe some sort of pan underneath that slides out?"

"If only that were a joke," Ida Belle said.

The pistol fired and even though I'd known it was coming, my hand whipped around my waist, and I caught myself just before I pulled out my nine. I watched the boats launch from in front of the dock, and as predicted, they sent a roost of bayou water hurling onto the dock. Gertie jumped up and down like a child playing in a fire hydrant, and I couldn't help but laugh. I hoped I found that much fun in life at her age. Hell, I hoped I found that much fun tomorrow.

And then the situation went all Gertie.

CHAPTER FOURTEEN

ONE OF THE RACERS HAD FORGOTTEN TO UNTIE HIS BOAT from the dock. Everyone started yelling as the rope uncurled off the dock and raced into the water behind the boat.

"Untie it!"

"Cut it loose!"

"Get off the dock!"

People yelled and scrambled for the bank, except for Whiskey and Gertie, who were trying to free the rope before the racer ran out of slack.

"Got it!" Whiskey yelled as he uncurled the last of the rope around the piling, and that's when I realized the end of the rope was looped into one of the straps on the harness life vest Gertie still had on.

The slack went out and Gertie got yanked into the water. The vest kept her on top of the surface, but it was clear that body surfing was not her forte. She bounced across the top of the bayou like a performer in the worst redneck water show I'd ever seen. Whiskey fired his pistol again to get the driver's attention, and when the man caught sight of Gertie, he whipped the boat around and came back for the dock but didn't decrease his speed.

"What the hell is he doing?" Ida Belle yelled. "Slow down, you idiot!"

The boat roared past the dock and the racer screamed out something about a stuck throttle.

"Kill it!"

A dozen people hollered as he went by, but I could see him twisting the key and the engine simply wasn't responding. This is what happened when you combined hopped-up engines, drunks, and a boat race.

Gertie flew by, arms spread out and whooping as though this was all part of the event.

"That woman has lost her mind," Ida Belle said.

"She's going to lose more than that if he doesn't figure out a way to stop that boat," I said.

Apparently, the racer had figured out the same thing, so he swung the boat around and headed for the ramp next to the dock. I understood his plan—a boat on land couldn't move—but I had to pray that the rope was long enough to allow Gertie to stop before she hit that ramp with any momentum.

The crowd realized about a second after I did what was going on and everyone scrambled to get out of the way. The boat hit the ramp at full speed and launched into the air a good fifteen feet high and propelled forward into the parking lot. It crashed into the back of a pickup truck just as Gertie hit the ramp. She flew up the incline and got airborne. If she hit the ground from that height and at that speed, there wouldn't be enough joint replacement surgeries to fix her.

I ran into her path and leaped in front of her as she dropped, breaking her fall. We both hit the ground and tumbled into a table—a table that held containers of seasoned fish, ready for frying. The table tipped over and the fish dumped over the top of us. I felt the cold, slimy water seep into my tennis shoes and tried to brush the salty mess from my face.

"Are you all right?" Ida Belle asked, leaning over us.

"I think so," I said. "Gertie?"

"That was epic," she said.

"That's good, because the two of you are walking home," Ida Belle said.

"Anyone get that on video?" Gertie called out.

At least a dozen people raised their cell phones and cheered.

Oh goody.

I jumped up and shook my arms, slinging fish juice everywhere, and that promptly dispersed the handful of people still standing around. The rest had gone over to the truck where the boat had landed and were now arguing over the best way to get the boat out of the truck, since the hull had gone through the back windshield. A man waving keys—who I presumed was the owner—was threatening to drive the whole thing down the ramp and let insurance deal with it.

"Is the driver all right?" I asked Whiskey, who was helping free Gertie from the life jacket.

He nodded. "Came up cussing and asking for a beer. I figure he's fine. He's not running that boat again, though. Not until he proves he knows how to hop it up without breaking it. Someone could have been killed. Several someones. Can you imagine explaining all that to my insurance company if someone had died? I'm already paying a fortune on this place."

"I can imagine," I said, thinking of some of the things that had occurred on the premises. "Well, if there's nothing else you need us for, I'd like to go home and shower for a week."

Ida Belle shook her head. "Still not getting in my SUV."

"Oh the hypocrisy," I said. "So it's okay for you to not want this smelly mess in your SUV but I'm weird for not wanting it in my boat."

"You're right," Ida Belle agreed. "And I am now firmly in your camp on not having fish in your boat."

"That's convenient," I said.

I reached down to give Gertie a hand up and she sorta rose, then stumbled into me.

"I think I twisted my leg or wrenched my hip or something when I hit the ramp," Gertie said as she clutched my shoulder to stand.

"Who would have thought?" I said and looked at Ida Belle. "Clearly, we can't walk home. Gertie wouldn't have made it even before she twisted her leg out of socket. It's definitely not happening now. And honestly, the next time the two of you invite me to go hunting, I'm going to Bermuda instead, or maybe Peru."

Ida Belle pulled out her cell phone and dialed.

"Hey Scooter, I need a favor," she said. "Can you bring your truck over to the Swamp Bar and pick up a couple of people that smell like fish?"

Then she sighed.

"Of course they're not dead," she said.

I looked at Whiskey, who shrugged.

Seemed a reasonable question to ask. This was Sinful.

———

DESPITE BEING HAULED around like an inner tube, Gertie's leg appeared to be more or less fine. Nothing was out of line and the scratches were mostly on her knees. She was already sore, and I was guessing walking would be a premium the next day, but since she could move it all directions and put some weight on it, she refused to go to the emergency room. Ida Belle followed us to Gertie's house and said she'd stay with her and check her leg out after Gertie got showered. If there was any swelling or other indication of a bigger problem, then she'd haul her to the hospital whether Gertie liked it or not.

Ronald was on my front porch when we pulled up in Scooter's truck, and I couldn't help but wonder what level of hell I'd dropped into this weekend. I climbed out of the back of the truck, gave Scooter a wave, and trudged toward my house.

"I got a call from a friend at the Swamp Bar who sent me a video of the whole thing," Ronald said. "Good Lord, woman, how do you manage to do such horrible things to your body? When you jumped on the car the other night with your gun out, that was supercool, but if that whole CIA agent thing requires you to get smelly and dirty so much, then I think I'm going to have to pass on this adventure."

I wasn't in a position to be excited about that news, but Carter would be thrilled that Ronald had nixed the idea of being me.

"What are you doing here?" I asked and pointed to a plastic bag he was holding. "And what's that?"

"Honey, we have to hose you down out back. I've got grease cleaner and Febreze. We have to get you decent enough to go inside because that old, cheap rug in there is not going to handle a cleaning, and I'm surprised that stair runner hasn't disintegrated from a mere vacuum."

I opened my mouth to say that I didn't like the rug or the stair runner, so they could both go, but then I thought about the hardwood floors. Even if they'd been sealed, how long ago had that been? And how many scratches would take on fish liquid and hold it? If this smell crept into my floors, I'd have to move.

So that's why ten minutes later, Carter walked around the side of my house and found Ronald spraying me with Febreze.

"Okay," Ronald said. "Now slip behind those bushes and take off those nasty clothes. I've got a garbage bag here and a cheap robe. Five-star hotel, my butt. That robe chafes. I suggest you wear it just inside the house then toss it back out the door. I'll make sure everything gets buried or maybe burned. Or both. And when you get inside, run straight for the shower and don't get out of there until next year. You might consider some diluted bleach. If things are dire enough, we can cut your hair."

"You're going to run naked through the house?" Carter asked.

Ronald rolled his eyes. "It figures all you took away from this situation is the naked part. I get that she's hot but we have a real situation here. Do you know how hard it is to get the smell of fish juice out of something? We'd have to burn that house down if she'd gone in the way she was delivered here."

"Yeah, I'm with Ronald on this one," I said.

Carter watched in amusement as I stepped behind the bushes with the robe. I felt like an idiot, undressing in my backyard, especially knowing Ronald was standing there like the EPA to collect my clothes and Carter was hanging around for his own personal entertainment. There was no point in even attempting to elicit sympathy from him as he'd just say we shouldn't have been at the Swamp Bar. And I had zero doubt that half of Sinful had already forwarded him the video.

Despite the fact that I'd been doused with grease cleaner and Febreze, my clothes still reeked as I pulled them off and tossed them over the hedges. I hesitated for a moment with my undergarments because, well, no one wants to go tossing their wares at their neighbor. Except maybe Gertie. If someone hot lived next door, she might participate in some ware tossing.

Finally, I sighed and flung the garments over. At least I was wearing a sports bra and hadn't been carrying a sandwich in it like some other people I know. I slipped my Glock into the robe pocket and would dump it in the kitchen sink as soon as I got inside. As I stepped out from behind the bushes, Ronald was shaking his head.

"We really need to go shopping," he said. "You need some sexy underwear."

Carter made a strangled sound, and his shoulders shook from trying not to laugh. My hand twitched a bit near the pocket with the Glock but I managed to control my supreme embarrassment.

"I can't have lace rubbing on me when I'm chasing bad guys," I said. "You hate chafing—you should know."

Ronald frowned. "That's a good point. Maybe just some sexy colors. I'll do some research on the matter. We can't have you strolling around in basic lingerie when you have a sexy man to show them off to."

Carter's amusement faded when Ronald made his 'sexy man' comment and I smiled at him, wondering how he felt now that the tables had turned. I headed up the steps without saying another word and slipped inside. I immediately tossed my Glock into the kitchen sink, then shed the robe and flung it outside. A wave of fishy smell flooded my nose, and I took off at a dead run, not wanting any of that smell to seep into the house, especially the kitchen, where I spent most of my time. I sprinted out of the kitchen and through the living room.

And that's when I remembered Ally was staying with me.

I barely caught her look of surprise as I streaked past her and up the stairs. I didn't stop running until I'd jumped into the shower. I grabbed the bottle of shampoo and took the top completely off, then dumped the entire thing on my head. Then I turned the water on as hot as it would go and scrubbed my hair and scalp until I started developing a headache.

Thirty minutes later, my headache was in full force and my skin was irritated from all the loofah scrubbing. I'd gone through two bottles of shampoo, an entire jar of body scrub, and a bar of soap. For good measure, I'd taken the shower curtain, the loofah, the towel, and the bathroom rug and tossed them all out the back window. They could either join Ronald in his burial/burning ceremony, or I'd double-bag them and put them in the garbage. When I walked downstairs, I could hear Ally and Carter talking in the kitchen, so I headed that way.

Ally was taking cookies out of the oven, and Carter had my gun in pieces on top of a garbage bag on my kitchen table. He'd located my cleaning kit in the utility room and was going over it with a brush. I took a big whiff, but the only thing I could smell was whatever heavenly goodies Ally had pulled out of the oven.

"Smell my hair," I said and bent down near Carter.

He leaned over and took a whiff. "Smells like shampoo."

"You're sure?" I asked as I sank into a chair. "Because I only had two bottles. I can go buy more."

"One, you're going to have to buy more anyway if you used both bottles," Carter said. "And two, you don't need to rush out and do it now. Your hair smells fine. But I saw your shower curtain hit the back lawn. You'll need to replace that."

"I have a spare," I said.

"Why on earth would you have a spare shower curtain?" he asked.

"In case I need to haul off a body," I said.

It was really because I'd accidentally ordered two online and was too lazy to return one, but it had been worth it just to see the look of concern that flashed across his face.

Ally grabbed a beer out of the fridge and put it in front of me. "I think you might need this."

"I'm not sure a keg can handle today," I said. "And I gave myself a headache scrubbing my head."

I started to get up, but Ally waved a hand at me and grabbed some aspirin from the cabinet. She set the whole bottle in front of me along with a bottled water and a plate of cookies so hot the chocolate chips hadn't hardened yet.

"Give those another minute or so," she said.

"That's just cruel," I said, staring wistfully at the cookies.

"So," Carter said. "You want to tell me what led to you bathing outdoors with Ronald, flashing Ally, and scrubbing yourself until you look like a tomato?"

"Don't pretend you haven't seen the video," I said.

"Oh, I saw it," he said. "Most of Louisiana and a good part of the country has seen it. It was probably on YouTube before you got up off the ground. But the part the video doesn't explain is why you were at the Swamp Bar."

I shrugged. "Nothing better to do."

He raised one eyebrow. "You expect me to believe that you volunteered to hang out at the Swamp Bar? You might as well fess up. You never go there without a reason."

"Yeah, but my reasons for going always fall under things you don't want me to do."

"Because they're often illegal."

I waved a hand in dismissal. "There's no proof that we've ever done anything illegal at the Swamp Bar."

"Because you've gotten lucky."

Ally laughed, and I remembered she was still in the kitchen.

"Sorry you're having to listen to us rehash the same old tired ground," I said.

"It wouldn't be old and tired if it stayed in the past," Carter pointed out.

"Look, all we did was go to chat with Whiskey," I said. "Then Gertie wanted to watch the boat race and all manner of problems began."

"The manner of most of your problems begins with the name 'Gertie,'" Carter said.

"You've lived here longer than me," I said. "And you're a deputy. If you haven't managed to get her in line, why should I bother to try? Quite frankly, if Ida Belle hasn't managed since the crib, I'm pretty sure we're all doomed if we head down that path."

"I have to side with Fortune on that one," Ally said.

"I thought you were both our friends," Carter said to Ally. "Doesn't that mean you're supposed to be the impartial one?"

"That statement *was* impartial," Ally said. "No one—not even Jesus—can tell Gertie what to do. My committed belief in that has nothing to do with being friends with Fortune or you. It just comes from two-plus decades of watching her in action."

"Hey," I said. "How about you tell me about the break-in at Miles's rental and I'll tell you why we went to the Swamp Bar?"

"You know that's not how it works," he said.

I smiled. "Exactly. You have to trust that if I get anything that you can use for an arrest, I'll let you know."

"That's exactly the part I don't trust," he said. "Every time a body pops up in Sinful, you have at least two near-death experiences."

"Correlation does not equal causation," I said. "And besides, you don't know how many near-death experiences I have when there's not a body, so you have no baseline for comparison."

He gave me a look of utter dismay, and Ally giggled.

"With that," he said, "I best get back to work. I have a ton of crap to write up and I'm not looking forward to it. Is Mannie supposed to finish up the alarm system today?"

Ally nodded. "He said he'd call when he was ready to show me how it all worked."

"Can you at least tell me if you found Miles's car?" I asked.

"Fine," he said. "I'll throw you a bone, even though I'm sure you already figured this would be the case. The car was dumped in a strip center parking lot up the highway. Nothing inside. Only prints belong to Miles. A scooter belonging to one of the tattoo parlor employees was stolen the same night and has not been recovered."

I sighed. "Another dead end."

He leaned over and kissed me, then sniffed my head. "Still smells like shampoo."

As he headed out, I looked over at Ally, who was smiling wistfully.

"You guys are so cute together," she said.

"I don't know that we're the kind of people who want to be described as 'cute.' I'm sorry I totally flashed you earlier. I completely forgot about you staying here. How, I have no idea since it all relates to why I was at the Swamp Bar in the first place."

"I figured you guys didn't go out there for the beer, especially as you have a case in your refrigerator. Did you find out anything?"

"No. Both Miles and Jasper were remarkably absent from the local population. There was a dude called Corndog that used to throw some back with Jasper, but the only thing we might have gotten from him was a lead on where Jasper retired to."

"What do you mean 'might'?"

"He called it Bar of Pots. I'm pretty sure that's not a real place."

Ally's eyes widened. "Maybe he meant Barra de Potosi. I had a distant cousin who studied fish or ocean currents or something there for a summer. That was when I was a kid, and I don't think it was much more than a village then."

"I'm not positive it's much more than that now, according to Jasper's description. Is Barra de Potosi anywhere near Acapulco?"

"I think so. I remember he sent Mama and Aunt Celia shot glasses from Acapulco."

"Why in the world would he send them shot glasses? Was he trying to make them mad?"

"Definitely in Celia's case, and it did. Then because Celia was so mad, Mama decided it was funny and that made Celia even madder."

"Smart cousin."

"What do you want to find Jasper for? Do you think he would know why someone would want to kill Miles?"

"Maybe. I don't know. There's not a lot to go on."

Now Ally sighed. "I'm sorry you're in the middle of this."

"That's not your fault. I was going to be in the middle of this as soon as Gertie pulled that body out of the bayou. You know me."

"Yep. You're easily bored."

I grinned. "That's one way of putting it."

CHAPTER FIFTEEN

ALLY MANAGED TO BAKE THREE DOZEN COOKIES BEFORE Mannie called and said he was ready to show us everything. I checked with Ida Belle, but she was making Gertie sit in an ice bath every hour, so they were going to pass. So far, it didn't look as if an emergency room visit was going to be required, but she said Gertie was moving worse than usual even though she was refusing to complain. Probably because she didn't want to be left behind when we went investigating again. That was a bridge Ida Belle and I would have to cross depending on how she was tomorrow and what we had on the docket.

It was around 7:00 p.m. when we pulled into downtown, and the only vehicles there belonged to sheriff's department employees and Mannie. I spotted the camera above the door of the building tracking me as we walked in, and relief coursed through me. Average criminals usually avoided a building once they saw security cameras. If someone went to the lengths to disguise themselves and break in again, then we were going to have to tear the place apart brick by brick. No one would take that kind of risk unless the payoff was huge.

Mannie smiled at us as we entered, and I noticed his gaze

lingered on Ally longer than me. Ally gave a hearty hello, but I noticed she couldn't look at him more than a couple seconds before lowering her gaze. I definitely wasn't an expert on the inner workings of romantic relationships, but even I couldn't miss the signs of attraction.

"How's Gertie doing?" Mannie asked me.

"I guess you saw the video," I said.

"Everyone has seen the video," Mannie said. "Big and Little got a huge charge out of it but told me to make sure Ms. Hebert didn't need anything."

"What constitutes 'anything'?" I asked, mostly out of basic curiosity.

Mannie shrugged. "Massage therapist, home nurse, hot supper, all the way to strong-arming the hospital to fit her up with a room that resembles a hotel and not a hospital."

"I think we're good so far," I said. "But please give the Heberts my thanks."

He nodded. "Let's take a look at the alarm system first. There's two keypads for arming and disarming—one next to the front door and one next to the back."

He had Ally pick a code and then showed us how to arm and disarm the alarm. Then he took Ally's phone and added the alarm app to it so that she could arm and disarm from her phone and check the status of the alarm at any time.

"Now, for the cool part," he said, and pulled up another app he'd installed on Ally's phone. "This is your camera system. I set this up to show all six cameras on one screen. Then you can select a camera for a closer look or to check history."

The system was essentially the same as what I had at my house, so I wandered through the building, only half listening as he explained how to access the information to Ally. What in the world could be hidden here? The place was basically empty. Or maybe whatever the killer was looking for was long gone and he knew that now. That was my hope, anyway, because it meant no more issues for Ally. But I still didn't believe there was any chance the break-in here and the one at Miles's rental home were a coincidence.

"Fortune?" Ally's voice broke into my thoughts. "Mannie wants to put the security camera app on your phone. Is that all right?"

"Is it all right with you?" I asked.

She gave me a somewhat apologetic look and said, "No offense to Carter, but since your reaction time and force are likely to be a bit better and far less restricted than the sheriff's department, I'm all for it."

"What you're saying is I'm readily available and don't follow the rules," I said as I handed a grinning Mannie my phone. "Load me up. I'd prefer to have eyes on the place anyway."

"Honestly, I'd be surprised if you had any more problems," Mannie said. "All this hardware tends to make people with two brain cells think twice about a break-in. But then, we're talking about Sinful and not much about all of this makes much sense so..."

I nodded. "I know. I figure hedge all bets because if living here has taught me one thing it's to expect the completely out of left field."

He handed me my phone back. "It says a lot when the place you live is more unpredictable than the Middle East. And even though this is one of the best you can buy, remember that no system is foolproof. Pros can get around them."

"I can't think of a reason for a pro to rob a bakery," I said.

"Probably not," he agreed.

"Have the Heberts ever been robbed?" Ally asked.

"Lord no," Mannie said. "But they have other things in place besides just a security system. There has been talk, though, over the years—you know how things filter back to them. Seems some with the illegal kind of pursuits were robbed somewhat regularly for a long stretch. It's settling down some now."

"Who would take that kind of risk?" Ally asked.

"Other criminals," Mannie said. "The Heberts always assumed it was an underlying result of turf wars. Tit for tat and all."

"I guess it's more profitable and less messy than a drive-by," I said.

Mannie grinned. "The app for the system is the same one you use for your own house. I just added Ally's location. You can choose which to look at with the drop-down at the top."

"Perfect," I said. "I really appreciate you getting all this done so quickly."

"Yes," Ally said. "I feel so much better knowing the place is covered. I don't figure I'll be allowed a minute alone after dark for a while, but I'd hate for someone to vandalize the place once construction starts. I have insurance for that sort of thing, but they tend to get testy if it happens more than once. Fortunately, nothing was damaged this last time."

"Except you," Mannie said. "The most important asset the business has."

"Oh," Ally said as she blushed and then stared at the floor.

Although I was a general lover of silence, this awkward kind was not my cup of tea.

"He's right," I said. "The most important thing is protecting you. Drywall and stuff can be repaired. Sometimes people can't be."

Ally lifted her head and gave me a nod before looking back at Mannie.

"Well, I really appreciate it," she said again. "How much do I owe you?"

He shook his head. "On the house."

"No!" Ally said. "I can't let you give me all this equipment, and then there's your time, and that just wouldn't be right."

"The equipment is courtesy of the Heberts," Mannie said. "And so is my time as they pay me very well regardless of what I happen to be doing for my employment. They have simply asked for a blackberry cobbler when you're up and running. It's Big's favorite dessert."

"Well, I can certainly do that, but a cobbler hardly covers all of this," Ally said, still looking anxious over accepting such a gift.

"I don't know," I said. "I've had your blackberry cobbler."

Mannie smiled. "The Heberts feel it's important to keep Sinful safe. They want this town to prosper and for the residents to feel they can be out after dark and alone in their businesses without worry, especially the women. They're very pleased that you've decided to open your bakery here rather than locating it in a bigger city, which you certainly had the option and talent to do."

Ally's face softened. "That's so nice of them. Please tell them how much I appreciate it and that I have a ton of frozen blackberries in my deep freeze. I picked them myself and they are huge and sweet. I'll be making that cobbler tomorrow."

"Well, you have my number," Mannie said. "Just give me a call when it's ready and I can pick it up. But if you have other things you need to be working on, the cobbler can wait. The Heberts are in no hurry. Well, Big might be in a little hurry, but that's just because of his relationship with food."

Ally and I both smiled and Mannie gave us a nod.

"You ladies stay safe and if you need anything else, let me know," he said, and then left the building.

Ally watched him go and let out a small sigh as the door

closed behind him. I doubt she was even aware that she'd done it.

"He's single, you know," I said.

"What?" She whirled around and stared at me. "I'm not...I mean, I don't..."

"Don't you?"

"Oh, Fortune, I just can't. What with getting my business going and all, I just don't have the time."

"Really? You're going with the old and tired time excuse? You can do better than that."

"Okay, well, maybe I'm not the best judge of men. I've dated some real doozies. And while I'll admit that Mannie is one hot guy, he's also the Heberts' right-hand man. I don't know for certain what he does for them but there's rumors, and everyone knows the Heberts aren't exactly law-abiding citizens."

Since Mannie had taken out one of Ahmad's men before he could kill Carter, I was well versed on just how far Mannie would take things if necessary. But given that we were cut from the same cloth, I couldn't fault him, and he'd saved Carter's life. That earned him permanent status with me, and even Carter had backed off his hard line on the Heberts and Mannie. He didn't exactly approve of the things they did, especially when they helped me with my investigations, but he couldn't argue with their intentions, which were always to help keep Sinful safe and weed out the bad guys.

And I had my own theories about Mannie's role with the Heberts. I had learned some time back that they were federal informants. That's exactly how they kept their toe in illegal business but never brought the heat on themselves. As long as they weren't running drugs or weapons or dealing in murder for hire, the Feds were quite happy to leave them alone with the loan-sharking and illegal gambling.

I had a feeling that Mannie might be their handler.

Which led to the interesting train of thought of who was really the boss—Big or Mannie?

Either way, I didn't so much as blink over the thought of Ally having a relationship with Mannie but on the surface, I could see where it might not be a good idea. I knew the truth, but the rest of Sinful only knew the gossip. There would be more than one raised eyebrow if the town's sweetheart started dating the local bad boy. And gossip in places like Sinful could tank reputations. With Ally just starting her business, it might not be a risk she could take right now.

"You're right," I said finally, and Ally looked relieved. "It's probably not good timing and likely not the best choice for a place that seems to survive on gossip. But I can tell you that Mannie is one of the good guys. I wish I could say more, but it's not my place."

"I believe you. I get a good feeling about him, despite all the talk. And I know I said I haven't had good luck with men, but I've also ignored my instincts. I'm not going to do that anymore. But still, now isn't the time. I need to focus on my business because I've only got the capital for one shot at this."

"It's going to be awesome. And I'm not saying that just because I get to taste-test everything."

"Are you sure?"

I laughed. "Pretty sure. What do you say we get out of here and swing by Gertie's house to see how she's doing? Ida Belle could probably use the diversion."

We found Gertie ensconced in her recliner, a bottle of Sinful Ladies cough syrup in one hand and a hot dog wiener in the other. Ida Belle came out from the kitchen carrying more snacks and two beers, which she promptly handed to Ally and me then went back to retrieve two more for herself. Apparently, it had been that kind of day.

"You should see what's been on television," Gertie said, her words slightly slurred. "There were cars going around in a circle as fast as they could go. Then there were dogs—all sorts of pretty dogs—and women with horrible shoes."

"Car racing and a dog show," I said. "It's been a busy evening."

Gertie nodded. "I had to sit in a tub of ice a million times. And Ida Belle wouldn't let me sit naked. I didn't see the point in adding to my laundry, but she said that ice might kill the nerves in my lady parts. Well, we can't have none of that!"

Ally giggled at Ida Belle's long-suffering sigh and I couldn't help but smile.

"I see you've reverted to the get-'em-drunk method of care-taking," I said to Ida Belle, and pointed to the cough syrup.

"She wasn't going to get in that ice without it," Ida Belle said. "I'm not sure which Gertie is harder to handle—the sober one or the drunk one."

"I'm not drunk," Gertie said, and tried to take a drink of the remote.

"Hmmmm," I said. "Let me get back to you on that one. You staying here tonight?"

"Yeah," Ida Belle said. "I'm afraid once she gets to sleep that leg is going to stiffen up and she'll need help walking. I brought a walker so hopefully, she'll be able to hobble around, but we'll see."

"I'm sure it would be much worse if you hadn't done the icing," I said. "Honestly, for someone her age and as little as she exercises, she's surprisingly sturdy."

"I am Iron Man!" Gertie yelled, and Ally laughed.

"Well, we're going to get out of your hair," I said. "I'm hungry and I think I'm going to get in another shower before I go to bed. Just in case I missed a fish glob."

"I heard about Cleanup Crew Ronald and you flashing

Ally," Ida Belle said. "Makes my time here feel a little better, anyway. At least I wasn't hosed down in my backyard and I didn't have to see any naked parts."

"I've got naked parts under these clothes," Gertie said.

Ida Belle shook her head. "While Naked Parts was soaking, I got hold of Cara. Carter said the house is released and she agreed to meet us there tomorrow at noon. But she triple-warned me it was a mess. I swear she almost sounded like she was about to cry. They must have really done a number."

I sighed. Talking to Cara would never be my first choice of things to do, but we needed to see the house. There was always the off chance that I would notice something the forensics people hadn't.

"If this one can move without that walker, I'll pick you up 9:00. We can grab breakfast at the café and ease into the day for a change," Ida Belle said.

"Sounds good," I said, and we headed out.

"What do you think they're looking for?" Ally asked as we got into my Jeep.

I shook my head. "I wish I knew."

———

AFTER THE MANY challenges of the day, I should have been wiped out, but despite the long, hot shower, a huge shrimp po'boy, and way too many of Ally's cookies, I kept tossing and turning, only managing to sleep in short bursts filled with restless dreams. Every time I woke up, I was more tired than when I'd gone to sleep. Finally, I threw the covers off and headed downstairs for my own bottle of Sinful Ladies cough syrup. If anything was going to get me over the hump, that would do it. And maybe one more cookie. Okay, two.

I stuffed my nine in my shorts and grabbed my cell phone,

giving the security cameras at Ally's place a check as I headed downstairs. No movement anywhere, which was good as it was 1:00 a.m. and well past when people should be strolling around downtown. And I hadn't really expected to see anything but mostly wanted to ensure that there were no problems with the system itself. Not that I expected any with Mannie acquiring the equipment and doing the install, but he didn't wire the electricity or internet for the building. Problems could crop up in either of those areas.

I was just lowering my arm when movement caught my eye. I clicked on the camera behind the building to expand and then zeroed in on the back door. I wasn't imagining it. Someone had just crept up to the door and was holding something in his hand. Maybe a knife or screwdriver.

CHAPTER SIXTEEN

I PULLED ON A HOODIE AND SHOES IN MY LAUNDRY ROOM, disarmed my alarm, and dashed into the garage. I saw a light flicker on in the guest room and cursed. I had hoped Ally would sleep through my exit but given her recent trauma and the fact that she was no longer taking painkillers, that probably wasn't likely.

I called Carter as I backed out of the driveway.

"Do not make a move on this guy before I get there," he said.

I didn't bother to reply because it was a waste of both our times. If I had an opportunity to tackle the guy, Carter was going to have to deal with it. Then I dialed Ally and told her that someone was on camera, I had already called Carter, and I was going to check it out. I didn't even give her a chance to respond.

I pulled over to the curb just short of downtown and ran down a series of hedges to the back of the row of buildings that constituted one side of Main Street. There were a few lights on the backside and not a single one was on. He must have disabled them. I inched my way toward Ally's building trying to cover by tucking in behind garbage cans and crates as I went.

Then I heard the gunshot.

I immediately hit the ground, trying to zero in on where the shot came from, and hoped to God it was Carter who'd fired it and not the bad guy. Then I heard someone running away from the building and I knew that couldn't be good. Only the bad guy would run away. If Carter wasn't in pursuit that meant he might have been shot.

I sprang up and twisted around the trash can I'd been hiding behind, my gun leveled toward the back door on Ally's building, but even in the dim light, nothing moved. I hurried down the building, squinting in the minimal moonlight that streamed through and trying to move as quietly as possible. If the shooter was still around, the last thing I wanted to do was provide them with another target.

As I approached the back door to Ally's building, I could see a lump on the ground in front of the door. All caution fled and I took off running. I dropped next to the body and pulled it over. My breath rushed out and relief swept through me when I realized it wasn't Carter. But it also wasn't someone I recognized.

"Hands up where I can see them!" Carter's voice sounded behind me and I held up my hands.

"It's me," I said.

He ran up and looked down at the guy, who was bleeding from the bullet hole in his stomach. I didn't think it was possible that he was alive, but I felt for a pulse and was shocked to find a really faint one.

"He's still alive!" I said.

Carter pulled out his cell phone and called 911 as I yanked off my hoodie and pressed it on his stomach to stop the bleeding.

"Where did it enter?" Carter asked after he hung up and dropped down next to me and checked his pulse.

"Through his back. This is an exit wound."

"I told you to wait!"

"I didn't do this! I wouldn't shoot unless fired on and you can't fire on someone with your back turned."

Carter ran one hand through his hair. "I'm sorry. You're right. So who shot him?"

"I heard someone running away after the shot, but they were going in the opposite direction so I couldn't see them. Who is this guy?"

Carter checked his pockets and shook his head. "No ID. I have no idea."

"Seriously?"

"He looks familiar—like one of those memories from a long time ago, but where it's not quite the same. He's not a Sinful resident, though, and hasn't lived here recently."

I studied the guy's face but didn't even get a glimmer of that familiarity that Carter had. He was probably around fifty years old, so not old enough to be Jasper unless Jasper was a really well-preserved alcoholic. But if it was Jasper, Carter would have remembered him, especially given the current situation.

"I got nothing," I said. "I know you're going to veto this, but I suggest you ask Ida Belle and Gertie."

He started to shake his head, then frowned. I saw that as an opening and took it.

"Unless this guy has DNA or fingerprints on file for some reason, you're not going to easily ID him."

"Well, given that he was trying to break into the building and could potentially be the person who murdered Miles, then I'm going to bet on both being on file."

"Maybe. But it's easier to get them to look at him now than

explain to the hospital why you need to parade people through his room later on. Or the ME, depending on how this plays out. At least let me take a picture of him. I'm going to have to send Ida Belle over to my house anyway."

"Do it before I change my mind."

He took over holding the hoodie on the bullet wound and I took a picture and sent it to Ida Belle. I was about to call to wake her up when I got a text right back.

Good. God. What the hell is going on? Let me show this to Gertie.

I waited for a bit and finally got a follow-up text.

Both of us think he looks familiar but we can't place him. Can we see him in person?

Voices sounded behind us and Carter yelled and waved his flashlight in the air as the paramedics rounded the corner.

I texted back.

Negative. Paramedics just arrived.

He's still alive?

For the moment. Can you head over to my house and watch Ally?

On it.

Carter and I stepped back and let the paramedics do their job. They got him up and into the ambulance in record time, working on stabilizing him as they went. Carter told them he'd follow to the hospital and a couple seconds later, they were gone.

Carter looked at the retreating ambulance and back at the building and sighed. "I'm going to need a statement, but it can wait. I guess I better head to the hospital."

"I have video as well," I said. "That's how I knew someone was here. I couldn't sleep and checked the cameras."

"Can you see if the shooter shows up on it?"

"Yeah, but I wouldn't count on it. He was at least thirty yards away in the opposite direction. Probably at the edge of the tree line where the woods start."

"That's a good shot to make in the dark."

"Good, but something that a whole lot of people in this town could manage, especially with a rifle and a scope."

He sighed. "True."

"Here," I said, and showed him my phone. "You can see our bad guy working on the door and it should be about now..."

The bad guy stiffened, then crumpled.

"Even if we slow it down, the most you'll get is the bullet entering the scene," I said. "If you didn't know where it came from, that would be one thing, but I'm telling you what I heard and saw."

He nodded. "I'm sure your assessment is accurate. I'll get a team down here to work the area you indicated. Why don't you head home? Try to get some sleep."

"Ha! 'We're putting you in a sleepy small town,' Morrow said. 'Nothing ever happens there,' he said."

"I swear, at one time, that was essentially true. But now..."

He didn't have to say anything else. I knew how upset Carter had been over the rash of violent crime that had swept through his hometown the past couple years. Most people would just blame it on society going downhill, but the reality was, a lot of the events had been in the making for years if not decades before the situation exploded.

"It's not on you," I said. "None of this is. You're just cleaning up other people's messes and a lot of them were started long before you could even drive a car, much less wear a badge."

He nodded, but it didn't appear as if my words had made him feel any better.

"I better get to the hospital," he said. "I need to run fingerprints and see if I can figure out who the heck this guy is."

I gave him a quick hug and then hurried to my Jeep. A

couple minutes later, Ida Belle met me at the front door and let me inside.

Ally was in the kitchen, serving up hot chocolate. Gertie was sitting at the table with a pair of crutches propped on the wall behind her.

"She was already in the kitchen when we got here," Ida Belle said, waving a hand at Ally.

Ally nodded and put the hot chocolate in front of all of us.

"No way I was going back to bed until I knew what was going on," she said.

I looked over at Gertie. "You should have stayed home and rested that leg."

"Or at least used the walker I brought her," Ida Belle said.

"Only old people use walkers," Gertie said. "And if you think I was going to stay home and miss out on the fun, then you don't know me at all."

Ally frowned. "You know I'm not against you guys having fun, but I wish it wasn't because of me."

Gertie looked chagrined and squeezed Ally's hand. "I'm so sorry, dear. I'm not excited for your misery. I just want all of this cleared up for you so you can focus on your bakery."

"I know," Ally said. "The only thing that makes me feel better is knowing you guys won't stop until things are back to normal. Not that Carter isn't great. But you guys get away with things he can't."

"His hands are tied by the law," I agreed.

Gertie nodded. "While ours are loose and just trying to avoid being caught."

Ally smiled. "I would tell you not to take risks on my account, but I know it's a waste of time. So I'll just say be careful. Whoever is behind this—whatever this is—has killed one person and just tried to kill another."

"Or the guy who got shot tonight killed Miles and someone else took a shot at him," I said.

Ally shook her head. "I really don't want to process two killers. I'll leave all the elaborate plans with multiple bad guys to you."

I pulled out my phone and passed it around for everyone to see the man again. They all studied it, sometimes enlarging the view, but ultimately, they all shook their heads.

"There's something," Ida Belle said. "But I can't quite place it."

Gertie nodded. "I know I've seen him somewhere before, but I also know it's not right."

"What do you mean?" I asked.

"Like, it's someone I've seen but something's different," she said. "Aside from age, because I guarantee you, the faint glimmer that I get is from some time ago."

"I agree," Ida Belle said.

"He doesn't look familiar at all to me," Ally said.

"That's not surprising," I said. "If it's someone who hasn't been seen around here for decades, then you would have been really young or maybe not even born then."

"There's something about his eyes, I think," Gertie said. "That's what I keep going back to."

"Then maybe it's not necessarily that you know him but you know a relative," I said, an idea forming. "When it's a decent time tomorrow morning, we'll go show this to Emmaline."

"Why Emmaline?" Gertie asked. "She's at least a couple years younger than us."

Ida Belle snorted.

"Because she's an artist," I said. "She's trained to notice things like eyes and might be able to tell us if anyone in town is a match."

"Oh, that's smart!" Gertie said. "So what do we do now?"

"Go to bed," I said. "I know it's late—or early—but we haven't slept worth crap lately and if I'm going to be creeping around behind buildings when shooting breaks out, I prefer to be in top form."

"She's right," Ida Belle said. "It's not going to be easy, but we all need to give it a go. Especially you, Gertie. That leg isn't going to heal with you walking around on it."

Gertie grumbled a bit and watching her attempts to use the crutches was somewhat painful, but she refused any help and finally managed to limp out. I locked the door behind them, turned on the alarm system, and looked over at Ally.

"Let's try this again," I said.

"Maybe we'll get lucky," Ally said as we headed upstairs. "Maybe he'll live and tell Carter what's going on."

"Maybe," I said, but I wasn't feeling optimistic about his survival chances or his willingness to talk. He had to have seen the security camera but chose to attempt to break in anyway. That showed desperation. And then there was the shooter— did the burglar know he was being followed? If so, it was another risk, going there at night and exposing himself that way.

The only thing I knew for certain was that the shooter wasn't a pro.

A pro would have made the headshot.

———

EMMALINE WAS one of those early-to-rise people, so I knew I didn't have to wait until 'acceptable' visiting hours to go see her. Plus, she was Carter's mother and knew what sort of things we got up to. And since we'd just figured out who'd almost killed her not that long ago, I was sure she'd be happy to help prevent another tragedy, especially as it involved Ally. Ida Belle picked me up and we headed over at 8:00 a.m.

I wasn't sure how I'd managed to do it, but I'd fallen asleep almost right away and had actually made it until 6:00 a.m. It wasn't a stellar amount of time, but it was doable. And I actually felt rested, so that was a bonus. Gertie was moving better, but Ida Belle still insisted on the crutches since she wouldn't go for the walker. She groused about it and didn't put much weight on them, but they were good for balance. The last thing we needed right now was for her to take another fall.

Emmaline was surprised to see us but had clearly been up for some time. She was wearing a sundress and her hair and makeup were already done. Short of the time she'd been in the hospital in a coma, I don't think I'd ever seen Emmaline when she wasn't 'fixed.' I couldn't imagine what she thought of me on that side of things, although she'd made it clear that she thought I was the perfect match for Carter.

"Ladies," she said as she waved us inside. "Let's get Gertie in a chair before she falls over. I saw that video and you're lucky you weren't killed. Now, what in the world is going on that you need me first thing in the morning? Because I know you're not here for my cooking when Ally is ensconced in Fortune's house. Whatever it is, I just made a fresh pot of coffee, so have a seat and I'll get it."

We all sat at her kitchen table and waited while she served up the coffee, then sat.

"There was a situation last night," I said and explained what had happened.

"Good Lord," she said when I was done. "What in the world is going on?"

"I wish I knew," I said. "Unfortunately, the three of us are coming up with nothing. All we can presume is one or more people are looking for something Miles had hidden. That's the only theory that works for both the house and the business being broken into."

"But what on earth could he have that's worth killing people over?" she asked.

"Money, drugs, weapons, Francine's banana pudding recipe," I suggested.

"You might be right about that recipe." She sighed. "I know Carter is doing everything he can, and I know the three of you won't quit poking the bull until it charges. And I'm relieved that Ally is safely in your care, but I really wish all this heartache would stop. We need a break."

"In more ways than one," I said. "Which is why we're on your doorstep first thing this morning. We need a break in this case."

Emmaline shook her head. "I don't see how I can help."

"We want you to look at a picture of the guy who got shot last night," I said. "Ida Belle, Gertie, and Carter get a twinge of familiarity but can't pin it down. And all think it's not a recent memory. I suggested that he might have facial features similar to someone local that could be driving that minimal recognition. With you being an artist, you automatically study and categorize those things more so than the average person."

"Oh," she said. "Well, I hadn't thought about it that way, but I suppose you're right. He wasn't...there's no damage to the face, is there?"

"No. He was shot in the back."

"Okay, then go ahead and show me."

I pulled up the photo and handed her the phone. She studied it, then tilted her head to the side, then enlarged the photo and moved it around some, studying all the features. Finally, she gave it back to me.

"I agree that pieces of the image look familiar," she said. "Mostly around the eyes."

"That's what I said!" Gertie exclaimed.

Emmaline nodded. "But what I'm about to say isn't going to help any."

"Why not?" I asked.

"Because those eyes belong to Dinah Benoit."

CHAPTER SEVENTEEN

WE ALL STARED AT EMMALINE, THEN I LOOKED AT THE image again.

"She's right," I said. "I didn't even catch it and I was just talking to the woman yesterday."

"But that's not possible," Ida Belle said. "Bart died over a decade ago, and Dinah didn't have any other children or brothers or sisters."

"I know," Emmaline said. "Which is why I said it wouldn't help. But the familiarity you're seeing is Dinah. I have no doubt about that."

"Oh, I'm not doubting you either," Ida Belle said. "And now that you've pointed it out, it's clear."

Gertie nodded. "Maybe Dinah had a child we don't know about...maybe before she came to Sinful."

"And her husband didn't know either?" I asked. "From what I learned from you, this guy is the right age to be her son. Could she have had another baby that close in age and her husband not noticed? Because he doesn't sound like the kind of guy who would have gone for a woman with a kid."

"Unless she gave him away?" Gertie suggested.

I shook my head. "I think it's far more likely that Bart Benoit isn't dead. At least, not yet."

"I attended his funeral," Ida Belle said. "And I can't fathom that Dinah's grief wasn't real. I saw it firsthand. Why would someone tell her that her child died if he didn't?"

"Because that child wanted to disappear?" I suggested. "Maybe he got into trouble with the law and death was the easy way out. Or worse, got in with the wrong people and death was an eventuality unless he took matters into his own hands."

"He was breaking into a building," Gertie said. "That lends credence to the criminal element theory. But why come back now?"

"Maybe he was into something with Miles," I said. "Or Jasper for all we know."

"Well, what the heck do we do now?" Ida Belle said. "We can't stroll over to Dinah's house and flash a potential picture of her dead son, then tell her he just got shot during the commission of a crime and might die again."

"This is what I'd call a real mess," Emmaline agreed.

"Mess doesn't cover the half of it," I said. "But on this one, we don't have to do anything but wait."

"We're not going to tell Carter what we know?" Gertie asked.

I shook my head. "If that man is Bart Benoit, his prints will pop because he was military. Carter will know for sure, if he doesn't already. Then notification is on him, and he won't be happy if we jump the gun. We just need to wait until he's performed his duties, then we can follow up."

———

WHEN WE LEFT EMMALINE'S, we headed for the café to get some breakfast and see if there was any loose talk. I didn't really expect much yet, given that only a handful of people knew what had occurred, but things had a way of leaping from paramedic or nurse to their sister to their brother's cousin to their neighbor and eventually everyone knew the major points. The story had usually grown in drama, so sometimes you had to cut through the weeds a bit to get to the real dirt.

In this case, I didn't need the dirt as I'd been standing on it myself. But I was curious to hear the speculation as to who the man might be and what he might have been doing. Unfortunately, the local population seemed to be at as big a loss as we were, and we finished up breakfast and headed out for our appointment with Cara, no closer to a guess than before we'd gone into the café.

"That was somewhat disappointing," I said as we climbed into Ida Belle's SUV. "Not the breakfast part but the lack of creativity on behalf of the residents of Sinful."

"This one does seem to have everyone stumped," Gertie said.

"That and they were all too interested in talking about your latest YouTube appearance," Ida Belle said.

My cell phone rang.

"It's Carter," I said as I answered. "You're on speaker with Ida Belle and Gertie. How's our burglar doing?"

"Still holding on but in a coma. Doctors are giving him a fifty-fifty chance at survival, but they aren't even talking about what surviving might look like."

"Then I guess it's too much to ask for him to confess so you can wrap this up."

"Probably so, but I'm about to break protocol and give you some information that I'm not supposed to. It's going to come out soon, but I'm hoping the Troublesome Twosome might be able to help with this one."

"You found out our burglar is Bart Benoit," I said.

There was dead silence and then Carter cursed.

"Where did you get that information?" he asked.

"Your mother. I showed her the photo because I figured with her being an artist, she'd recognize body features and be able to place them on a relative. She recognized the eyes as Dinah Benoit's."

"I waited all this time for a fingerprint match to come back, and all I had to do was ask my mother?"

"Apparently, although the fingerprints are likely to stand up better with the DA than 'my mother said so.' Unfortunately, I don't think we're going to be any help. None of us has any idea why Bart has returned from the dead or why he was pretending."

He sighed. "I figured that was what you were going to say. Good Lord, how do I tell Dinah that her dead son is actually alive but might die again? This is not what I signed up for. There's Sinful weird and then there's this—weird and awful."

"I'm really sorry you're in this position," I said. "I can't even imagine."

"I'm going to put some feelers out," Ida Belle said. "I'll let you know if I hear any scuttlebutt, but honestly, I'm not expecting any."

"Me either," Gertie said. "Bart was one of those kids that just cruised through school under the radar of teachers, bullies, and most everyone else. He was quiet, passed everything, never caused a raised eyebrow, graduated, and was gone."

"Yeah," Carter said. "I don't really remember him but then I was a kid when he went into the military, and I didn't spend much time thinking about adults unless they were calling me down for something."

"Is there anything we can do regarding Dinah?" Gertie asked.

"I guess you could do one of your casserole runs after I talk to her," he said. "She will probably need the company. And someone to talk this out with."

"And maybe she'll tell us something that she doesn't want to tell you," Ida Belle said.

"Always a possibility that a woman would rather confide in other women, especially women from her same generation," he said. "I'll let you know after I've spoken with her. Unless you have unearthed any more clues, I've got to go meet with the forensics team and see if they found anything."

"We are completely out of clues," I said. "And overwhelmed with bodies. I prefer the other way around."

"Me too," he said and disconnected.

Ida Belle pulled up at the curb of the house Miles was renting and I spotted Cara's car in the drive. We headed up the walk and helped Gertie up the steps while Cara scrutinized her use of the crutches.

"Ms. Hebert, you might want to wait in the front room," Cara said. "It's going to be hard for you to get around in there."

Ida Belle scanned the front of the house as if she were actually interested. "No garage?"

Cara shook her head. "All the bedrooms were on the second floor, so the owner enclosed it to create a master suite on the first floor."

Cara unlocked the front door and paused.

"I know I warned you about the condition," she said, "but I feel I have to do it again. The place is really a mess. It's going to take so much money to fix this that I'm wondering if this is the thing that finally gets the heirs to sell. If that happens, I won't be relisting it as a rental, but I can try to help your friend find something else."

Ida Belle nodded. "That's fine. And if the heirs decide to sell, let me know. I might want to pick it up at a significant discount, handle the repairs myself, and then either flip it or rent it myself."

Cara perked up a bit at the potential of continued business, then stepped back and waved us in. As we walked inside, Gertie gasped. Cara hadn't been lying. The place was trashed.

"I tried to warn you," Cara said, looking contrite.

Ida Belle waved a hand at her. "You told us just fine. But it's still a bit shocking to see the extent of the damage."

Cara nodded and sniffed, and I wondered if she was going to cry. "I just don't understand why anyone would do this. I get that the house was outdated but in a charming way. I don't even know if those old moldings can be saved."

I looked around what was probably the living room with what had likely served as an office off the side of it. The drywall had been torn out every couple feet, the ceiling contained the same damage, and pieces of the floor had been ripped out and the subfloor beneath littered with holes.

"Is every room like this?" I asked.

Cara was apparently too upset over the house to be miffed at my being there because she just nodded.

"The kitchen is actually a little worse," she said as she started down the hall.

Ida Belle motioned to Gertie to stay put and for once, Gertie didn't argue. Playing hopscotch with crutches would likely get her benched for the day, so she wasn't taking any chances.

"They pulled out the appliances but didn't unscrew them first and most of the cabinets have been ripped out," Cara said as we walked. "The bathrooms are just as bad. They even knocked the surround out of the tubs. Some of that tile had historical significance and none of it can be matched. The whole thing is just sad."

I was a little surprised to see this other side of Cara. I knew she did well as a Realtor, but I hadn't taken her for someone who was actually into her product. But based on her obvious emotions about the destruction, it was clear she had a lot of respect and knowledge of older architecture and building materials.

"When was the last time you were here?" I asked. "I mean, before this happened?"

"Thursday evening," she said. "I didn't have another showing until Sunday morning and since no other agents had shown it since then, I assumed everything was still as I'd left it."

"That's a lot of damage in a short amount of time," I said.

"How did they get in?" Ida Belle asked.

"I'm not sure," Cara said. "Carter said there was no sign of a break-in."

"Did he say anything else?" Ida Belle asked.

Cara shook her head. "I guess it's just vandals, but I don't know why they picked this house. There's several others empty in town at the moment and even more outside of town. I would think it's far less risky to tear up something out in the middle of the marsh or the woods rather than doing it right here where someone might see or hear."

"And did anyone?" I asked as we started a tour of the rest of the rooms.

"Not that Carter could find," she said. "None of the neighbors have security cameras either. This used to not be that kind of place, you know? But between this and what happened to Ally, I'm going to get my house outfitted as soon as I can."

Ida Belle gave her a sad nod.

Cara tried to pull herself together by the end of the tour but I could tell that walking through the house had depressed her. Ida Belle took some information from her and told her to call as soon as she knew what decision the heirs made. Cara said a quiet goodbye and headed for her car. We climbed in Ida Belle's SUV and sat for a bit as she drove away.

"She's really upset," I said.

"I can't blame her," Gertie said. "What was done to that house was awful. Could one person do all that damage in two days?"

"I suppose, but they'd be hammering and sawing," I said. "How did someone not hear all that?"

Ida Belle had been staring at the house next door, then pointed to the roof, which had a bright blue tarp covering it, and a fence that was partially finished.

"Maybe they didn't do it at night," she said as she started up the SUV. "Maybe they did it during the day, using the construction next door to hide the sound. And with the house being unoccupied, even if people realized sound was coming from here, they might have figured some repairs were being made."

"Talk about ballsy," Gertie said as we drove off.

I shook my head. It was ingenious but risky as heck.

What in the world was worth all that risk?

"We're not giving any credence to the vandal theory, are we?" Gertie asked.

"No," I said. "And I'm guaranteeing you that Carter isn't either. If it was vandals, the damage wouldn't have been so repetitive and deliberate. And think about it, not a single window was knocked out. Nothing spray-painted on the walls."

Ida Belle nodded. "The way the walls, ceiling, and floors were cut, it definitely looked like they were searching for something. The cuts were spaced just far enough apart to give them access to check for anything hidden."

I nodded. "I think our original theory is sound—either Miles or Jasper had something hidden and someone else is looking for it."

"And they're willing to kill for it," Gertie said.

"I think we should swing by the bank and ask my friend about those bills," Ida Belle said. "Money is the most logical guess at the moment since we found those bills with the body and they were old issue."

"Sounds good to me," I said. "I don't suppose you've had any takers on your information request on Bart?"

"Not so much as a peep," Ida Belle said. "I was afraid that might be the case."

"At some point after Carter has informed Dinah of her son's resurrection, we need to revisit with her," I said. "But before we do, I'd like to talk to Sharon Parker. Bart faked his death for some reason, and if Sharon's mother was around Dinah a lot, maybe Sharon overheard things."

Gertie nodded. "Kids hear everything. They just don't always realize what it means."

"Exactly," I said. "I don't know that anything she remembers will necessarily help us with the case, but she might be able to shed some light on Bart, in general. He returned here for a reason, and I don't think the timing is a coincidence. Something was going on with one or both of the men who owned the cleaner's after Dinah."

"But what did they have to do with Bart?" Gertie asked.

"I don't know," I said. "But he knows something. The question is, will he talk when he wakes up? *If* he wakes up."

"Given that the man faked dying to get away from this town, I doubt he's going to just offer up why he returned," Ida Belle said.

"Especially if he's the one who killed Miles and attacked Ally," Gertie said.

"Maybe we'll get an answer to one of the questions here," I said as Ida Belle pulled into the bank parking lot.

We headed inside, and Ida Belle waved at a pretty young woman sitting in a glass office. I recognized her as Felicia Woods, one of the assistant managers who'd helped me open my bank accounts once I was the real me. She smiled and came out to clasp Ida Belle's hand.

"It's so good to see you up and around after that horrible boat incident, Ms. Gertie," she said, then turned to me. "And Ms. Redding. I'm almost afraid to ask what brings the three of you into the bank today."

"That's because you know us," Gertie said, and she laughed as we followed her into her office and took seats.

"We came across something odd during one of our investigations," Ida Belle said. "And even though it's not really related to the work we were hired to do, we got intrigued and I thought you might be able to help us out."

"Now I'm intrigued," Felicia said.

"It was some old bills," Ida Belle said. "I'm talking should-have-been-retired old. And we had some beers and got into some creative thinking and wanted to know if you could run a couple of them in that database you guys have."

Her eyes widened. "For stolen money? Wow! That would be something. Do you have the bills with you?"

"No," Ida Belle said. "I only have pictures. They were part of the evidence so they had to be turned over to the police. Like I said, it's not really part of our case anymore, but curiosity and cats and all."

"I can work with pictures," she said. "Just as long as you don't tell anyone I did this. I'm not sure on the rules given that the bills are part of a police investigation. Regardless, I don't want to get on Carter's bad side. He's let me off of speeding violations too many times and since I have a lead foot, I'd like to stay in his good graces."

I passed her my cell phone with the shots.

"Trust me, the last people who will tell Carter when we're poking our nose into his business is us," I said.

She laughed as she looked at the pictures and typed. "Yes, I guess dating him would give you more to lose, right?"

"I'd definitely get more grief than a speeding ticket," I said.

Her computer beeped and Felicia stared at the screen, frowning at first, then her eyes widened. "Oh my God," she said.

"I take it you got a hit?" Ida Belle asked.

She nodded. "Let me just run this other one." She tapped furiously on the keyboard and a few seconds later, another beep.

"I can't believe it," she said. "These bills were part of a huge heist of Bayou Bank & Trust in New Orleans. The robbers got away with over a hundred thousand dollars."

"That's a big take, isn't it?" I asked. "I didn't think banks stored that much cash anymore."

"They don't," Felicia said. "But this was thirty years ago, and Bayou Bank & Trust was the holding company for all the Louisiana branches. The overflow of cash was taken there, then transferred to their vaults."

"Did they catch the robbers?" I asked.

"No," Gertie said. "I remember this case. Probably everyone around here over the age of forty does. It was on the news for weeks. The police suspected it was an inside job because that amount of cash was never in the bank for more than twenty-four hours and the day varied."

"Was any employee ever indicted?" I asked.

"They looked hard at the bank manager," Ida Belle said. "I

remember that much but not anything else. It was on the news every day for weeks but then when the cops couldn't come up with anything, it eventually faded away."

"I guess thirty years ago, it would have been easier to launder the money," I said.

"Easier, yes, but not simple," Felicia said. "It's true that the databases were nothing like today. A lot of things were still being done by hand and if the bills were distributed throughout the public, then they could have wandered into anyone's grasp, really. But that's about the time that the databases started to get updated and shared more, and I'm sure this case would have been one of the first loaded and shared given the size of the job."

"Well, that's sort of exciting," Gertie said. "We've never been involved with a bank robbery. You know what I mean."

"Neither have I," Felicia said. "Promise me that once this is all said and done with the cops, and it won't get you into trouble, you'll fill me in."

We promised her we'd be back if or when we could tell her anything, then headed out.

CHAPTER EIGHTEEN

"So what do we make of that?" Ida Belle asked as we pulled away from the bank.

"I'm not sure what to make of it," I said. "It's possible to get hold of some stolen bills if they were put out there. It's kind of odd to have them thirty years after the fact because bills that old are usually taken out of circulation in half that time due to wear and tear. But then, there are people who keep cash stuffed in their mattresses as their retirement plan, so anything is possible."

Gertie nodded. "It's possible one of the suspicious old coots around here hauled out some money from their stash to pay for something. Miles sold most everything off before he moved. He could have gotten hold of the bills that way."

"It's certainly possible, but that wouldn't have gotten him killed." Ida Belle said.

"Are you going to tell Carter?" Gertie asked.

"Yes," I said. "I'm sure he'll run the bills but he has a lot of other things to manage as well, so I think we need to give him a heads-up on this so he can start collecting information about that robbery. I'll text him the info."

"So I guess we have to look into the bank robbery now," Ida Belle said. "I swear, this case has us checking out distant possibilities but nothing concrete."

I nodded. "It does seem like everything points to the fringe."

"Lots of stuff can collect in the fringe," Gertie said.

"Well, let's talk to Sharon first," I said. "Then if we haven't heard anything from Carter regarding Dinah, we can head back to my house and dive into this bank robbery. Hopefully we can find some stuff online. If not, we might have to make a drive to NOLA and dig through the newspaper archives."

"Sharon's a nurse at the hospital," Gertie said. "Let me call and see if she's at work."

Gertie got hold of Sharon, who was, indeed, at work. But she was taking her lunch break in thirty minutes and said if we could make it there by then to meet her in the cafeteria. We headed out and pulled up in front of the hospital with minutes to spare. Which was a good thing because I'd forgotten about Gertie's less-than-stellar pace.

"Those crutches aren't going to cut it for this," Ida Belle said as Gertie teetered, trying to gain her balance, then managed one tiny step forward.

A nurse rushed out of the ER entrance with a wheelchair and hurried over. "Ma'am, please sit down. We don't want you to get a bigger injury before the doctor sees you."

"You don't have to worry about that, because the doctor's not going to see me," Gertie said.

The nurse stared, completely confused, and Ida Belle chimed in.

"We're here to meet a friend," Ida Belle said. "This one has already refused treatment, so we're just tolerating her stubbornness by walking like turtles."

Clearly not convinced, the nurse shook her head. "Well, do

you want to borrow this while you're here? I'll need it back, but we have a couple more."

Gertie was shaking her head when Ida Belle pointed at the chair. "Climb in. The cafeteria is on the other side of the building and with the construction, I can't park any closer than this."

"I don't need a wheelchair," Gertie argued.

"If we want to make this meeting you do," Ida Belle said. "It's this, or you wait in the car. But either way, Fortune and I are not missing this."

"Fine," Gertie groused and plopped into the chair.

I thanked the nurse and grabbed the chair and pushed it into the building and into the maze of hallways that would lead us to the other side. We were only a couple minutes late and Ida Belle pointed out a pleasant-looking woman with a sandwich, sitting in a back corner of the cafeteria.

Late forties. Five foot five. A hundred sixty pounds. Solid arms and back—probably from lifting patients. Likely deadly with a needle but no immediate threat when armed with what looked like turkey and cheese on wheat.

She looked up as we approached and her eyes widened when she locked in on the wheelchair. She dropped her sandwich and jumped up.

"Ms. Hebert, are you all right?" she asked as she hurried over.

"I'm fine," Gertie said. "I just wrenched my leg a bit and we had to park on the other end of the hospital. These two didn't want to miss your lunch hour, so I agreed to this indignity."

Sharon's lips quivered as she sat back down. "Well, I wish I had someone pushing me around. Lord, what a shift here does to your feet."

Ida Belle introduced me to Sharon and she nodded. "I've heard a lot about you—I'm sure a lot is exaggerated."

"I wouldn't bet on it," I said, and Sharon laughed.

"I don't suppose you're working the ER?" Ida Belle asked. Sharon nodded.

"Have you seen the guy who came in with the gunshot wound?" Ida Belle asked.

An angry look flashed across Sharon's face. "You mean Bart Benoit?"

We stared.

"You know who he is?" I asked.

"I spent enough time over at his house when I was a kid," Sharon said. "And I've got a good memory for faces. It's what makes me an excellent nurse. I remember my patients and every ailment I've seen them for. Oh, he tried to change things up, but that man is Bart Benoit."

"What do you mean by change things up?" Gertie asked.

"Plastic surgery," she said. "He's had a nose job and a cheek and chin implant. The surgical scars are easy enough to locate if you know what you're looking for."

"That explains why you guys didn't recognize him right away," I said. "You've got an *excellent* memory for faces, Sharon."

She looked pleased with the compliment. "When I first saw him, I thought, no way in hell, right? Then I eased his shoulder up a bit and there was that heart-shaped mole. I knew I was right. But how did you guys find out?"

"Well, I caught him on security camera behind some buildings downtown and went to check things out," I said. "He got shot before I could confront him about lurking around. I took a picture but since Ida Belle and Gertie didn't recognize him, we took it to Emmaline."

Sharon nodded. "That's smart. An artist of Emmaline's skill would catalog things differently than most people. I assume Carter ran prints and has confirmed this?"

"Yes, but that information hasn't been released," I said. "He doesn't want it public until he can talk to Dinah."

"Of course." The angry look returned. "What is wrong with that man? Like his poor mother hasn't been through enough in her life. Why would he do this to her?"

"We don't know," I said. "We were hoping you might be able to tell us more about Dinah and Bart. I understand your mother was Dinah's best friend."

"Her only friend, truth be told," Sharon said. "Dinah wasn't one to mingle. She was an introvert and said she didn't see the point in flitting around town doing things. I suppose given how things have gone with her back, it's just as well she wasn't a social butterfly."

"Can't miss what you never had," Gertie said. "I'm going the other direction. Do everything and miss it all. But the memories will be awesome."

"And with so many of them on YouTube, even future generations can relive the horror of some of your decisions," Ida Belle said dryly.

"How did they become friends?" I asked.

"My mother babysat for her," Sharon said. "Until Bart started school and they had an after-school program for him to stay in. She sat for several families over the years, but Dinah was different. They clicked for whatever reason even though they didn't have much in common."

"Sometimes the differences are the reason for the clicking."

"That could be true. Can I ask why you want to know about Dinah and Bart?"

"You heard about Miles Broussard being murdered, right?"

She nodded.

"And then there was a break-in at the building and Ally was attacked," I said.

She frowned. "Yes, but what does that have to do with Bart being alive? You think all those things are connected?"

"Well, they all seem to center on the dry cleaner's, or at least the building where the dry cleaner's was located," I said. "Obviously, I never knew Dinah, and it sounds like she was so private that most people didn't know her well. I'm just trying to fill in all the backstory, especially now that her son has returned from the grave and went straight to the dry cleaner's and got shot there."

Sharon shook her head. "I guess when you think about it, the whole thing does seem to be wound around in the same weird tangled ball. Well, I have no idea if I can help but I'm happy to tell you anything I know. Dinah is going to be devastated by this, and I want whatever is going on stopped before someone else winds up hurt or dead."

"What can you tell me about Dinah's husband?" I asked.

Her eyes widened. "Bertrand? I can't tell you a whole lot as I was only seven when he died. He was a commercial fisherman. Usually on the Gulf when we went to visit Dinah, so I wasn't around him much. When he was there, he was the give-you-a-nod type, then he'd disappear in his shop, usually with a beer in his hand."

"How was the marriage?" I asked.

"Oh, well, I was just a little girl then, so that's not the kind of thing I would have paid attention to."

"Yes, but you're an adult now and have an excellent memory, so I'm guessing some things fell into perspective over the years."

"Or your mother mentioned things after the fact," Gertie said.

She pursed her lips and stared at the table for a bit.

"You're not betraying anything by telling us your thoughts," Ida Belle said.

She sighed. "I guess I just don't see how this could help, but I told you I'd do anything, so here goes—the truth is, I was afraid of Bertrand. He never did anything to me or in front of me to make me feel that way, but every time he was around, I just had this overwhelming urge to flee. I know that sounds like little-girl drama, but I promise you, I don't have an ounce of drama in me, or I couldn't have worked the ER all these years. I was one of those scary practical kids."

"Do you think he was abusive?" Gertie asked.

"I'm sure of it," she said. "Mom hinted at such but wouldn't specify even when I got older and pushed for more. I do remember that Dinah sometimes had bruises on her arms. She wore long sleeves a lot, even when it was hot as heck. We'd stop by and she'd come out of that barn wearing long sleeves and sweatpants when it had to be a hundred degrees closed up in there. But a couple times, we caught her working in her garden wearing a T-shirt and I saw bruises. I remember my mom asking and her saying she'd had this accident or that one. I never thought much of it at the time because I was a rough-and-tumble sort of kid and always had a bruise somewhere."

Gertie nodded. "When you're young, you have this idea that everyone is doing the same things you're doing and with the same result."

Ida Belle looked at her with raised eyebrows. "Some *old* people are still doing the same things with the same results."

"So now that you've aged, you think differently?" I asked.

"I do," Sharon said. "I never saw anything that looked like a punch, you know? No black eyes. No spots that would have indicated a hard strike from a solid surface. But the marks on her arms looked like fingerprints. The first time I got an abuse victim in the ER, I saw those same marks and I had a flash of memory back to standing in Dinah's garden and her weak answer about how she got them. God knows, I've seen them far too many times in here—on kids and women. I know what I'm looking at now."

"I'm sure you do," I said. "And I seriously doubt those fingerprints were the extent of the damage. You probably just couldn't see the rest of it. What about Bart? Was he abused as well?"

She blew out a breath. "That's a tough one. He was a boy, and he was a typical Sinful boy—always out in the bayou or the woods or falling out of a tree—but he was also a few years older than me and at that age, a few years is a lot. Mom was keeping another girl my age after school when she kept Bart, and no way was he interested in playing little-girl games so we didn't interact all that much. When Mom and I visited when I was older, he usually made himself scarce. No boy wants to hear a bunch of hens talking, but he'd hang around long enough for my mother's cookies to come out. If his dad was there, I never saw him, and if his dad showed up, Bart disappeared like the wind."

"So what you're telling me is that no one was overwhelmed with loss when Bertrand died," I said.

"I don't know that I saw either of them shed a tear," Sharon said. "A lot of people don't cry at funerals—it's just their way—but my mom was around a lot right after to look in on Dinah and to help her with meals and around the house. She never so much as sniffled. I remember asking my mom about it at the time and she just told me that Dinah was tough and everyone grieved their own way. When I got older, I realized my mom probably suspected it was more of a relief than anything."

"Too bad Bertrand didn't do them all a favor and die sooner," Gertie said.

Sharon choked on her soda. "Oh my God, the things you say, Ms. Hebert. Not that I disagree, mind you. Still, it wasn't easy on Dinah, keeping the business going and getting Bart through school, plus finishing that old wreck of a house they lived in."

"We were just over there yesterday and it was really nice," I said. "I guess she managed to get it all fixed eventually."

"It took years and she wouldn't let us help—my mom always offered," Sharon said. "She always said she'd pay contractors and do it a little at a time. Every time we visited something else had been upgraded. It took a while, but it is a really pretty place."

"Do you see her much anymore?" Gertie asked.

She shook her head. "I tried to keep up visits after Mom passed, but when I took that job with the hospital in New Orleans and had my own kids, I'd find it had been weeks since I'd even called. And I noticed the times I did make the trip to Sinful to see her that she didn't really seem to want me there. She wasn't rude at all, but she didn't appear to get anything out of my visits. Until last week, I'd been on the night shift for three months and never could get my sleeping right. It's been that long or better since I've been by."

"What can you tell me about Bart?" I asked.

"Probably as much as I can about Bertrand," Sharon said. "I didn't really hang out with him. Too much age difference and Bart didn't really go in for parties or school events. He went into the military right after high school and we all figured he'd make a career out of staying overseas given that it was as far from Sinful as he could get. Then he got that discharge—something to do with his knee maybe—and he was back home for a couple years. He worked on the rigs during that time, then took off for Alaska, saying he had a good offer to work on the pipeline up there. I don't think he visited but maybe once. Then one day, Dinah tells Mom he was killed."

"Who contacted Dinah?" I asked.

"Someone from the company, I think."

"And obviously, they didn't forward the body."

"No. They claimed the accident was a bad one and a viewing wasn't an option. They suggested cremating him there and sending her the ashes. She told my mom there was an insurance check for twenty thousand. Probably the base amount the company took out on employees, but now that we know it's all a lie, that seems really odd."

"How was Dinah's relationship with her son?" I asked.

"It was obvious it wasn't great even before he died, or faked his death I should say. He was always well mannered and when he came back from the military for that bit, he'd check on her to see if there was something he could do, but he didn't live with her for more than a couple weeks. As soon as he picked up a job, he moved to a garage apartment in town. I ran into him a handful of times at her house back then. Sometimes he seemed caring and then other times, I'd see him eyeing her like there was something whirling in the back of his mind that he didn't like."

"He might have been trying to settle on his own feelings about the matter," Gertie said. "It's hard to be an abused child and watch your mother's abuse as well. There's this whole other part where you're sad for her that she was being abused but also mad at her for *allowing* it to happen to you. I would imagine it's hard to find a balance there."

"I think you're right," Sharon said. "And it looked to me that while Bart cared about his mother, his solution to dealing with those feelings was to care from a distance. At least, that's what I used to think. Now I just can't even imagine. I mean, I can get harboring some resentment for the way he was treated by his father, but faking your own death is beyond the pale."

"It does seem an extreme response just for holding a grudge against your mother," I said. "I have to think there's more to it than that, especially as he's returned. Was Bart ever in any trouble?"

Her eyes widened. "You mean with the law? No. Not that I ever heard of. But then, I guess we don't know what he got up to overseas with the military or in Alaska. Can I ask what you think is going on?"

"I wish I knew," I said. "But I'm as confused by it all as you are."

"Do you think Dinah's in danger?" she asked.

"I don't have a reason to believe she is, but I didn't have a reason to believe Ally was, either," I said. "Until we figure out what's going on, I think it's possible, at minimum, for people to be in the wrong place at the wrong time."

Sharon frowned. "I don't like her living out in the middle of nowhere and all alone. And with her mobility issues, she'd be hard-pressed to make a retreat if something were to happen."

"She has a good security system," I said. "I noticed it when we visited. Hopefully she's smart enough to carry a phone or remote alarm button on her at all times. Does she have a firearm?"

Sharon laughed. "Everyone in Sinful over the age of five has a firearm. But yes, I know she keeps a gun in the house. Said she's had to run coyotes away from her chickens."

Sharon glanced at her watch. "I'm sorry, ladies, but I need to head back to my shift. Is there anything else?"

I looked over at Ida Belle and Gertie, who shook their heads.

"Well, if you have any other questions, just give me a call," she said. "I wish I knew something that would help."

"I appreciate you talking to us," I said. "I think Carter was going to inform Dinah about Bart sometime today, so if you'd just wait to see her until after..."

"Of course," Sharon said. "Honestly, I dread that visit. I have no idea what I'm supposed to say, and Hallmark hasn't made a card that covers this one."

"They should start a 'sorry your kid's a butthole' line of sympathy cards," Gertie said. "Would probably do well."

Sharon nodded. "Based on the things I've seen in the ER, you have no idea."

She hurried off and I looked at Ida Belle and Gertie. "I'm not sure if that helped at all."

Ida Belle shrugged. "It confirmed our abuse suspicions and explains why Bart was so dead set on leaving Sinful and didn't bother to visit much."

"But it doesn't explain why a company would say he died when he didn't," Gertie said.

"Because it probably wasn't the company who called Dinah," I said. "If Bart was serious about disappearing forever, then he could have gotten a friend to do it."

"And the insurance check?" Gertie asked. "That's a lot of scratch."

"He had a lot of years to put it together," I said.

"And it made the whole thing more legit," Ida Belle said.

"But why go to all that trouble?" Gertie asked. "He left for Alaska and only came back once. It's not like he was required to visit. Why go to the trouble and expense to fake his death?"

"That part might have had nothing to do with anything here," I said. "My guess is he got into trouble there, and since he didn't have much of a relationship with his mother anyway, this was the best way to disappear permanently and make it look really legit. She had a funeral service for him, right? And people know she got a check from an insurance company. If he was in deep with the wrong element, that's more than enough evidence of death for them to focus their attention elsewhere."

"So we'd also have to assume he moved at that point," Gertie said. "So where's he been all this time?"

I shook my head. "Maybe Carter can find out. But in the meantime, the number one question is still why he's back in Sinful. Because clearly, he never meant to return."

CHAPTER NINETEEN

WE SPENT WHAT WAS LEFT OF THE AFTERNOON AND INTO the evening researching the bank robbery, but I wasn't sure it forwarded the case any. The general talk was that there had to be inside knowledge, but the Feds hadn't been able to make anything stick on the employees, so it was just speculation. Likely good speculation, but with no proof to back it up, it didn't matter how logical it was.

Ida Belle and Gertie headed out fairly early, arguing over whether or not Gertie needed to sit in another ice bath, and Ally and I had some dinner and settled in for a marathon night of television. We were in the middle of a late-night snack when someone knocked on my kitchen door. Since Mannie always let himself in and Gertie and Ida Belle had a key and came in the front, I figured it was either Ronald or Carter. I wasn't sure which one would take more energy to deal with at the moment, but at least Carter wouldn't stress us out with his wardrobe choices, so I was leaning toward hoping it was him.

I peered out the blinds and Carter waved.

He walked in and slumped into a chair, looking beat. Until he saw the cookies. Then he perked up.

"I don't suppose you have another serving of those for a poor, overworked detective?" he asked.

I shook my head and grabbed him a beer from the fridge while Ally put together a plate of cookies.

"I know you invest everything and your house is paid for," I said, "so I'd argue the poor comment. Overworked, I'll give you. This week anyway."

"So I found out some information this evening and against my better judgment, I'm going to tell you," he said. "But you can't tell anyone except the Troublesome Twosome."

"Scout's honor," I said.

"You weren't a scout," he said.

"So I swear on Ally's baked goods," I said.

"Trust me," Ally said, "she thinks my baked goods are spiritual."

"Miles Broussard was a petty criminal," he said. "He's had multiple arrests for everything from jaywalking to fencing stolen goods. He's only ever held minimum wage jobs and rarely for very long. I swear the guy must have been arrested every time he committed a crime because he's spent a ton of time in jail, and some of his arrests were due to his beyond-stupid choices. He's no criminal mastermind, that's for sure."

"So how did he buy the dry cleaner's?" I asked.

"Good question. According to his bank records, which usually showed an overdrawn account before purchasing the cleaner's, fifty grand was dumped in there a week before closing."

"Where did it come from?"

He shrugged. "Can't trace it. It came from a foreign bank account and they won't disclose. He is originally from France, so I suppose it's possible he inherited something from a relative over there."

"But not overly likely," I said.

"I definitely wouldn't bet on it," he said. "After purchasing the dry cleaner's, he regularly shifted money from the dry cleaner's account to his own."

"How much?" I asked.

"Nothing that would raise eyebrows," he said. "Looked like he was moving the profits. No other big deposits on record but he wasn't a big spender either, so he had put together five thousand in his checking and had twenty thousand in his savings account before selling the building to Ally for thirty thousand."

"That doesn't seem like a lot to retire on," I said. "It's not like he was anywhere near Social Security age."

"Maybe he wasn't going to retire," Carter said. "Maybe he was going to move to Florida and take up his old profession again. At least he'd amassed some bail money."

"Did you find where he was moving to?" I asked.

He nodded. "He'd signed a lease on a condo near Orlando. It overlooked a lake, and the rent was way higher than I'd take Miles for paying."

"Sounds more and more like Miles had a stash somewhere," Ally said.

"Or found a stash somewhere," I said. "The question is where did it come from and where is it now."

Carter nodded. "I also did some background work on Jasper Cummings and found out he doesn't exist."

Ally and I both stared.

"But I did some more digging and found out that Miles did a stint with a Jasper Comeaux, who was in twice for robbery—once at a jewelry store and once at a payday loan place. And there was another arrest for the distribution of stolen money, but he claimed he got the stolen bills from selling an old motorcycle and produced a bill of sale."

"And you think Jasper Cummings was really Jasper Comeaux," I said.

"I'm certain of it," he said and pulled up a picture on his phone. He showed it to Ally and she nodded.

"That's definitely the dry cleaner's Jasper," she said. "Wow! I wonder why theft didn't increase in Sinful while he was living here."

I shook my head. "The dry cleaner's was his cover—he could push stolen cash through as legit. He wouldn't risk stealing in Sinful. Better to do it in bigger cities, probably during those weekend trips he took. For all we know, Miles was up to the same thing, assuming he got better at criminal escapades."

"I agree," Carter said. "Anyway, for the obvious reasons, I can't have this get out. But I wanted you to know, Ally, so you could be certain that the attack on you was a wrong-place-wrong-time thing and not personal. It looks like either Miles or Jasper was hiding something valuable, and someone else is looking for it. They checked the house and have attempted to check the dry cleaner building."

"That does make me feel better," she said. "Fortune kept saying as much, but it's nice to have proof."

"So how does Bart Benoit factor into all of this?" I asked.

"I have no idea," Carter said. "So far, I haven't been able to locate a single thing on Benoit after he left Sinful that second time. I verified his military service dates and his employment with the oil company after he came back home. But I can't find any record of him living in Alaska or working with the pipeline. In fact, I can't find a record of him working anywhere after he left."

"Well, we probably know what that means," I said.

"Shady business," he said. "The problem I'm having is

connecting him to Miles or Jasper. And unless he comes out of that coma and talks, I don't know that I ever will."

"He came home for that one visit right after Dinah sold the dry cleaner's," I said. "So he could have met Jasper then, but a visit seems like a short amount of time to establish a criminal network or even grudges."

"How is Bart doing?" Ally asked.

"About the same," Carter said. "The machines are running the show right now."

"Did you talk to Dinah?" I asked. He'd never contacted me about it and I wondered if he'd withheld that conversation for some reason.

He nodded. "I'm not even a little ashamed to say that I put it off until this afternoon. I've done notifications before, and they're never a good thing, but I went rounds with myself for hours on how to even approach this one. I'm flinging an impossibility, followed by a tragedy, followed by zero answers at this poor woman. They don't train you for this in the military."

"How did she take it?" I asked.

"Let's just say I was glad I had asked the paramedics to stand by," he said. "She collapsed and they had to give her oxygen. Then she insisted on seeing him. I told her it wasn't a good idea. I don't want her hopes up given how bad his chances are, but she insisted. The paramedics drove her so they could continue the oxygen and I followed. She collapsed again when she walked into his room. That was two incidents in less than thirty minutes, so they admitted her. That's why I never called to let you know. She definitely wasn't fit for visitors."

Ally shook her head. "I just can't even imagine."

I remained quiet on that one. I could sort of imagine given that my father had "died" twice now. He'd only come back from the dead once but I figured if I lived long enough, he'd pop up again at some point. Still, your kids weren't supposed to die before you did. But then, they also weren't supposed to fake their own deaths.

"If she's still there tomorrow, maybe we can pay her a visit at the hospital," I said.

Carter nodded. "I don't think there's anything to be gleaned from her necessarily. I think her shock was real, but it wouldn't hurt my case if you talked to her and it would probably help her, so go for it."

He rose from the table. "I better head out. I need to feed Tiny and I still have a ton of things to get into notes tonight while it's all fresh." He pointed a finger at me. "If that alarm goes off or you see anyone on camera downtown, call me. Do *not* head out to the scene of another attempted murder. I can't keep your name out of the official police documents and at some point, people are going to start to wonder."

"It's not like I'm trying to find bodies," I said. "I can't help it if they're attracted to me. I figure it's the universe telling me this is what I'm supposed to do."

He leaned over to kiss me and smiled. "I guess it's better than you attracting other things."

"Like what?" I asked. "Stalkers? Terrorists? Cats? Crazy people?"

He cringed. "Yeah, never mind."

Ally laughed as he left and I locked the door behind him and turned on the alarm because I knew he'd stand out back until he heard it. Ally and I made quick work of the dishes and headed upstairs. I was just about to crawl into bed when I got a text from Ida Belle.

Ida Belle: Walter saw Dirk Richard driving through downtown super late Friday night. Said he wasn't in his Mercedes. It was a late-model blue Ford truck.

Me: He's sure it was Richard?

Ida Belle: Yeah. Walter can't stand him. It's like Gertie seeing Celia.

Me: Then I guess we need to check on Richard tomorrow. Carter told Dinah about Bart and she collapsed. She's stable but they admitted her. We need to talk to her first thing tomorrow, either there or at home if she's been released.

Ida Belle: I'm sorry to hear that but not surprised. Will be there bright and early.

I checked the security cameras at the bakery one last time before turning off the light and crawling into bed. Maybe tomorrow would provide the clue that put all of this together. Because now, more than ever, I wanted answers. For myself. For Miles. For Ally.

And most of all, for Dinah.

————

We met for breakfast at my place. Ally whipped up crepes stuffed with strawberries and cream cheese, and I fried up a pound of bacon and life was really good. Then we had to leave and go to the hospital to talk to Dinah. Ally was headed to the bakery to meet with the contractors.

Dinah was awake when we arrived and a mostly uneaten breakfast was on her tray table. She looked a bit surprised to see us but didn't give off any signs of not wanting us there.

"Carter filled us in," I said. "I hope you don't mind. He thought you might need some support."

"How are you feeling?" Gertie asked.

She shrugged. "All the tests are good except my blood pressure, which is way too high. Lord only knows why that's the case, right?"

"Stands to reason," Ida Belle said. "I know this is probably a pointless question but is there anything we can do?"

Dinah's eyes teared up. "Unless you can tell me whose ashes I have up on my mantel, or why my only child did this to me, then no. Because right now, there's nothing else I want except the answer to those two questions."

Her despair was so palpable that I could feel it, and I desperately wished I had answers even though I figured they wouldn't help as much as she thought.

"We can't help with those questions," I said. "But we're going to try to find out who shot him and why. Maybe that will lead us back to other answers. Or maybe he'll pull through and have to explain himself."

"What the hell explanation is good enough for this?" she asked.

We all shook our heads.

"Do you know his status?" Gertie asked.

"Not good," Dinah said. "The doctor said he has a fifty-fifty chance of pulling through but he's almost certain he will never walk again. He can't say yet about the upper body, but it might be a no-go as well. I have limited mobility, but I can't even fathom having none and then possibly no use of my arms. I just...it's overwhelming to consider."

"Has he regained consciousness?"

She nodded. "After my spell yesterday, they gave me some meds and I rested for a while then asked to see him again. I was sure, but I wasn't...if that makes sense. I had to get a longer look."

"Of course," Ida Belle said.

"I was just standing there staring down at him while the nurse did her thing, and his eyes popped open," Dinah said. "He looked right at me and said, 'I had no choice...you made me—' And then he dropped back unconscious again. What the hell does that mean? He was an adult living in another state. What could I possibly have made him do?"

"Those words could have been the start of most anything," Gertie said. "You made me angry. You made me feel guilty. He's just been shot and he's in critical condition. We don't even know that he's in his right mind."

"But why pretend to die and come back now?" she asked. "What is going on?"

Ida Belle shook her head. "All we know is that Miles must have been up to something. His rental house was trashed, and people keep trying to get into the dry cleaner's building. We have no idea how Bart factors into that, but since he returned and went straight for the cleaner's, we have to assume he's involved somehow."

"But how?" she asked, putting her hands up in the air. "He never had anything to do with that dry cleaner's. He was long gone to Alaska before I sold it to Jasper, and he came back for only one brief visit, and that was after I'd sold. I don't recall him ever meeting Jasper, much less having issues or some collusion or whatever you think is going on. And he'd already faked his death long before Miles appeared. Even if both of them were up to something nefarious, how can Bart be tied up with men he never came in contact with?"

"Maybe he met one of them somewhere other than Sinful," I said. "We don't really know what Bart did after he supposedly died. And neither Miles nor Jasper offered up much to locals about their personal lives, so it's hard to know what they might have been up to as well."

She sighed. "I guess you're right, but I just don't get it. And no matter how hard I try to make sense of it, the only thing I keep coming back to is that my son let me think he was dead."

For the first time in a long time, I couldn't think of a single word to say. There simply weren't any that would help and none would convey my empathy for her despair and outrage.

The only thing I could do was figure out what happened on the likely chance that Bart didn't make it.

"Did you receive a payout from the company?" I asked.

She frowned and nodded. "Good Lord, I hadn't even thought about that part. I got a check for twenty thousand. But if Bart wasn't really dead... Oh my God, did he send that money just so I'd believe it all?"

"Maybe he felt guilty about what he was doing and that was his way of trying to make up for it," Gertie said.

"He *should* feel guilty," Dinah said. "And how in the world would money make up for the death of your child? If it bothered him so much, why do it?"

"Maybe he really didn't think he had a choice," Ida Belle said. "I hate to put it out there, but what if he got caught up with the wrong kind of people and the best way to protect himself, and you, was to no longer exist?"

Dinah stared at her for a bit, then shook her head. "Bart always did struggle with trying to protect me. I'd asked him not to with his father—it only made things worse for him and he was just a little boy—but I could still see the clenched fists and jaw when his father lit into me. I should have done more. I should have left my husband before he started on Bart. I can make excuses and say it wasn't all that easy a thing to do at that time, but that's all it would be, an excuse. Maybe that's what he meant by having no choice. Maybe he couldn't deal with my lack of backbone. How did I do everything so wrong?"

"It was a different time," Ida Belle said. "Communities didn't talk about such things, much less take action against them, so domestic violence victims were very much on their own unless they had family who were paying close attention."

Gertie nodded. "You got past the bad times and managed to raise your boy and run a business, even when your health started to decline. You've got a beautiful home and a nice retirement. I know it doesn't seem like it at this moment, but you're an accomplished woman, Dinah."

"For all the good it's done me," Dinah said quietly.

"Do you remember the name of the company Bart was working for?" I asked.

Dinah was silent for a bit, then finally nodded. "Northern Atlantic Services. I probably still have a copy of the check. I kept everything..."

"When you get a chance, that would be great," I said. "I'm sure Carter would appreciate it as he might be able to do some backtracking through the bank account."

"I'm hoping to get out this evening," she said. "But if they don't cut me loose today, I'm checking myself out tomorrow, even if it's against doctor's orders. Never did like hospitals. Always seen them as places people went to die."

"Well, we're going to get out of here and let you rest," Ida Belle said. "Is there anything we can get for you? Can we bring you anything from your house?"

"I really appreciate the offer, but I'm fine," Dinah said. "There's a woman who does a deep clean for me once a month and she dropped by earlier to get the keys. She'll bring me some things since I might be here longer than I originally thought."

"Well, I'm going to send someone over with food from the café," Gertie said. "Whatever that is on that tray looks awful."

"It was pretty bad," Dinah said. "I really appreciate everything you ladies are doing. I wish I could do more to help."

"You just get better," Gertie said. "You've got enough on your plate right now. Let us handle the rest."

We headed out of the hospital and were all somewhat somber as we drove away.

"That was something I'm not anxious to ever repeat," Gertie said.

"It's rather an extreme situation," Ida Belle said. "I can't imagine it can happen too often."

"It *is* Sinful," I said.

"True," Ida Belle said. "I called that commercial Realtor last night and left a message. He called back while we were in with Dinah and said he can see us anytime this afternoon after two."

"What did you give as a reason?" I asked.

"I said Walter and I were tossing around some business ideas, and I wanted to talk about commercial space in the area," Ida Belle said.

"Perfect," I said.

Gertie clapped her hands and bounced up and down. "Road trip!"

I slouched down in my seat, getting comfortable for the ride, but I couldn't get my mind nearly as relaxed as the rest of my body.

Things had reached a boiling point and the water was spilling over.

Someone was going to get burned.

CHAPTER TWENTY

DIRK RICHARD HAD A RITZY OFFICE IN THE BUSINESS district of downtown. It was one of the older buildings that had been completely gutted and remodeled, leaving only the exterior as a historic reference to what it once was. But when you stepped inside, everything was polished marble and chandeliers and expensive plants. A snooty receptionist completed the entry.

"We're here to see Dirk Richard," Ida Belle said as we stepped up.

"Do you have an appointment?" she asked, giving us a once-over. I had a feeling we were coming up short in her mind.

Ida Belle nodded and gave her name.

Snooty sniffed once, dialed and gave the message, then hung up and frowned as she pointed to the elevators. "He's on the second floor. Take a left off the elevator, and his office space is all the way to the back of the building."

We headed up and I took in the business names on the other doors as we walked down the hall. Mostly attorneys and investment sorts. It made sense to occupy that type of space given what Dirk was into. You had the potential for picking up clients through the investment brokers, and attorneys right on hand to help with any legal wrangling. Nice and tidy. But I was betting the rent on the space wasn't cheap.

His office lobby was small but elegant and I had no doubt that the rug, leather couches, and paintings probably cost more than all of my decor put together. It just had that expensive look to it. There was an old, ornate desk in the center of the room but no one occupied it. We stood for a couple seconds and I was about to go on a hallway tour to find someone when a man stepped into the lobby and hurried over to Ida Belle to shake her hand.

Late fifties. Six foot one. A hundred eighty pounds. Good lean body mass. Built like a runner, but he wasn't skipping weight training. The smile was as fake as his capped teeth and if he kept pumping Ida Belle's arm that hard, he might raise oil from the floor. To me, low threat. But I wouldn't trust him any further than I could throw him. He just gave off that vibe.

"It's so good to see you," he said to Ida Belle when he finally released her hand. "It's been a long time. I heard you and Walter finally tied the knot. I didn't believe it at first, but my sources were solid, so I finally had to."

Ida Belle nodded. "Well, we weren't getting any younger."

He laughed and turned to Gertie. "And Ms. Gertie, how are you doing? I saw that boat race video on YouTube. We need to get you in a chair."

He turned quickly to me and stuck out his hand. "Dirk Richard. I don't think we've ever met."

"Fortune Redding," I said.

His eyes widened slightly, and I knew he'd heard the gossip. Despite being located in NOLA, he appeared to be up on what was happening in Sinful. I wondered briefly who his source was but then, it could be any number of people. Plenty of residents didn't have enough to do and were always looking to talk smack with someone.

"Come to my office," he said and looked at Gertie. "I have to tell you, I'm surprised to see you walking at all. I'm not sure I would be."

"I'm pretty sore but Ida Belle forced me to sit in ice baths half the night," Gertie said. "I'm probably still frozen in most parts."

He laughed as he pointed her to a comfy-looking couch in his office. "Well, if that's what has you walking today, I would consider doing another round. I'm glad that situation didn't turn out worse."

I sat on the couch with Gertie, and instead of sitting at his desk, Dirk turned the two chairs for visitors around to face the couch, and he and Ida Belle sat.

"So tell me what you're looking to do," Dirk said to Ida Belle. "I was both surprised and excited to get your call. There's not a lot of movement in the smaller towns. Are you and Walter looking to expand the store?"

"Not really," Ida Belle said. "At least, not the General Store, per se, but we've been toying with the idea of a sportsman's sort of shop. Something with some good fishing tackle, ammo, that sort of thing. He carries a little in the General Store, but there's not really room there for a big variety."

"How big a space are you thinking about?" he asked.

"Nothing huge," she said. "We don't want another large store to run. We were just thinking of a place where we could keep the staples, so to speak, for the most common activities to keep people from having to drive up the highway just to pick up some shotgun shells or new lures."

He nodded. "Given how successful the General Store has been, I have no doubt you two would be able to stock the right inventory for solid revenue. Unfortunately, there's nothing for sale in Sinful right now and nothing that I'm aware of that's coming up."

"Oh well, that's a shame," Ida Belle said. "I was hoping since you were in town late the other night that there was something new on the radar."

His jaw tightened slightly but he just shook his head. "You must be mistaken. I haven't been to Sinful in a week or better."

Ida Belle waved a hand in dismissal. "My mistake. Walter and I were working late on inventory, and I thought I saw you drive by. Wasn't your Mercedes, though, so I should have known I'd gotten it wrong. Probably eye strain from looking at those bar codes all night."

"That does sound like tedious work," he said. "Unfortunately, the dry cleaner's was the last building that went up for sale in Sinful, but I don't think it would have been a good space for a store, even though you're not wanting a big one."

Ida Belle shook her head. "It wouldn't have worked, and honestly, this is just a whim that Walter and I came up with. If it came down to having ammo on Main Street or Ally's baking, I'd go with the baking any day."

The fake smile was back. "I've been fortunate to enjoy some of her products and I can agree with you on that one," he said. "I think she's going to do very well. I tried to get her to consider a space in the French Quarter because I think her quality is in line with or superior to most of what I've had here, but she wouldn't even consider it. Our loss. I guess I'll just have to visit Sinful more often to get my fix."

"It would be worth the drive," Ida Belle said. "Of course, that's assuming she gets everything up and running without more incidents. I suppose you've heard that she was attacked in the building this past weekend."

His fake smile shifted to a frown. "I did hear that. Is she all right?"

"She's fine," I said. "And has a military-grade security and camera system now, so I don't think we'll have to worry about that happening again. Although a guy was shot trying to break in last night."

His eyes widened. "What? I hadn't heard that. Who was he?"

I shrugged. "The police aren't saying. Probably have to notify family and all that."

"Did he die?" Dirk asked.

"No, but we heard through the grapevine that he's critical," Gertie said. "The outlook is apparently grim."

Dirk looked confused and stared at me for a couple seconds. "I don't understand—aren't you dating Deputy LeBlanc?"

"Yes," I said. "But Carter is really strict about that 'not talking about police business' thing. I get more information through the Sinful gossips than I ever get from him."

"Well, I suppose you can't fault the man for doing a good job," Dirk said. "Although I'm not sure I could stand to be so close to someone and not be in on all those juicy secrets."

"Like Miles Broussard's murder," Gertie said. "That's another one that he's not talking about."

Dirk shook his head. "I had heard rumblings, but no one has ever confirmed. So it's true? You're certain?"

"On that one, we're definitely sure," Gertie said. "We found the body."

He sucked in a breath. "You did? How horrific!"

"It definitely wasn't what we were looking to do when we went hunting," Gertie said. "But sometimes life throws you a curveball."

"So Miles is really dead," Dirk said. "What a shame. He was so happy when he signed the contract for the sale. All ready to go off on his big adventure. Who would want to kill him and why? I didn't know the man very well, but he seemed rather innocuous."

"Which makes it all the more strange," Ida Belle said. "Was anyone else interested in the dry cleaner's when he bought it?"

Dirk shook his head. "Not that I'm aware of, but it was never really on the market. Jasper came to me and said he was selling and had a guy interested and asked if I could just take care of the legal documents. It's a fairly common practice."

"Did he ever say where he met Miles?" I asked. "It's sort of strange—the guy lived in Sinful for five years and yet no one seems to know anything about him. I was there five minutes, and I'm pretty sure the locals were cataloging me."

He smiled. "Well, you're a lot more interesting than Miles. And significantly more delightful to look at. A beautiful young woman will always attract attention while nondescript older men tend to fade into the wallpaper. But to answer your question, I don't think Jasper ever told me how he met Miles, or if he did, I've forgotten. But then, Jasper and I weren't friends either. I just handled his purchase and sale of the business."

"I don't suppose you've ever heard from Jasper after he left, have you?" I asked.

He looked somewhat surprised at the question. "I have no reason to. Why do you want to know?"

"A question came up about some modifications to the building that happened after he took over," I said. "We asked around, but no one seems to know where he went except Mexico, and it's a pretty big country to try to track down a guy without a starting place."

He shook his head. "I wasn't made aware of any structural changes, and none were disclosed in the sale that I can remember, but I'll check my records to be sure. It has been a while. I'm afraid I don't recall where he was off to, assuming he even said."

I gave Ida Belle 'the look' and she rose. "Thank you for your time, Dirk," she said. "If anything comes down the pipeline in Sinful, let me know. We're still at the talking stage anyway."

"Of course," he said, and rose with us. "I don't suppose you'd consider other areas."

I walked over to the window and looked out at the parking lot behind the building. I spotted a white Mercedes in one of the reserved slots and figured that must be Dirk's car that Ida Belle had mentioned, as it was the only Mercedes in a reserved space. I didn't see any sign of a Ford truck, but then, if he had a backup car for his criminal pursuits, he probably wouldn't keep it at the office.

"I don't think we're interested in any location but Sinful," Ida Belle said. "The whole point was to keep locals from having to go up the road to purchase things."

"I understand," Dirk said. "Well, it was great to see you ladies, and please let me know if I can help you with any other commercial real estate needs."

"This is a really nice building," I said as I turned around. "It's amazing what they can do remodeling these old structures."

Dirk nodded. "I'm really glad I moved my office here. If you know anyone in the market for an office lease, they still have some space available. I can do the deal."

"Thanks," I said, and we headed out, not speaking until we were in the SUV.

"I never liked him," Gertie said.

"I can see why," I said. "I feel like I need to shower. He was lying about not being in Sinful."

"I know," Ida Belle said. "Walter is rarely wrong about that sort of thing."

"You think he's lying about any of the rest of it?" Gertie asked.

"Yeah," I said. "He's definitely hiding something. And for someone who clearly stays in the know on Sinful gossip, he sure didn't have a bunch of questions for us."

"That *is* weird," Gertie agreed. "His type usually wants to know everything."

"Well, I can only think of one reason he'd be going against type," I said.

"He already knows the answers," Ida Belle said.

I nodded. "I think Dirk knows far more about Jasper and Miles than he's letting on, and I have to ask, how lucrative is his business? Because I don't know jewelry but that watch looked expensive."

"They can do quite well," Ida Belle said. "But that watch is six figures. I saw it on one of those lifestyle shows."

"Holy crap!" I said, and Gertie whistled.

"You think he's making that kind of money?" I asked.

"I wouldn't think so, but it could be inheritance or something else," Ida Belle said.

I nodded. "Like robbing banks and whatever else and laundering the money through the dry cleaner's—which he sold to one person who doesn't exist and another who is a documented criminal."

"You think he has anything in those file cabinets in his office?" Gertie asked.

"Like what?" Ida Belle asked. "A confession? A bag of stolen money?"

"I was thinking more like Jasper's forwarding address or bank account information," Gertie said. "Something we could trace."

"Something we could trace if we were cops," Ida Belle said.

"The Heberts have helped us out before on that sort of

thing," Gertie said. "Or maybe we will find something that makes a connection between them outside of just the sales transactions."

"Did you see the security cameras in that lobby?" Ida Belle said. "You'd have to be a ghost to get by them all. And there might be a guard after hours."

I grinned. "I unlocked his office window when I looked outside."

CHAPTER TWENTY-ONE

WE WERE HAVING SHRIMP PO'BOYS WHEN CARTER CALLED.
I'd sent him a message earlier saying that we'd visited with
Dinah but hadn't gotten anything except she might be able to
come up with a copy of the insurance check when she got
home, but he hadn't replied. I figured he'd call when he got an
opportunity.

"So it was a no-go with Dinah," Carter said.

"Total no-go," I said. "That woman was as shocked as the
rest of us. Probably more so because it was her son."

"And she doesn't have any idea why he'd do this?" he asked.

"Nothing that we would find interesting, but I'm guessing
the fact that his father abused them both is probably lurking
in the back of her mind. Still, it seems a big leap to take just
because you're holding a grudge."

"I don't think it has anything to do with old grievances—
not the death faking or the return. At least not grievances with
his mother. There's something a lot bigger at play here."

"I agree, but I have no idea what it is."

"What are you up to?"

"Eating an excellent shrimp po'boy."

"At the café?"

"It *is* a café, but not *the* café," I said. "We're in NOLA."

"What are you doing there?"

"Probably wasting time, but when we finish eating, we're going to try to find out where either Jasper or Miles spent some of their off time. We're going to start by cruising the casinos."

"That's the longest shot ever."

"Well, I might be able to fire at closer range if I was working with all the clues…"

"Nice try, but it's still a no. Try not to get into any trouble in the casinos."

"Gertie won a motorcycle that one time. That wasn't trouble."

"Don't forget the part where she assaulted a guy and ended up in the hospital."

"Well, he was there to kill me, sooooo…"

"Details, details. I've got to run. That's my contact on the other line."

"Doesn't sound like he's any help," Gertie said. "Big surprise there."

"Honestly, I don't think he has much more than we do," I said. "I can hear the frustration, and when he's on track to an end of an investigation, his voice is different."

"You think we're going to find anything in the casinos?" Gertie asked.

I shrugged. "Not likely, but there's no point in driving back to Sinful when we need to be here after dark, especially since we don't have anything in Sinful to follow up on either."

Ida Belle nodded. "You never know. We might get lucky. Stranger things have happened."

"Stranger things happen to us all the time," Gertie said. "Just not always in the positive column."

I grinned. "Are you calling yourself a 'stranger thing'?"

"I'd probably put Ronald in that category," Gertie said.

"Don't even get me started on Ronald," I said. "He's been messaging me underwear pics all day."

Ida Belle froze, her mouth open for a bite. "*His* underwear?" she finally asked.

"God, no! Underwear he wants me to buy because apparently I should be deadly and sexy at the same time."

"Ah," she said. "This is because he burned your clothes the other night."

"And we thought our mothers were joking when they made comments about being careful what underwear you wore out of the house," Gertie said.

"I don't think any of our mothers had Ronald in mind," Ida Belle said.

We finished up our sandwiches, made a quick stop at a store to pick up a cane for Gertie since she was refusing the walker and her armpits were hurting from the crutches, then headed out to the casino. We figured we'd start at the biggest venue offering the most vices first, then branch out to bars only. The casino wasn't very busy, but then it was late afternoon on a weekday. A lot of people were at work and a good bit had probably done all their losing over the weekend. And the Halloween tourists that flocked to the French Quarter every year were long gone.

"You have a method for this?" Ida Belle asked.

I nodded. "I want to find an older waitress—think forties and up—see how long they've worked here, and then flash the pictures. The younger ones aren't likely to remember or have been here long enough to have seen either Miles or Jasper."

"I'm not sure I like forty being considered 'older,'" Gertie said.

"That's because you couldn't see forty in your rearview

mirror even if you had binoculars," Ida Belle said. "Why don't you sit here and let Fortune and me comb the area? If someone comes by who fits the bill, then run them through the questions."

"Fine," Gertie said. "I'll just pop some money in the machines and grab a drink and you two do all the work."

"Do *not* get into any trouble," Ida Belle said. "A tortoise would outrun you at the moment."

"How much trouble can I get in just sitting here?" Gertie asked.

Neither Ida Belle nor I answered before walking away.

"Looks like the bar at the back is where the servers pick up their drinks for this section," I said. "Let's stake that out for a bit."

Ida Belle nodded. "Saves us walking all over, chasing people around."

We took seats at the end of the bar where the bartenders passed drinks to the servers and each ordered a soda. Then we waited. The first couple servers were early twenties, so they didn't fit our profile, but then one approached who looked like a good one to try.

Midfifties. Five foot five. A hundred eighty pounds. Decent muscle mass but carrying too much weight. Probably deadly with that tray. Facial expression somewhere between bored and done with life. Zero threat unless you grabbed her unmentionables. Then you'd probably get the tray.

"Excuse me," Ida Belle said after she gave her order to the bartender. "Have you worked here long?"

"Ten years," she said, and gave Ida Belle a once-over. "Don't do it. I'm only forty-eight and I look eighty. You're a little longer in the tooth. Would probably be worse."

"I'm not looking for a job," Ida Belle said. "I'm looking for a man."

The server snorted. "Aren't we all, honey. And he needs to be rich and look like Thor."

"Thor works for us," I said. "Actually, I'm a private investigator and this is my assistant. We're looking for information on a man who died. I'm trying to run down next of kin."

Her expression shifted from bemused to serious. "Oh. Well, that sucks. At least I don't have to tell people their weird old uncle died. Who's the man?"

"Miles Broussard," I said.

She shook her head. "Doesn't sound familiar."

"Here's a picture of him," I said and showed her my phone.

She stared at the picture, squinted a bit, then gave me a pensive look. "I can't be sure, but he kinda looks like a guy who used to come in here on the regular. Haven't seen him in a couple months though. He used to play the slots and get sloshed."

"Is there anything else you can tell us about him?" I asked.

"Afraid not. I never talked to him. He liked the higher-dollar slots and I usually work the lower ones. Believe it or not, the people betting less tip more. The higher-dollar ones are too often addicts. They don't like spending money on tips. But there is someone who might know more—it's a long shot though."

"Long shot is my middle name," I said. "What you just told me is the extent of what I have to go on at this point, so anything more would be great. Is there another server who would know him?"

"Maybe, but I was thinking about another vice," she said. "There's a pro, if you know what I mean. I've seen him leave with her more than a few times."

"Do you know where to find this pro?" I asked.

"Tuesday night the casino's not that busy," she said. "And management has more of an opportunity to see that kind of play is going on and get it out of the building, so the pros don't usually come in on slow nights. I've been out with friends and saw her once on Bourbon Street during the week, but I don't know if she was working or out for fun. Dress code on Bourbon is kinda the same for both."

"Do you know her name? And what does she look like?"

"She goes by Spice. Has dyed red hair. Green eyes. She's really tall and thin. I mean model tall and thin. Probably close to six feet tall and then the heels on top of it. If she's down there, you won't be able to miss her."

"Thanks," I said and passed her some bills. "I really appreciate it."

Her eyes widened as she looked down at the money, and she nodded.

"Thank you!" she said. "This might be more than I make the rest of my shift. Tuesdays suck, but you have to do a rotation to get weekends. There's my drink order. You ladies have a good one."

"From the casino to Bourbon Street to breaking into an office building," I said. "You think we can swing all of those without trouble?"

"Not if we keep taking Gertie everywhere," Ida Belle said. "Every place we take her decreases our odds of getting out of town without mishap."

"Maybe we can talk her out of Bourbon Street. No way she can walk very far, and we don't know where Spice will be, assuming she's even there."

"Face it, we just need to buy a wheelchair to have on tap."

"Probably not the worst idea. In fact, I can probably use it as a business expense."

"There's a medical supply store a couple blocks from here," Ida Belle said. "I saw it when we drove by. It's not quite five o'clock, if you want to try to swing this purchase now."

"Do we want to take Gertie down Bourbon Street at all?" I asked. "I was thinking maybe we could leave her here for a bit."

"Do you think we're better off with her in a wheelchair that we're pushing or alone in a casino with her purse?"

"Wheelchair it is!"

As soon as we hopped off our barstools, we heard a commotion on the other side of the casino—the side we'd left Gertie on. There was yelling and bells sounding and something that might have been weird crying or might have been a wild beast telling the crowd it was a buffet.

We both took off running and there was Gertie, locked in a fight with a woman who looked too old to even be breathing.

"That was my machine!" the woman yelled and swung her walker at Gertie's head with surprising strength, although the balance was a little sketchy.

"You left it ten minutes ago and were at the other end of the row," Gertie said. "Stop swinging that thing, or I'm going to have to fight back."

Gertie was standing but given all our movement today and the extent of her injury, it wasn't going to last long. Not that it mattered since Gertie would never retreat, but she also couldn't defend herself as well as she could if she were completely mobile. Unfortunately, I didn't want to have to take out a disabled senior either, especially with an audience. YouTube was the devil. The woman lifted the walker and swung again, but this time, Gertie lifted her handbag up to block it.

I don't know what was in the handbag, but the weight of it swinging combined with the bum legs was enough to send Gertie off-balance and pitching forward into the Walker Woman. Gertie lost her grip on the handbag as she fell, and it went sailing right into the face of a security guard who had arrived to control the scene. The security guard looked as if he'd been hit with a sledgehammer. He staggered backward into a man on a stool, who toppled over, sending the whole line of people with him like dominoes.

By this time, Gertie and Walker Woman were grappling on the floor like an MMA fight, and I was praying that Gertie didn't manage an arm bar because that would only make a bad situation worse.

"Arm bar!" Gertie yelled.

Ida Belle jumped into the fray, and I hurried for the purse before someone else snatched it up and left with God only knew what. I found it under a barstool along with a woman with bright purple hair. I helped the woman up, grabbed the purse, and hurried back to the fray.

Ida Belle had managed to break up the arm bar but now, Walker Woman was swinging her purse backward at Gertie's head. As I ran up, Gertie pulled half a shrimp po'boy out of her bra and clocked the woman across the face with it. I turned and grabbed a pitcher of beer off a server's tray, then spun around and flung the whole thing on the fighting seniors.

Right as the security guard bent over to break up the fight.

CHAPTER TWENTY-TWO

"THE SINFUL JAIL CELLS ARE A LOT NICER," GERTIE SAID. "AT least they mop."

"The least of our worries is our shoes resting on a dirty floor," Ida Belle said. "If you're concerned with hygiene then I wouldn't advise thinking about that bench you're sitting on."

"Or the air you're breathing," I muttered.

Some of those sharing our cell could do with a mopping themselves.

I flopped down on the bench next to Gertie, not remotely concerned with germs. I had spent most of my CIA career in dirty places. Clothes could be washed or sent to Ronald for burning.

I groaned at that thought. "Man, I hope Ronald doesn't hear about this before we get home. He'll have me showering in my backyard again."

"Still wearing basic underwear?" Ida Belle asked.

"That's better than none," I said.

"Not if you're going to have to keep burning them," Gertie said.

A big woman, who looked like an MMA fighter, rose from

her bench across from us. "If you're burning clothes, must mean you got money. Maybe you should hand it over."

I stared at her, confused by the utter stupidity.

"They take everything before they put you in here, remember?" I asked.

"I've got a couple fried shrimp in my bra," Gertie said.

MMA Fighter frowned. "Then you can pay me after you get out."

"Sure," I said, not wanting to get into another fight since that's why we were here in the first place.

"You don't sound sure," MMA Fighter said as she moved closer.

"I suggest you sit back down," Ida Belle said. "And I mean that for your own benefit."

MMA Fighter snorted. "You think that skinny bitch is going to take me down?"

"I'd bet my life on it," Ida Belle said. "Why do you think we're in here?"

Ida Belle's tone must have had her wondering because she stared me up and down for a bit. Finally, ego must have won out because she shook her head.

"Ain't buying it," she said.

"Just sit down and mind your own business," I said. "We all want to get out of here and starting trouble in a jail cell is a direct pass to an extended stay."

MMA Fighter shrugged. "Ain't got nothing better to do."

"There's a shocker," Gertie mumbled.

MMA Fighter started toward Gertie. "What did you say, old woman?"

I stood up and got in between them.

"I'm begging you to just go sit down," I said.

She let out some expletives that were usually only appropriate in jail and lunged. As she did, I grabbed her wrist, twisted it, and twirled and slammed her into the bars, her arm bent so far up her back it might not come back down. She yelled in agony but no way I was letting go until the cops let us out.

"All right, break it up."

I peered around the mountain of woman I had pinned to the jail bars and saw the sergeant who'd locked us up standing there looking as though he had no idea what to make of this. Next to him stood Detective Casey, a sharp female detective we'd met on our previous big case. She looked amused.

"Let her loose, Redding," Casey said, then looked at MMA Fighter. "Consider yourself lucky that you're alive and don't have anything broken. That woman, who is a third your body weight and has you pinned, is a former CIA operative. She could kill you in her sleep."

I let MMA Fighter go and she whirled around to stare at me, her eyes wide, then hurried silently back to her bench.

"Let's go, Redding and company," Casey said and motioned to the sergeant to let us out.

We followed her into an interview room and all took seats at a table. The sergeant disappeared and returned with Walker Woman. She gave us a dirty look and sat at the far end of the table. A couple seconds later, a captain came in and I said a quick prayer of thanks that it wasn't Casey's boss but a captain of another division. Casey's captain had a problem with PIs.

He looked at all of us and frowned. "I would think women of a certain generation could show more decorum than starting a brawl at a casino."

"I didn't start it," Gertie said.

"That's true," the sergeant said. "The security guard sent the footage over. This woman swung her walker at the other lady. That's how the fight started."

"That's not how it started," Walker Woman said. "That hussy stole my seat and won my prize."

"You'd moved minutes before," Gertie said. "You can't claim a whole row just because we can smell your cheap perfume all the way down it."

Walker Woman turned red and was gearing up for another fit when the sergeant held up his hand. "That is also correct per the footage. I asked for twenty minutes before the fight broke out to see if there was an inciting incident. I saw Ms. Hebert arrive and take a seat. The two women had no interaction until Ms. Hebert hit the jackpot."

The captain looked at Gertie. "Would you like to press charges?"

Gertie shook her head, and I could see his shoulders relax with relief.

"Let the old coot go," Gertie said. "She's not worth making a trip back here to testify against. Might already be dead by then."

"Who are you calling old?" Walker Woman asked.

"Can we just skip the Battle of the *Walking Dead* and get to the releasing us part?" Ida Belle asked.

"I'm not so sure about that," the captain said and pointed to me. "This one assaulted a security guard."

"Not intentionally," Ida Belle said. "She was just trying to break up the fight like everyone else."

The captain looked over at Detective Casey. "You sure you want to vouch for them?"

She nodded. "She's a well-respected PI. And you know that's saying a lot coming from me. She's also former CIA. These two are her assistants, and since gambling is not their vice and they're a ways from home, I have to assume they're working."

The captain blinked at the former CIA statement but

finally shrugged. "Hell, I don't care, and the security guard doesn't want to bother either. Turn them all loose. Saves us the paperwork."

"I'm not giving up my prize," Gertie said. "It's on the film. I won it fair and square and that casino is going to pay up."

"The casino manager has instructed us to tell you to come by anytime to claim your prize," the sergeant said.

"It's not her prize!" Walker Woman yelled.

"What the hell is so great that you'd fight over it?" the captain asked.

"VIP tickets to the upcoming Chippendales show," Gertie said.

The captain's expression shifted to total dismay. Walker Woman took one look at him and pointed her finger.

"You try getting a glimpse of hot men mostly undressed when you're my age and using a walker," she shouted as the captain hurried out of the room.

"Let's go," the sergeant said.

"You take her and I'll get these troublemakers," Casey said. "Bring their things to my desk."

We followed Casey to her office and took a seat.

"You working on anything I can help with?" Casey asked. "Anything that won't get me in hot water with my captain, who is not nearly as easily deterred from pressing charges as the beat captain."

"We were just leaving the casino and headed to Bourbon Street to find a prostitute," I said.

Casey raised one eyebrow. "Statements like that usually get you arrested by people like me. Is this pro involved in anything I should know about?"

"Not that I'm aware of," I said. "I'm looking for background on a murder vic, and she might have spent some time with him. It's a long shot, but we don't have a lot to go on. In fact, at the moment, this is all we have to go on."

She nodded. "Been there before. Good luck then, and try not to get into any more fights."

"I didn't start it," Gertie said.

Casey grinned. "I have a feeling you never do."

As I stood, I looked out the glass wall of Casey's office and saw a cop hauling in a tall, lanky red-haired woman who was dressed the part we were trying to find.

"Something wrong?" Casey asked, noticing my expression.

"That might be the woman we're looking for," I said and pointed to the pro as the cop directed her to a chair. "She fits the description, anyway. Goes by Spice."

Casey nodded and picked up her phone. The cop who had brought the woman in answered.

"Does that pro go by Spice?" Casey asked. "Cool. I was going to do a sweep for her later. Can you drop her off in my office for a minute? I need to ask a couple questions related to a case. Shouldn't take long."

The cop delivered Spice to Casey's office, and she scanned the room, clearly confused.

"What do you people want with me?" she asked. "I told that cop I didn't do nothing."

"I'm a private detective," I said. "I'm looking for information on a man that I think you might know. I'm not looking to run you up on anything."

She shrugged. "I know a lot of men."

"This one would have been more regular," I said. "Miles Broussard?"

She frowned. "I don't usually get names. Not first and last anyway. Better for everyone."

I pulled up the picture of Miles and showed it to her. I

could tell she recognized him, but she was still too wary to say anything.

"What did he do?" she asked.

"He was murdered," I said.

Her eyes widened and she shook her head. "Wow. I didn't see that one coming."

"So you knew him?" I asked,

"Not really," she said. "I did entertain him a couple times a month. He was nicer than most. Even bought me dinner sometimes."

"What do you know about him?" I asked.

She shrugged. "Not much. Like I said, safer. He said he lived in one of those bayou towns around here. Came to NOLA on his days off. He spent more time in the casinos than with me, so I can tell you that women weren't his first or only vice."

"He tell you what his job was?" I asked.

"No. But one time he had to meet some guy. He got a call at his hotel room just after we finished, you know, and said he had to meet a business partner downstairs. I was headed out for second shift anyway, so I took off. But then I saw an old friend in the bar and stopped to chat with her. Miles came in and went to a back table where a guy was already sitting. He was only there a minute or so, then left, but this time he was carrying a backpack."

"And you're sure he didn't have it when he went down?" I asked.

"No. And there wasn't one in his room." She shrugged. "I usually give rooms a once-over when they're in the john. Miles always came with the same old duffel bag."

"You ever see that backpack again?" I asked.

"Maybe."

"And what was in it?" I asked.

She was silent for a while, then blew out a breath. "Money, okay? It was full of hundred-dollar bills."

"Did you get a good look at the guy Miles met in the bar?" I asked.

"I guess, but it's been months, and if Miles was killed over that backpack, then maybe I should just stop talking. Like I said—better not knowing stuff."

"Well, Miles is dead, so unless the man he met saw you together at some point, you're in the clear."

She bit her lower lip and I could see her weighing the odds of this turning out badly. "You said he was murdered?"

"Yes."

She sighed. "He didn't deserve that, even if he was mixed up in something stupid. He was a nice guy, really, but never struck me as overly smart. I guess that turned out to be true since he got himself dead."

She was silent for several seconds, then nodded. "The other dude was a basic white guy. He was sitting down but his head was above Miles's, so I figure he was fairly tall. Brown hair. Regular build—not fat, not thin, but seemed fit, if that makes sense. And...well, I didn't like his smile."

"What do you mean?" I asked.

"He smiled at Miles right before he took off with the backpack. It was one of those big-mouth, full-teeth sort of smiles. The kind used-car salesmen have, you know?"

I nodded. I did know. And I'd just met a broker who fit that description.

IT WAS close to nine o'clock before the parking lot behind Dirk's building completely emptied out and the streets were left with only the occasional car driving past. I'd already filled

Ally in that we'd be in NOLA late, and she'd agreed to lock up the bakery before dark and secure herself in my house. I'd told her to call Mannie if something happened as I might not be in reach. Then I'd called Mannie and let him know I was hot on a trail and that if anything went down in Sinful, Ally was under orders to call him for backup. Finally, I'd texted Carter that we were staying in NOLA for a while, still chasing down leads.

Now I studied the back of the building from the front seat of Ida Belle's SUV, which was parked at the rear of the lot in a shadowed area where no parking lot lights reached.

"You sure you want to do this?" Ida Belle asked. "We've already got a pretty solid lead on Dirk from Spice. Combine that with Walter seeing him in Sinful late and him denying it, and I think we've got enough for Carter to push for a search warrant or an asset check or whatever might be able to pin him with something."

"She's right," Gertie said. "You know me, I'm always up for an adventure, even an illegal or dangerous one, but we've already been in jail once today. We might want to pace ourselves."

I considered this for a bit. They weren't wrong, but then I wasn't convinced we had enough for Carter to get a warrant by a judge. He could certainly do a more intensive look at Dirk, but his review of Dirk's business practices would be limited to public records and bank accounts. Mine would only be limited by what Dirk didn't keep in his office.

"I still want to do it," I said. "As soon as I head up, you guys will jet up the street and park. If anything goes wrong, I'll run for it and call you from a pickup place. You'll back away quietly and wait for a call."

Ida Belle nodded. "And if we see anything moving your direction, we'll text. So far, it doesn't look like the building has a night guard."

"Let's hope it stays that way," I said. "Okay, I'm off."

I hopped out of the SUV and hurried across the parking lot, keeping to the darker areas just in case anyone was in a nearby building. I had donned my emergency breaking-and-entering gear that we kept in Ida Belle's SUV, so was currently sporting a black hoodie, yoga pants, and tennis shoes, black gloves, and a black ski cap. I figured a full-blown ski mask would get a police call straight off but all black and a ski cap might make me look like an edgy teen. At least from a distance.

I'd already spotted the drainpipe that ran on the side of the building next to the window and that was going to be my way up. I grabbed hold of it and tugged, making sure it was sturdy enough for my weight, then I clutched it with both hands and started my climb up the building. When I was next to the window, I leaned out from the pipe and pushed the unlocked window up. Then I stretched one foot onto the window ledge and pushed off the drainpipe, and in one fluid move, braced my hands on both sides of the window casing and thrust myself inside.

I started with the desk, looking through all the paperwork and checking all the old-school hiding places—back of drawers, stuff taped underneath the desk—then moved to the file cabinets. I'd seen several USBs in the desk but didn't have time to cue them up and couldn't take them or the potential evidence wouldn't be there when the people who could pursue legal action showed up. That was the problem with technology —it eliminated the need for old-school hiding of documents.

I flipped through the files, my aggravation growing as I saw nothing of value. Why did I think Dirk would be foolish enough to keep evidence of shady transactions in his office? If he had a secondary vehicle to handle off-the-books business in, then he probably also had other places to hide things. He was a real estate broker. For all I knew, he could be hiding things in his listed properties.

I frowned. Including the dry cleaner's.

But surely he would have removed anything before the closing happened. Unless he missed something. I shook my head. That didn't make sense. If Dirk and Miles had been laundering money through the dry cleaner's, which was my current guess, and they'd never been caught, then he had to be far more organized than to lose track of a bag of cash. And besides, the bills found on Miles were old and couldn't be easily laundered.

At least, not in the US.

Which meant maybe the money predated Miles, and all of Jasper's trips to Mexico weren't about boozing and finding a retirement place. He couldn't have brought much money at a time or traveled there weekly or it would have raised flags with customs. But a small haul every six weeks or so might work— at least enough to cover the cost of the trip and the risk, and have some left over.

But that meant the laundering would have been going on for a long time. Fifteen years, assuming Jasper and Dirk were in bed together from the beginning. The files were in alphabetical order by buyer name. One file cabinet was all corporate purchases and the other individuals. We knew Jasper Cummings was actually Jasper Comeaux, but I had to assume he used the fake name to conduct his business, so I went to the CUs.

I spotted the file for Jasper Cummings and pulled it out. There was paperwork for the dry cleaner's but that was it. I frowned. Maybe I was completely off track. I dug in the files again and couldn't help smiling when I caught sight of another folder with the name Jasper Comeaux on it. I'd been right. The dry cleaner's wasn't the first business transaction Dirk had taken care of. Prior to the dry cleaner's, Jasper had owned a pawnshop and a bar. Both easy businesses to run cash through. And these two files proved that Dirk knew Jasper had a fake identity, which meant he was in it up to his eyeballs.

Maybe one of Jasper's businesses had started to pull heat from the NOLA cops, and given Jasper's record, they would have looked harder at him than usual. If that was the case, a new name and relocating to a place like Sinful was a smart idea. I took some pictures, then closed the file and put it back in the cabinet. I thought I had enough to go to Carter with. Maybe enough to get him a warrant—at least to get all records associated with Jasper and Miles.

My phone vibrated, and I pulled it out but didn't recognize the number. Still, not that many people had my number so I figured I better answer.

"It's Spice," the woman said.

I'd given her my card at the police station and told her to call if she remembered anything else. Now I could hear panic in her voice.

"That man is here," she said. "The man from the bar. I knew I shouldn't have talked to you."

"Where are you, and where is he?"

"I'm in my apartment. He's parked in the lot out front, just sitting there. I know he didn't follow me because I'm careful about that stuff. And I change apartments every six months. I've only been here two. So how did he find me?"

"He's in the real estate business and has connections all over town," I said. "If he knows where you live, then he'd already called in favors to find out. Talking to me didn't make a difference. He was already looking for you. In fact, talking to me is probably about to save your life."

"Oh my God! He's getting out of his truck. I think he has a gun!"

"Is there a back door on the apartment?"

"No. But there's a window in the bathroom I can crawl out of. I've done it when I didn't have all the rent money."

"Go! Get to a nearby business—a café or something—and make sure you're around people. Do you have a place?"

"Cup of Joe is two blocks over."

"Give me the street. Get there and stay put. I'll either get you myself or have someone pick you up. I'm in the middle of something right now."

My phone buzzed again and my pulse rate shot up as I saw the message at the top of my phone.

Cops headed your way. Security guard just went in back of building.

CHAPTER TWENTY-THREE

"SPICE, I'VE GOT TO RUN," I SAID AND PEERED OUT THE window. "Get out of there and stay put."

Someone must have been burning the midnight oil nearby and seen me climb in the window. Which meant the cops and the security guard knew exactly where I'd accessed the building. The elevator and stairs were off the hallway, but the security guard could cover both by just standing at one end. And I couldn't go back the way I came because the cops had just pulled up behind the building. The only thing I did know was that I couldn't remain in Dirk's office.

I headed into the hallway, called the elevator, then ducked behind a big plant in the corner near the staircase. A couple seconds later, a tall lanky guy ran up the stairs and I could see the flash of metal at his waist. Not good. This guy looked like a runner, and the downstairs door was probably locked from the inside with a key.

But I was out of options. I had to get to the first floor and find another way out.

As soon as he'd passed me, I crept out from behind the

plant and hurried down the stairs, but even my breaking-and-entering tennis shoes couldn't stop the historic staircase from creaking. I heard him running back for the staircase as I launched onto the first floor. The cops were beating on the back door, announcing their rank and requesting entry, so I ran for the front of the building.

The front door was locked from the inside, as I'd suspected, and there was no key in sight. So I did the only thing left to do. I grabbed a potted plant and swung it at the door, shattering the glass, then whirled around and tossed it at the security guard, who was running straight for me. At the end of the hallway, the cops had just entered and were now headed for us.

I darted out of the building and ran across the street just as Ida Belle's SUV squealed around the corner and took off in the opposite direction. I heard the cops and security guard yelling behind me and wished I'd had more of a head start on them. I might be able to outrun them all, although the security guard was a wild card, but no one could outrun a bullet and sometimes people got overzealous on the job.

As I bolted toward a building with a revolving door, Gertie waved me inside. I had no idea what she was up to, but at least I didn't catch sight of her handbag when I ran into the turnstile. A second later, I knew why she didn't have her bag. There was an explosion behind Dirk's office building, and I had a good guess that a dumpster had just taken one for the team. The cops, who were running across the street behind the security guard, changed direction and headed back into the building. The security guard was having none of it and continued across the street.

I couldn't be certain that the guard had seen where I went, but no way he could miss me in the plate-glass windows, so I ducked behind a plant near the revolving door. At least there was no security guard in the lobby, but I expected one would show up soon.

I peered through the plant leaves and saw Gertie dart out of the door and behind a trash can. As the security guard approached, she pushed it over, hitting him right in the stomach. He doubled over and fell but hopped right back up, scanning the streets and poised to take off again at first sighting.

"Thank God it's the police!" I heard Gertie say. "I just walked out of the building and a man stole my purse and shoved me down."

"Ma'am, I'm not the police. Did someone wearing all black run in this building?"

"Of course not or they'd have run me over," Gertie said as she dug her phone out of her bra. "What are you going to do about my purse?"

"I'm not the police. I'm a security guard, and I need to find the guy who ran out of that building across the street. You're sure no one ran inside?"

He moved closer to the glass and peered through. I made myself pencil thin and froze.

"No one went in there," she said. "Are you really not going to help an old lady?"

"You just dug your phone out of your bra," he said. "Use it to call the cops."

I heard the elevator ding behind me and cringed. Crap! Gertie needed to get this guy off that glass window and away from the building.

"Of course it was in my bra," Gertie said. "This is the new iPhone. Done had two purses grabbed this year. Ain't no one grabbed my boobs in decades, so tell me where it's safer? I saw a guy run off that way when I was walking out. Wearing all black, like those young hoodlums do."

"Hey, you!" A voice sounded behind me and I slowly rose

up as the guard sped off. "What are you doing there? This building is supposed to be closed."

"The door was unlocked," I said. "I was walking down the street and heard a huge bang. I thought maybe it was a gang war and jumped in here."

The guard looked me up and down and frowned. Given that I was dressed more like a cat burglar than a tourist, I could understand his dilemma.

"Well, get moving," he said. "It was probably fireworks or something. You knock that trash can over?"

"No. That was some other guy."

"Uh-huh, well go ahead and go. I need to lock this door."

He didn't believe for a minute that the noise was fireworks, but he also didn't want trouble in his building because then he'd have to deal with it. I didn't want him to commit my face to memory, so I headed into the revolving door and inched forward, scanning the street for the security guard.

I didn't see him anywhere, but that didn't mean he wasn't lurking in a doorway or couldn't pop around the corner at any moment. Gertie had limped down the block in the opposite direction of the guard as soon as he'd hurried off, and I couldn't see her either. I stepped out and took off in the direction Gertie had gone, and when I got midway down the block, I heard her call from an alley. I ran through the narrow passage to the other end and as soon as I exited, Ida Belle's SUV slowed at the curb.

"Stop!"

The security guard yelled behind me and I dived in the back seat of the SUV where Gertie had opened the door. Ida Belle punched it and I sprang up to get the door. I peered over the back seat as the security guard ran out of the alleyway.

"I hope we're far enough away that he can't read your license plate," Gertie said.

"I took it off," Ida Belle said. "But I need to stop as soon as it's safe and put it back on. Then we can get back to Sinful where half the town isn't looking for us."

My phone buzzed and I saw a text from Spice.

I'm still at the café. What do I do?

I sent a text.

On my way.

"I'm afraid we have one more stop to make," I said. "Well, maybe two."

———

BECAUSE I WAS DRESSED to be the least recognizable, I headed into the café that Spice had indicated. I spotted her in a corner with a full glass of water in front of her and wearing a panicked expression. When I came in, she glanced at me, then looked back down, then a second later, her head popped back up and she zoned in on me and I could see her shoulders relax slightly.

"I didn't think you were coming," she said as I slipped into a chair across from her.

"I got caught up in a bit of a police chase," I said.

Her eyes widened. "The police were chasing you? And you came here?"

"Don't worry. I ditched them. But we have to get you out of here. Do you have anyone you can stay with for a couple days?"

"This isn't exactly a profession that gets you friends who have the means to put you up, you know?"

"Okay, then we'll get you a motel room while I sort this out."

"Ha. Yeah, so whatever Miles was up to has probably been going on for years. I don't think you're going to fix all that quickly, and I can't afford a motel room for even two nights if I'm not working. I have to make rent—not that I can go back to that apartment now. What a mess."

"Do you have a lease on your current apartment?"

"Month to month. Like I said, I don't stick in one place for very long. It's not smart. Maybe I should just get out of NOLA. He'd have a hard time following me to another city."

It wasn't the worst idea in the world, but I got the impression that she didn't really want to leave New Orleans. An idea was floating around in my mind, but it was something I'd have to check on. In the meantime, we needed Spice safe somewhere, at least for tonight. And I couldn't risk bringing her to Sinful when a killer was lurking around.

"Here's what we're going to do," I said. "Me and my friends are going to take you to a hotel on the other side of town. One with room service. We'll get you registered and you'll stay put until I can work out something else. My agency will foot the bill. All you have to do is not leave your room. Order in food and check the door before you open it. Keep the drapes closed."

She shook her head. "Look, I know how to hide. Done it enough times. But that doesn't solve the problem of work. I can't make rent on the first if I'm not out. And I just don't see how you're going to fix something this big in a couple days."

"Don't worry about rent," I said. "I'll make sure you're covered."

She raised one eyebrow. "What are you—rich?"

"More like motivated. I don't like when people are murdered in my town. And I really don't like it when one of my best friends is attacked, likely by the same man."

Her eyes widened. "And you think that guy did it?"

"He's definitely at the top of my list."

She studied me for a long while, and I knew she was trying to get a read on me, something she was likely very good at out of necessity. She must have clued in on my honesty because she finally nodded.

"I can do it a couple days, but after that, I have to figure out something else."

"Great, then take this." I handed her a baseball hat and a New Orleans Saints hoodie. "Pull the sweatshirt on over your other clothes and stuff your hair under the cap. That's the one thing that would definitely give you away."

"You think he's around here?"

"He saw you go in the apartment and if he was approaching, he likely broke in and realized you'd given him the slip. Whatever he has in mind was important enough for him to track you down and then go to your apartment, so yeah, I think he's probably still looking for you."

"This is some bullshit," she said as she pulled on the hoodie. "I barely saw the guy and only once."

"It's not fair," I agreed. "He probably thinks you know something you shouldn't. Either Miles told you or you found out something snooping."

"You know, the funny thing is, most regulars do tell us things they shouldn't, but Miles never said hardly anything about his personal life."

We rose and headed out of the café.

"I get that," I said. "But right now, this guy only sees you as a loose end."

WE GOT Spice situated in a hotel and headed home. I'd gotten two texts from Carter and given one brief reply. Now I sent another, asking him to meet me at my house when we got back to Sinful. I let Ally know we were on our way and then, with all my notifications issues handled, I told Ida Belle and Gertie what I'd found in Dirk's office and my suspicions about what it meant.

"That's a good theory," Ida Belle said, "but where does Bart fit in?"

"That's the thing that has me stumped," I said. "And then there's still the case of the disappearing Jasper. I called in a favor with a CIA contact, and she wasn't able to find any record of him even leaving the country after he sold the dry cleaner's. No sign of him in Barra de Potosi now or ever."

"Maybe he's here," Ida Belle said. "Maybe the whole thing started with him and Dirk. The Mexico story was probably a fake the whole time. Jasper probably moved to a different city with a new name to set up shop again and Miles took over here."

"Then why wouldn't Dirk continue business with Jasper rather than use Miles?" Gertie asked.

"How do we know he wasn't using both?" Ida Belle said. "Maybe Dirk's illegal activities extended beyond robbery. A commercial broker can do a lot of business under the table if he's dealing with questionable clientele. Simple to write up a contract for one amount and collect a different one. Then the seller shows less profit on the sale and Dirk gets off-the-books cash for handling the transaction."

I nodded. "Or Dirk could be handling laundering for some of those unsavory sorts."

Gertie sighed. "Poor Spice. That girl's life is already hard enough and now she's in trouble for being in the wrong place at the wrong time."

"I doubt it was just the once that Dirk saw her," I said. "A man like Dirk wouldn't trust someone like Miles. If Dirk is the criminal we think he is, then he's gotten away with it for a lot of years. We know from Miles's arrest record that he wasn't nearly as successful, so it wouldn't surprise me if Dirk hadn't followed him before, just to make sure he knew what Miles was up to."

"Spice is lucky we talked to her at the police station," Ida Belle said. "If we hadn't put her on notice, no telling what might have happened tonight."

Carter wasn't at my house when we pulled up, so I told Ida Belle and Gertie to head home. If he was still working and he hadn't contacted me, then something big was going on, and I was unlikely to hear from him until morning. I trudged inside and Ally handed me a drink and a couple of cookies. I plopped down in my recliner and let out a huge breath. What a long day with too much running, too many cops, too much drama, and not nearly enough answers.

"I'm almost afraid to ask how it went," Ally said. "But I'm going to anyway."

"It...went. I was hoping Carter would be here so I could fill you both in at the same time, but I haven't heard anything from him for a while now. Is anything going on that you're aware of?"

She shook her head. "No one has called me with anything, but then, I'm not in any of the good gossip chains. I'm too young."

My phone buzzed and I checked. Carter.

"You still working?" I asked.

"Yeah. There was a situation at the hospital."

I straightened in my chair. "What happened?"

"Someone tried to kill Bart. Tried to smother him with a pillow."

"Holy crap! You said tried...is he all right?"

"He flatlined, but they got him back."

"Did you get the attacker on security cameras?"

"Yes and no. The construction here knocked out the security cameras. They got the most critical ones back online, so the hallway cameras in ICU were working, but as soon as he exited the area, it's a black hole."

"But you got him on camera in the ICU?"

"Yeah, but he was wearing surgical scrubs and a mask with thick black glasses and never looked up where we could get a clear look at his face. No one working the ICU could identify him or recall seeing him. A window was open in the break room but the ground outside is all mulch, so I can't tell if anyone went out that way."

"No one saw him?"

"I'm sure they did but there was an explosion on an oil rig and they Care Flighted a bunch of men in right before it happened. Everyone was focused on getting them stable."

"So he was intentionally avoiding the cameras. Combine that with the way he was dressed and the Care Flight arrival and no one would even look twice if they passed him in the hallway or even the parking lot. Just ditch the mask close to the exit and he'd be golden."

"Exactly. I asked two of the nurses to see if scrubs were missing from the employee locker room, which is supposed to always be locked, but they weren't sure about it. Not that it matters. You can buy them a ton of places, which is the smarter move rather than hoping you can find them on-site."

"What time did this happen?" I asked.

"About two hours ago," he said.

I frowned. Two hours ago, Dirk was sitting in front of Spice's apartment.

Maybe the Jasper-lurking-around theory wasn't a big stretch after all.

"I need to talk to you," I said. "How much longer are you going to be there?"

"Probably another hour at least."

"I'll be up. The time doesn't matter."

"You got something?"

"I've got a lot. I'm just not sure how to put it all together."

CHAPTER TWENTY-FOUR

IT WAS THE WEE HOURS OF THE MORNING WHEN CARTER finally slumped into a chair at my kitchen table. He looked beat and I wasn't sure I looked much better. The only advantage I had was the thirty-minute shower I'd gotten and Ally's cooking, of course.

"You want something to eat?" I asked.

"I do, but I'm not sure I have the energy to chew."

"I have Ally's meat loaf and mashed potatoes."

"I'll work up the energy."

"How's Bart?"

"The same. I put a guard on his room and Dinah's. She heard the commotion and kept calling for the nurse, so I finally told her what happened. She didn't take it well."

"It doesn't look good for Bart, does it?"

"I wish I could say differently, but no. He was already in serious condition and now this. But the doctors are remaining optimistic. They said he's strong and doesn't appear to have any other health issues... I guess we just have to wait and see. So what did you overturn with your trip to NOLA? I kept waiting for the police to call and say they had you in handcuffs."

"Oh, Detective Casey vouched for us, and we got out of jail. I am sorry to say, we *did* arrive there in handcuffs. You know how things with Gertie go."

He stared at me for a bit, then blinked.

"You're not joking," he said finally.

"I wish I was, because the NOLA jail houses some very unpleasant people and I had to put one of them in her place. But trust me, our arrest had nothing to do with the investigation and there are no charges, so we're all good."

He didn't look convinced, and I probably wouldn't either if I were him, but he was probably too tired to work up to upset. Which meant I needed to fill him in on everything before he dozed off in his mashed potatoes. He ate while I recounted what we'd found, stopping only occasionally to ask a question. When I was done, he sat his fork on the empty plate, leaned back, and blew out a breath.

"What do you think?" I asked.

"I definitely don't like the way Dirk looks and I think you're onto something with the Dirk and Jasper partnership. But I don't see where Bart fits in or who pulled the attack on him tonight unless the theory about Jasper and Dirk cleaning house is accurate and Bart has been involved somewhere in the shadows all these years."

"There's only a couple reasons to fake your death, and being a criminal is the most popular. I know it sounds crazy but it fits. We know Jasper did time for robbery, and laundering is just the flip side of the business, so that part isn't a stretch. And I have no doubt Walter saw Dirk in Sinful the other night in a different vehicle, but why lie about it unless he was up to something?"

"Like tearing up the rental house?"

I nodded.

"But let's just say this whole thing is about that bank robbery thirty years ago. That robbery was clearly done by a pro and Jasper's police record made his skill level clear, so I can't see him for it. But if Dirk was the pro, then he would have known how much of the take had been cleaned. If there was any left, he could have easily removed it from the building when it was sold to Miles or when Miles had it listed for sale and he had a valid reason to be inside. Why wait to break in after it had changed hands?"

"It only makes sense if Dirk didn't know the money was there."

"But why wouldn't he?"

"What about this—when that robbery happened, the databases for stolen money were just starting to come online. So even if Jasper was hauling money to Mexico, or somewhere else for that matter, he couldn't possibly take much at one time. What if Dirk decided the money got too hot to mess with and told him to destroy it?"

"But Jasper sold the business and left the money in its hiding place instead? Why?"

I shrugged. "Maybe he couldn't bring himself to destroy money. Or maybe he figured it was unlikely to ever be found and even if it was, he didn't care because he was leaving Sinful and would likely be a different person wherever he landed next."

"And then Miles found it," Carter said.

"Exactly," I said. "He had bills on him when he was killed, so I have to assume that finding the money was the catalyst for his 'retirement.'"

"But how did Dirk find out? Miles would never have told him. He wouldn't have risked his newfound riches, especially knowing Dirk's real line of work."

"He'd been meeting with Dirk about the sale of the building, and I have to figure that Dirk was already suspicious about Miles's retirement as Dirk would have known better than anyone else exactly how much money Miles had coming in. So what if Miles handed over one of those bills to pay for drinks or dinner? Dirk would have known right away that the bill was too old to be in circulation. He might have nabbed a shot and checked it out, just like we did."

"But wouldn't Miles have known the bills were too old as well?"

"Sure, but what server remembers which customer gave them which bill? Even a hundred on a nice dinner or several rounds of drinks isn't going to stand out. Granted, it's the slowest way possible to put money into circulation, but it's also a good way to spend it and not get caught."

"True. As long as you don't disperse it wide enough to be zeroed in on or, as in Miles's case, you're about to leave town."

I nodded. "And then Dirk realized he had a problem. If Miles got caught, he might offer up Dirk to get a lighter sentence. I'd bet anything it was Dirk who supplied the money for Miles to buy the dry cleaners."

He nodded. "So Dirk and potentially Jasper are cleaning things up."

"Well, someone is helping Dirk because he couldn't have been at Spice's apartment and at the hospital at the same time. And if we assume that Jasper is the one who hid the money in the first place, then he's the only other person with a vested interest in making it go away, especially if he lied and told Dirk he'd destroyed it."

"It still doesn't explain why Bart came back from the dead. If he's mixed up with them somehow, why not let Jasper and Dirk handle it? He was too young to have committed the robbery."

"I have no idea why he's back, but it had to be important to risk his whole fake death over it. And he went straight for the dry cleaner's, so I have to think he knew about the money somehow. But unless Bart wakes up, we may never know. So, do you have enough to get a warrant? There's a paper trail somewhere or digital one, whatever. If you could get a forensic audit of Dirk's records versus his lifestyle, I'd bet anything you'd find discrepancies."

He frowned. "I don't know that it's enough. We have some damning things and some speculation, but none of it puts Miles's murder on him. I'll do some poking around—the kind that doesn't require a warrant—and see if I can come up with enough to convince a judge. I might be able to work with the second vehicle—you know, a tip that it was seen leaving the scene of a crime, based very loosely on Walter's account. If I find something questionable in it, then I should be able to get one for his home and business."

"I like that idea. What about Spice?"

He blew out a breath. "She's sure she saw Dirk outside her apartment? She couldn't be mistaken?"

"Of course she could be mistaken, but the girl is terrified and it's no acting job. And the vehicle matched Walter's description. Besides, what are the odds that right in the thick of this Miles investigation, a man who was never a client shows up at her apartment with a gun?"

"I agree and would rather err on the side of caution. Tell her to stay at the hotel. Let me see what I can come up with in the next two days, and if it's still not enough, then we'll figure something out."

He leaned forward and gave me a hard stare. "But you have got to back off Dirk. Security is going to tell him about the break-in, and the fact that you were in his office today isn't going to escape him because he most certainly knows who you are and what you do. If he's really managed to stay below radar all these years, then he will know you were fishing and he'll suspect you're the one who broke in."

My stomach dropped. I hadn't even thought that far. "I screwed this up, didn't I? He's probably destroying evidence as we speak. Crap, Carter. I'm so sorry. I just didn't plan on getting caught."

"That's what they all say."

———

I SLEPT RESTLESSLY and awakened at 5:00 a.m. feeling just as bad as I had the night before. In my haste to find evidence for Carter, I'd put his investigation in jeopardy. It was stupid and showed a complete lack of thinking on my part, which had to change. The fact that Carter hadn't dressed me down for it made me feel even worse. He could have spent the rest of the night chewing me out and it still wouldn't have been enough.

I sat up in bed and sighed. My intentions were good and my dedication to the truth was as much a part of me as breathing, but I had to start thinking harder about execution. I trudged downstairs and found Ally putting coffee on.

"You're up early," I said.

"I could say the same thing to you. Too busy thinking about the case?"

"Among other things," I said.

I told her about the attack on Bart the night before.

"Oh my God," she said as she poured us coffee. "What a time for the cameras to be down."

"It definitely made things easier for him, but for all we know, he walked out of the hospital that way and never looked up. I'm sure the hospital's not advertising that their security system is mostly down, so unless it was an employee, he couldn't have known about that advantage."

"What in the world does Bart know that's so important someone would take that risk?"

"That's the question of the hour. I have a feeling that when we know the answer to that, all of this will break wide open. Did you have any issues at the building yesterday?"

She shook her head. "Had some delays with some of the workers finishing up another job and getting the permits in line, but we're making a dent in demolition. Got all the cabinets removed and that weird ceiling out as well as the counters. I double-checked everything to make sure there weren't any valuables, just in case. The crew knocked off about six and I locked up right behind them and came here. I checked the cameras several times but everything was quiet."

"That's good."

"Do you think I can go home? Not that staying here isn't great but with the construction starting, I keep needing things from my house that I've collected over the years—you know, paint swatches, furniture pictures, upholstery fabric styles—I have a bunch of stuff I've put together as I ran across things I like."

"Can you give it another night at least? Just to make me feel better."

She smiled. "Of course. You're a great friend, Fortune. I just hate causing you trouble."

"What trouble? As you can see, I'm rarely here, and while I'm gone, you cook. Trust me, I'm the one cashing in on this one."

"You're sweet to say so, even though we know that's not true. And since I'm up so early, I think I'm going to run by my house and grab some of those items I was talking about and then have breakfast at the café. You interested?"

I shook my head. "I need to get with Ida Belle and Gertie and bring them up to speed, then go over what we have and figure out what direction to go next."

"Okay," she said as she rose. "But please don't push yourself to exhaustion. You look tired. I don't want something to happen to you."

I nodded as she left and sent a text to Ida Belle letting her know to round up Gertie and head my way once they were up and about. I had a feeling that everything was just on the verge of opening up but had no idea what we needed to do next. Definitely another visit to Dinah was in order, but that was about decency, not the investigation.

My phone signaled an incoming text and I checked it, thinking it would be Ida Belle, but it was from Carter.

Got a line on Dirk. Do not go anywhere near him or his properties.

I typed in an answer.

10-4. Good luck!

I sat the phone back on the table and blew out a breath of relief. If Carter was already making a move on information this early, he must have found something to urgently pursue. I said a quick prayer that he'd be safe and another that he'd bust the whole thing wide open, then headed upstairs to get dressed. Ida Belle and Gertie wouldn't be sleeping in either.

CHAPTER TWENTY-FIVE

I brought Ida Belle and Gertie up to speed on everything while we whipped up some breakfast. It was just after 9:00 a.m. when we headed out for the hospital to see if there was anything we could do for Dinah. She was awake when we got there, though to be honest, it didn't look as if she'd slept at all. Her laptop was open on her lap but she was staring at the wall, her expression one of overwhelming exhaustion. It took her a couple seconds before she seemed to realize we'd entered the room. Finally, she turned her head toward us and blinked a couple times, then gave us a nod.

"How are you doing?" Gertie asked.

She shrugged. "About as good as expected, I imagine."

"Have you gotten any updates on Bart?" Ida Belle asked.

"Not really," she said. "That doctor came by earlier and said he was doing about the same, but that's it."

"We're really sorry," Gertie said.

Dinah's eyes misted up a bit. "I just don't understand what's happening. It's all just surreal. My mind keeps whirling, trying to figure out what is going on—*why* it's going on—and what my Bart has to do with it, but I don't come up with anything. Have you found any answers?"

"We're not sure," I said. "There's some things that we thought were questionable and we've turned over our evidence to Carter. He's working day and night on this. He'll get those answers."

She nodded. "I don't know him much to speak of, but no one has ever had anything bad to say about him. And I know his mother is the best kind of people. I'm sure he's doing everything he can. It's just such a mess. I hope it's enough."

"We all do," Gertie said. "But I believe in Carter, and I believe in Fortune. Neither of them will stop until they have answers for you."

Dinah nodded. "I appreciate it. More than you can ever know."

"All of Sinful is praying for you and Bart," Ida Belle said.

Dinah sighed. "So they all know?"

"I think it's pretty much made the rounds," Gertie said. "You know how things are."

"I do." Dinah nodded. "Guess I can't really complain about the gossip when I've been looking forward to getting my fill of it at delivery time." She stared down and then asked, "What are people saying?"

"Not much," Ida Belle said. "Everyone is shocked."

"They'll be saying I was a bad mother," Dinah said. "I guess that much is true. Being a mother begins with choosing the father, so I came out of the gate failing. My father was a terrible person and I married someone just like him. Then compounded it by staying with him. I know we all have regrets but letting that man lay a hand on me and my boy is my biggest one."

"You didn't *let* him," Gertie said gently. "And as we've

already discussed, options back then weren't at all what they are now."

"And hindsight is twenty-twenty," I said. "Trust me, I've made plenty of bad decisions. I think it's the nature of being human."

Gertie nodded. "Mother always said if we were perfect then Jesus would have been unnecessary."

"Ha," Dinah said. "Well, our need is greater than ever about now. I really appreciate you ladies trying to help with this and checking in on me. I know I more or less cut myself off from society years back when my mobility got so bad. But I'm starting to wonder if I was wrong for doing so. All that isolation leaves a lot of time for thinking, and I'm not so sure I like the topics I'm dwelling on these days."

"When all this is over and you're feeling better, we'll get you out to some town events," Ida Belle said. "The Sinful Ladies do plenty of volunteer work that lets you sit while you're doing it—fixing up stuff for festivals or church events and the like. And we'd love to have the company. We won't even make you join."

Dinah gave her a small smile. "I'd like that."

———

WE HEADED BACK to Sinful and spent the better part of the day helping Ally demolish stuff at the new bakery. I will be the first to admit, it was somewhat cathartic as they let me take a sledgehammer to the tile floor. There was an electric scraper thingy that would have made the job easier, but once I picked up the sledgehammer and had a go at it, no one seemed to want to tell me to stop.

I hadn't heard from Carter all day, which wasn't necessarily unusual when he was hot on a case, but given that I might have compromised that case, I was anxious to find out something on that front. I'd told Ida Belle and Gertie about how my break-in at Dirk's office might be a problem and they tried to make me feel better, but I could tell they were as remorseful as I was that our good intentions might cause an issue with the case.

Since we all felt properly and rightfully chastised, we'd voted to take the day off from investigating altogether, although to be honest, we didn't really have another avenue to explore. So aside from the visit to Dinah, which wasn't really investigating, and a call to make sure Spice was still good, that was the only action that related to the case that we'd taken all day.

So while I broke tile, Ida Belle and Gertie attempted to remove the wallpaper on that one sad papered wall. But it was stuck on so well that they only managed a tiny bit at a time. The construction foreman said a steamer would help and so now, Ida Belle was steaming and Gertie was scraping everything she could reach from a chair as her legs had started protesting about ten minutes into standing. Gertie had called dibs on the steamer but been outvoted by Ida Belle, me, Ally, and the construction crew, who either knew her well or had seen her YouTube exploits. The foreman had mumbled something about liability insurance before promptly setting the device in Ida Belle's hands.

It was getting on toward 5:00 p.m. and the contractors were just knocking off when Carter called. I stepped out the back door to take the call so no one could see my face if Carter told me that I'd ruined everything.

"I've made an arrest," he said.

"Holy crap! That was not at all what I expected to hear, but fantastic!"

"This is obviously not for public consumption but I've

arrested Dirk. He's being held in New Orleans and the DA is reviewing everything."

"What is everything?" I asked. "And please don't tell me you can't say because we visited Dinah this morning and I almost cried."

"I'll give you the highlights," he said. "I got an email in the middle of the night from an anonymous source. They claimed they'd seen Dirk haul something big and wrapped in a tarp into the back of a blue Ford truck the night Miles was killed. They even had the license plate on the truck."

"Good Lord!" I said. "Could you trace the email?"

"No. He hid his tracks. But the information was solid. I tracked the license plate and found out it was stolen off another vehicle so nothing doing there as far as identifying the owner, but I put out a BOLO for the truck with the NOLA police and got a phone call an hour later. The truck had been dumped in the Ninth Ward, in an abandoned neighborhood. It was in an empty lot and burning."

"Crap! That means no forensics."

"That's where I caught a lucky break. It was spotted by firemen who had just left a warehouse fire a few blocks over. They put it out before the fire got past the engine. The bed smelled of bleach but we recovered traces of blood from the bumper, and the DNA test was a positive for Miles. I tracked down the used car lot that is the last registered owner of the truck and the salesman identified Dirk as the purchaser."

"But unless you find this witness, Dirk is just going to say that the salesman is mistaken or someone stole it and used it. I know we have Spice's word that he was driving it when he went to her apartment but they'll kill her character on the witness stand. And they'll claim Walter saw him at a distance and at night and he's old so probably bad eyesight."

"He can say all he wants, but we pulled hair out of the cab.

No prints, so I assume he wore gloves while driving it, but he couldn't wear a bubble suit."

"I just love Locard's exchange principle."

"Me too," he said. "And three individuals, unknown to one another, putting Dirk in that vehicle carries plenty of weight regardless of who they are. Add to that, I got a warrant to search his financial records as far back as he existed. I think we're going to find that Dirk has assets his tax returns don't explain. And another interesting thing, do you know what the first commercial deal Dirk ever closed was?"

"What?"

"The Bayou Bank & Trust building."

"Inside knowledge," I said. "That's what the news stories hinted at, but they focused on employees. But the broker would know the building inside and out as well."

"Exactly. I doubt we'll ever be able to make it stick, even with the bills found on Miles, but I thought you'd find it interesting."

"I assume Dirk isn't talking."

"Right on that. He asked for his lawyer and hasn't said a word since."

"Then we still don't know how Bart figures into this. And who's lurking around helping Dirk clean up old business. My money's on Jasper, but with Dirk arrested, my guess is he'll disappear again."

"Unless he's planning on taking another run at Bart, that's probably the case."

"But why bother? If no one has located Jasper all these years, why not just bow out again?"

"True, but has anyone been looking for Jasper all these years?"

"That's a good point. I suppose no cover is foolproof forever. Do you still have guards on Bart and Dinah?"

"Unfortunately no. With Dirk arrested, the state police didn't feel it was a good allocation of their assets any longer. I'm going to have Deputy Breaux cover tonight but he can't make it there for a couple hours because he's handling other things. It should be all right though. I have less fear of things happening during the day, and with everyone at the hospital on alert, he'd be foolish to take another shot anyway."

"What about Spice?" I asked. "I assume the DA is going to want to speak with her."

"Definitely. I would say she's good with Dirk in custody, but since he might have a partner still running around here, I wouldn't advise returning to her apartment just yet. You can tell her about the arrest and that the DA will be contacting her, but don't give her any other information, other than he might not be working alone."

"Sounds good. I made some calls today about her living situation and got her a better option lined up. But I don't want her right back out working until things are more concrete. She's too easy to spot and he probably knows her areas."

"Agreed. I've got to go sign off on some paperwork before I can leave but I'm heading back to Sinful as soon as I'm done here."

"Great. We're still at the bakery doing some work. The construction guys just cut out but we wanted to finish a little more before we leave. The demolition has been cathartic and the more we do, the more money we'll save her."

"I'll check to see if you're there when I get to town. If not, I'll head to your house. Please tell me you have leftovers."

"Ally is living with me. Of course I have leftovers. What can I tell my people?"

"Everything. But they can't repeat it."

"Great. And Carter, thanks for not yelling about my

screwup. I promise that I will think harder about chain of evidence and all before I do stuff in the future."

"Hey, if you didn't butt in, some of these cases might not have been solved. PIs are allowed a little more latitude than cops, but if you could keep things to mostly legal, I'll admit, it would be less stress for me."

"Mostly?"

"I'm a realist. Asking for always is akin to begging for disappointment."

I laughed as he disconnected, then headed inside to bring the girls up to speed. We didn't have all the answers, but a killer was behind bars.

That was good enough for now.

CHAPTER TWENTY-SIX

ALLY HAD BROUGHT COOKIES WITH HER, AND IDA BELLE HAD the forethought to snag a cooler of beer from her house when we'd gotten back from the hospital, so now we all sat around on old cabinets, eating cookies and having a beer while I filled them in on Carter's call. Everyone was stunned that an arrest had happened so quickly but happy that at least part of things had been settled.

"So Dirk killed Miles and hauled the body to the bayou in his truck, then came back for Miles's car, ditched it at the strip center, and stole a scooter to get back to his truck?" Gertie asked. "Why not just haul Miles's body away in his car? That would be more efficient."

"It would," I said. "But remember, Miles's car was already stuffed with all his belongings and he didn't have a garage. So Dirk would have had to unload the trunk or back seat before even hauling the body out. He was already taking a big risk of being seen with just carrying the body out and then retrieving the car later, but if he started moving things around outside at night, it would have set off dogs."

Ida Belle nodded. "Which would have had people looking out their windows. His method took longer but was the safer route."

"So do you think it was Dirk pulling those robberies?" Ally asked.

I shrugged. "We'll probably never know for sure because Dirk won't ever admit it. But given his connection with Bayou Bank & Trust, and the fact that he had plenty of business dealings with the questionable sort who got robbed, I'd say he was on the ground floor for knowing not only who to target but what systems they had in place."

"Might have been him and Jasper," Gertie said. "Heck, could have been Bart too for all we know."

Ida Belle nodded. "He faked his death for a reason and is back for a reason. I just wonder how much of this will never be explained."

"Probably far too much for our liking," I said. "But at least we'll have a killer off the streets and we'll know people are safe in Sinful, especially Ally."

"Thank the Lord," Ally said, and looked at me. "So what is that Locard thing you were talking about?"

"Locard's exchange principle," I said. "Basically Edmond Locard, who was a pioneer in forensics, said that anyone present at a crime scene leaves something behind and takes something with him."

"So Dirk's hair and skin cells are part of that," Ally said.

I nodded. "And I have no doubt his financial records, or lack thereof, will also help build the case. Dirk doesn't have to talk. The evidence will pile up against him."

"Do you think Carter will be able to find the anonymous tipster?" Ally asked.

"Hard to say," I said. "With some smarts, it's easy enough

to hide on the internet. I know he'll try because the DA would love to have the testimony, but his success will depend on how good the tipster was at burying their identity."

"Who could it possibly be?" Gertie asked. "I can't see any of Miles's neighbors not coming forward when they had the opportunity. Anyone decent would have as soon as they heard about Miles's murder."

"I had a thought about that one," Ida Belle said. "What if it was Jasper? This whole thing has gotten out of hand. Miles's body was found, Ally attacked, Bart turning up after supposedly being dead. Their carefully constructed lies are falling apart. Since Jasper has ways of disappearing, maybe he decided to let Dirk hang for it all and vanish with the wind. Maybe both of them were at Miles's house that night and Dirk left with the body and Jasper left with Miles's car?"

I nodded. "It's risky but clever. Even if the cops manage to find Jasper and trace the tip back to him, he'll just use his testimony for a commuted sentence. As long as he's not the one who killed Miles, he's not looking at the death penalty."

"So are you going to try to find Jasper?" Ally asked. "Or are you going to let it go?"

"What do you think?" I asked.

She grinned. "I think Jasper should be very concerned."

"Darn skippy!" Gertie said.

I smiled. "I don't like loose ends either."

Ida Belle jumped up from her cabinet and headed for the door. "Walter's locking up the store. Let me tell him we're staying put for a while."

We watched as Walter broke out into a huge smile as he caught sight of Ida Belle crossing the street. He gave her a hug and a kiss and we all smiled.

"I am so happy that she finally married him," Ally said. "Ida

Belle is awesome and Walter is...well, Walter's just the best. I hope I can find someone like that someday."

"Maybe you've already met your Walter," Gertie said.

"Oh, I don't think so," Ally said. "I know everyone in town and no one's made me feel that way."

"Please," Gertie said. "There were more sparks between you and Mannie the other day than there are here on July Fourth."

Ally blushed. "I can't...I don't..."

"Don't you?" Gertie inquired.

Ally huffed a bit. "Okay, so he's a good-looking man. Everyone can see that, but I can't get mixed up with him. Not as long as he's working for the Heberts. You know how that would go over in Sinful, and I've got the bakery to consider."

Gertie frowned for a moment, then shook her head. "Honestly, I don't think it would stop a single person from coming into the bakery. Except maybe Celia, but that seems more like a perk than a disadvantage."

"Ha!" Ally said, then she was quiet for a moment. "You really don't think people would talk?"

"Good Lord, girl," Gertie said. "This is Sinful, not heaven. Of course people will talk. But I just don't think anything they say is going to change their minds on buying your wares. Oh, maybe a few more stick-in-the-muds like Celia will turn their noses up, but the eventuality is they'll either get over it or keep driving into NOLA for decent—but not stellar—baked goods."

"Hmmm," Ally said. She didn't have another comment, but I could see that Gertie had her thinking, which tickled me. I wouldn't mind seeing Mannie and Ally together. Maybe it couldn't work long term, but it would probably be a fun ride in the meantime. And Ally deserved some fun. Mannie did too, for that matter. Keeping the Heberts in line couldn't be a stress-free job.

Ida Belle popped back inside and handed Ally a long cardboard box. "Delivery was outside the door. Looks like it was for Miles though."

"Oh," Ally said. "Then we shouldn't open it, right?"

I tapped the side of the box. "Says on this sticker that they're apologizing for losing this. Likely something he ordered a while back and just turned up. It's not like there's any forensic evidence on it, so I say open it because I'm nosy."

"Definitely," Gertie said.

Ally tore open one end of the box and tilted it up to slide out the contents. It was a roll of wallpaper. A roll that looked like the one on the back wall. I picked up a slip that had fallen out.

"Past Time Papering," I said. "Looks like they specialize in re-creating old wallpaper."

"It's probably a decent niche market," Ida Belle said. "All those remodeling shows on television have people buying up those run-down historical homes. And a lot of them are looking to keep some of it original."

I shook my head. "I'm not sure why someone chose that wallpaper once, much less twice. And look at this—two hundred bucks a roll. That's a lot of money to look so ugly. Good Lord, and looks like this wasn't the only roll. He ordered two of them. I wonder if the other is lost as well."

I frowned at the ticket. Something was bothering me, but I couldn't figure out what. Then my phone rang and I saw it was Carter again.

"You finish up there already?" I asked. "That was quick."

"No, I'm still here," he said. "But I just got a phone call from the FBI requesting an explanation of events and medical status on Special Agent Bart Benoit."

I jumped up from the cabinet. "Holy crap! Well, that's one I hadn't put on my guess list."

"Me either."

"Was he here on a case? Do they know he faked his death?"

"Apparently, he's supposed to be undercover, but not in Louisiana. They found out he was here when I ran his prints, and since they didn't call right away, I can only assume they are well aware that he is supposed to be dead to everyone here and were trying to figure out how to handle this since obviously, they don't know what's going on either. But when I asked for information, I only got silence."

"What the hell, Carter? Then the FBI must have been in on him faking his death. If that's the case, he's been deep undercover for a long time. Why resurface now?"

I stared at the ugly wallpaper that was now half on, half off the wall and then back at the receipt and suddenly a flood of things went through my mind—Miles and the money from the old bank robbery, Jasper disappearing, the destruction at Miles's house and the break-in at the old dry cleaner's, Bart's return, and the roll of wallpaper. And then the comments.

I had no choice...you made me—

Kids hear everything. They just don't necessarily realize what it means.

Done doing other people's bidding.

A cash-only-no-invoices sort of deal.

Nondescript older men tend to fade into the wallpaper.

And with everyone at the hospital on alert, he'd be foolish to take another shot anyway.

I grabbed a scraper and went furiously at a section of wallpaper on an inside corner that Ida Belle had steamed earlier. A large strip came right off, and I could see the drywall patch beneath it.

"You've got to get to the hospital!" I said to Carter. "Bart is in danger!"

"The hospital staff aren't going to let anyone into his room," he said.

"They'll let one person in. I'm on my way."

CHAPTER TWENTY-SEVEN

THE OTHERS HAD JUMPED UP WHEN I DID AND HAD remained silent during my exchange with Carter, but when I'd made the comment about Bart being in danger, Ida Belle had dashed out and started her SUV, Gertie close on her heels. As I rushed out, Ally yelled for me to be careful, then I jumped in the SUV and we were off.

"Is it Sharon?" Ida Belle asked. "She's the only person I know for sure can get into Bart's room."

"No. It's Dinah," I said.

"Dinah?" Gertie gave me a shocked look. "Why on earth? She can't possibly be so angry over him faking his death that she'd actually kill him."

"Not that alone, but I think it factors in," I said. "Along with him being paralyzed if he survives and the biggest reason, because Bart is an FBI agent and Dinah is our thief."

"What!"

"No way!"

They both yelled at once.

"The woman is disabled, remember?" Gertie said. "She can't walk across the living room without a walker. How the heck was she breaking into high-security facilities—scaling walls and climbing through windows and through vent shafts and the like—because those burglaries the Heberts heard about had to be done by a pro. The bank robbery definitely was."

"I think she was disabled at one time and that's when she sold the business to Jasper," I said. "I'll bet if we check the timing, she had back surgery after that. She said it didn't work but I think that was a lie. She probably had a long recovery, but after that, I think it worked fine for a long time. It probably started giving her problems again about the time Jasper sold to Miles."

"So she never did business with Miles," Gertie said.

"Probably not," I said.

"If she was faking all these years, it was the perfect cover," Ida Belle said. "It not only ensured she was never under suspicion, it allowed her to disappear from society without anyone questioning it."

I nodded. "Dirk said something when we were in his office —'nondescript older men tend to fade into the wallpaper.' But so do nondescript older women. And when Bart said, 'you made me,' he wasn't talking about faking his death. He was talking about coming back to turn her in. And think about it— Dinah's house got repaired slowly but very nicely, and Ally made that comment about the contractor preferring cash and that would have been the perfect way to funnel some of her spoils without raising an eyebrow."

I saw their looks of disbelief and blew out a breath. "Look, I know it's mostly hunch and a lot of speculation, but it works."

"You really think it's Dinah?" Ida Belle asked.

I nodded.

"Do you think Bart knew what she was doing all this time?" Gertie asked.

"Remember, 'kids hear everything,' so at the very least, I think as he got older, he suspected," I said. "And dying was the perfect way to cut ties and not have to give up his own mother for an investigation. Maybe he thought when she sold the dry cleaner's because of her back issues, it would stop. And if he agreed to take on a very subversive role with the FBI, then faking his death was the best way to ensure no one would come looking for him and he wouldn't be called for testimony if she was ever caught. He already had a conflicted relationship with Dinah anyway because of the abuse, but taking a law enforcement role with a criminal for a mother was probably somewhere he didn't want to dwell forever."

"But when the man who took over the dry cleaner's turned up murdered and Carter ran those bills, he realized old business might not be so old," Ida Belle said. "That means that he's kept tabs on things here all this time."

"That's the only thing that makes sense," I said.

"Do you really think Dinah would kill her own son just to avoid going to prison?" Gertie asked. "I realize we're talking about someone who robbed a bank, but the other robberies were of questionable sort of people, so it seems she changed her strategy at some point."

"But did she change strategy because she thought those people deserved to lose their money or because she knew they wouldn't report the thefts?" I asked. "And remember what Dinah said about Bart's quality of life if he pulled through? Since she's only had a taste of what he's looking at, maybe she thinks he'd be better off not pulling through. And then add her hurt over his faking his death on top of it and coming back to turn her in, it might be the perfect storm."

"I still can't believe it," Gertie said. "But then, it fits, especially since Dinah is right there in the hospital with him. Oh my God, do you think she faked passing out to get admitted?"

"Not the first time," I said. "But when her first attempt to kill him didn't work and she knew they were going to release her, I think she faked the second to stay in there. Being on-site made it far easier to steal the scrubs and get into the ICU."

"So you think she's perfectly capable of walking normally?" Gertie said.

"I think she mostly is," I said. "I think it hurts more the longer she's mobile and that's why she stopped gardening. But she has plants in her bathroom shower on a ledge that could only be reached using a stepladder. Does that sound like something a disabled woman would do? And there's no sprayer in there, but those plants are healthy as heck. I just didn't zero in on the discrepancy because I was too busy thinking about how I needed to remodel my own bathrooms."

"Call Sharon and see if she's on shift," Ida Belle said to Gertie. "Tell her to make sure no one gets into Bart's room, not even Dinah."

"Are you sure we can trust her?" Gertie asked. "She was awfully mad about Bart faking his death..."

I blew out a breath. "And she *did* recognize him straightaway."

"And she lived in NOLA for years," Gertie said. "Maybe Dirk's not the only one with a partner."

Ida Belle cursed. "Then call the nurses' station. But get someone to guard that door."

Gertie dialed and waited and waited. "No one is answering. It's just ringing and ringing."

"It is the ICU," I said. "If they've got emergencies with patients, they're not going to answer the phone. And they're full up right now from the rig explosion. If the hospital needs staff, they call over the PA. Incoming calls are almost always family checking on something."

"So not a priority," Gertie said.

Ida Belle was already driving close to the speed of light, but she found some more horsepower and the SUV jumped forward again.

I prayed it was enough.

———

IDA BELLE SLAMMED to a stop in the circular drive of the ER and I bolted inside. The charge nurse yelled at me as I ran right past the desk and grabbed the door to the ICU as it was closing after an orderly who'd just entered. The orderly, hearing the yelling, spun around and tried to block me but I shoved him out of the way and kept running. Apologies could wait. Preventing another murder couldn't.

I burst into Bart's room just as Dinah placed a pillow over his head. She froze, staring at me, then grabbed the plug with all the medical equipment on it and yanked it from the wall. As I leaped forward to put the plug back in, she sprayed me with Mace and ran out of the room. I wiped at my burning eyes and struggled to find the plug. I heard a nurse yelling and realized she thought I'd done this.

I finally found the socket and got the plug back in place, then grabbed a pitcher of water from the table and dumped it in my eyes. The nurse frantically worked on the equipment as another nurse and a doctor rushed into the room.

"Which way did Dinah go?" I asked.

At that moment, a security guard burst into the room.

"Secure her," the nurse said and pointed at me. "She unplugged his equipment."

"I didn't do it," I said. "His mother did. Which way did she go?"

"Get her out of here!" the nurse yelled.

"Ma'am, you're going to have to come with me," the security guard said and reached for my arm.

So I did the only thing I could do.

I pulled out my nine and the screaming started as I directed it at the security guard's head.

"You're going to get out of my way now," I said.

He threw his hands in the air and backed away from the door. I bolted out just as Ida Belle ran up.

"Handle that!" I yelled as I sprinted down the hallway in the opposite direction of the exit. There were only two directions to go, and no way Ida Belle passed Dinah coming in or she would have stopped her.

At the end of the hallway, my options were left or right and both sides were empty. Gambling that she went for the quickest way out, I turned right and headed for the door marked *Break Room*. I threw open the door, startling an orderly who was about to exit.

"Did an old woman come in here?" I asked as I scanned the otherwise empty room.

"Yeah," he said, his eyes wide. "She jumped out the window. I was going to get security. Is she a patient?"

"Sort of," I said as I dashed for the window and jumped through.

I landed in mulch and slid a bit but regained my footing and stopped to try to hear which direction she'd gone. I got my answer a second later as a shot rang out and the bullet whizzed right by my head, striking the wall. I hit the ground and crawled along the side of the building behind the hedges until I could make a clean break for a parked truck. No other shots were fired, so I assumed she'd taken the opportunity to flee.

For a disabled woman, she was doing a darn fine job getting away.

I peered around the truck and into the woods at the back of the parking lot. That had to be where she'd gone. I gauged the distance from the truck to the tree line at about twenty yards. Plenty of room to get shot in. But it was go after her now or risk her getting away. And I had no doubt that a woman who planned as well as Dinah did already had an emergency exit plan in place. Complete with new identity and all the documents required to get out of the country with a stash of money she likely had tucked away in offshore accounts.

I took a breath and sprang up from my hiding place and sprinted toward the tree line. When I heard a car engine roar, I realized my mistake.

The headlights blinded me as the tires squealed and the car launched toward me. I could have leaped out of the way—at least I think I could have—but that would have been too easy and too final. No way this woman was getting away.

I had no time to get my weapon out and it wouldn't have stopped her anyway, so I just waited the two seconds it took for the car to get to me, then jumped onto the hood. I clutched at the back edge to hang on, but Dinah wasn't about to stop the way Timmy had. Instead, she punched it and swerved from side to side, trying to toss me off.

I clung to the back edge of the hood and spread my legs up and out like a frog, toes dug in, to hold my balance. But it wasn't going to last. I had to be able to pull my weapon or I was going to wind up in the parking lot, and Dinah was going to be halfway to South America before I could even dress my wounds.

I heard a bang and felt something wet hit the back of my

head and suddenly, the windshield was covered with something blue.

Gertie's paint gun!

Dinah slammed on the brakes and I lost my grip on the hood. I slid off the front of the car and took a single roll backward, pulling my nine as I went, then popped up and fired into both her tires, then put two more into her engine before creeping around the side of the car. When I got to the driver's door, I yanked it open with my left hand, then swung around, gun leveled, just in time to see Dinah exit through the passenger door and take off running for the tree line.

I dashed around the car after her and saw a delivery service taking wheelchairs out of the back of a van nearby. I caught a glimpse of Ida Belle grabbing one of the wheelchairs and a second later, it flew past me at the fleeing woman.

And it was a direct hit!

The wheelchair slammed into Dinah and she fell to the ground. I ran up and kicked her hand as she pulled her weapon. The gun flew across the parking lot and I leveled my weapon at the now-defeated Dinah. A couple seconds later, Carter's truck slid to a stop beside me and he jumped out. He took one look at me and another at the crumpled Dinah, then pulled out his handcuffs.

"Dinah Benoit," Carter said as he stepped forward. "I'm arresting you for the attempted murder of Bart Benoit—"

I turned around and walked away. I couldn't watch.

It was all too sad.

CHAPTER TWENTY-EIGHT

IDA BELLE, GERTIE, AND I PICKED UP SPICE AT THE HOTEL the next morning and filled her in on the basics of what had happened. We still couldn't say for certain that Jasper wasn't around, but with Dinah on the hook for Bart and Dirk on the hook for Miles, everyone thought Spice was in the clear. She was relieved but there was still that tiny bit of hesitation when I said we were there to take her home. Ida Belle headed toward the area she lived in, but when she should have made a right to go to Spice's apartment, she turned left instead.

"My apartment is in the other direction," she said.

"Not anymore," I said.

"What?" She flushed red. "Did that butthole kick me out? I paid this month's rent."

"He didn't kick you out," I said, and handed her an envelope of cash. "I acquired you a better situation and a partial refund."

She took the envelope and stared at it. "How? Places like that never give refunds, and how did you get me another place without me signing anything? What about my stuff? I don't understand."

"Friends of mine own the building you lived in as well as the one you're moving to," I said. "They had some employees box up your stuff and move it to the new apartment. I figured you'd feel better about not returning there, even though it should be fine."

Ida Belle turned into an apartment parking lot and Spice's eyes widened. The apartments were older but so much better maintained than her previous one and located in an area that wouldn't have nearly the safety issues that her old location did.

"This is way too expensive," she said. "I can't afford this."

"My friends have agreed to rent to you at the same rate as the other place for a year and then only small increases for inflation after that," I said. "But you're unlikely to ever pay market."

Her eyes widened, and I could tell she was afraid to be happy about her good fortune.

"Wait." She stared at me. "I heard that Big Hebert owned my last apartment building."

"He does," I said.

"You're *friends* with Big Hebert?"

"Very good friends," Gertie said.

Spice shook her head. "Girl, you have game that I would never have guessed. Friends with Big Hebert. That's something."

I handed her the keys. "Go take a look at your new place. I think you're going to like it. It's on the second floor, so safer, and overlooks the pool."

"There's a pool?" She asked it almost reverently.

I grinned. "And the furniture is way better. Maybe with a safer place to live at a good rate, you might think about changing other areas of your life. Your current profession doesn't fare so well in the long run."

"I've been thinking about going back to waitressing," she

said. "I don't make as much but I felt better about myself. And that way, I could go back to school."

"You were in school?" Ida Belle asked.

She nodded. "I was studying to be a nurse. Got another year to get my license, but there was a guy and things went south, and my parents were just as bad... Anyway, things got sideways."

"Well, this is your opportunity to get them straight," I said.

She smiled. "I don't know how to thank you. It's all so much. I just, I never, you know... No one's ever done anything like this for me."

I smiled back. "Then it's long overdue."

———

TWO DAYS LATER, Ida Belle, Gertie, and I were back at the bakery building, helping Ally pick out flooring, paint, and fabric from the swatches and pictures she'd collected. The drywall had been removed from the entire papered wall, but no more money was hidden behind it. I figured Miles had packed it all up to go to Florida and Dirk had acquired it when he killed Miles. Whether he'd kept it or destroyed it, no one could say as it hadn't surfaced yet in the search of Dirk's properties.

Everything had been quiet in Sinful since the arrests, especially since Dinah's arrest. People were floored by Dinah's attempt to murder her son but most didn't seem to be fazed by the accusations against Dirk. Apparently, others didn't like the slimy salesman act any more than I had. Of course, he still wasn't talking, but according to Carter, the evidence against him was piling up so high, the DA was going to need a ladder to climb on top of it.

The evidence against Dinah was even easier, at least on the

attempted murder charge, as I'd caught her red-handed. The fact that she'd tried to kill me when fleeing in a stolen car kind of sealed the deal. The keys had been lifted from one of the employee lockers, but that would have been child's play for Dinah. I suspected she'd planned on killing Bart and then disappearing. Fortunately, Sharon had turned out to not have a part in any of it and was as upset as the rest of us about how things had played out.

Carter seemed to think Dinah's attorney was going to go for a mercy killing angle on Bart, but I still believed if they looked, they'd find evidence that Dinah was the real burglar, not Dirk. Carter agreed with me, as the evidence against Dirk supported his laundering money but not stealing it. But he wasn't sure how to pursue an investigation into a thirty-year-old bank robbery or with a bunch of robbery victims who weren't going to talk to the police.

Of course, the big question that everyone wanted an answer to was why. Why would Dinah risk everything to rob a bank? To steal from hardened criminals? Obviously, the money helped raise her son, gave her a nice home, and left her with plenty to deal with her health issues when they arose again, but it had to be more than that.

Unfortunately, Dinah was refusing to talk as well and wasn't allowed visitors. So even if Ida Belle or Gertie or I could have gotten something out of her, we weren't going to get the opportunity. And while Bart was improving, he still hadn't woken up and started explaining everything. FBI agents had paid Carter a visit, but they were even more in the dark than Carter over why Bart had chosen to break his carefully created and requested cover and return to the place he'd left behind.

The contractors had knocked off an hour before, and the sun was already cruising down. But none of us had anything else to do, so we were still hanging in.

"I can't believe the money was in that wall all those years," Ally said.

"Miles thought he was being smart repapering with the same wallpaper and then aging it by staining it and putting heat on it," Gertie said. "Then if Jasper or whoever hid it there returned to check, he would think it was still there."

"Sure, but then he must have gone and flashed those bills in front of the worst person possible," Ida Belle said. "Not nearly as smart as he thought he was."

"Well, this turquoise paint is going to look so much better than that old ugly crap," Gertie said. "Now, what about the fabric on the booths and chairs?"

We were in the middle of a discussion on fabric swatches when Carter walked in. I could tell by his stride and his excited expression that something had happened.

"Boy, have I had a day," he said as he took a seat on a stool. "You guys are not going to believe what's happened."

"Well, it's got you all excited," Gertie said, "so spill!"

"Okay," he said. "But you—"

"Can't tell anyone."

We all spoke at once and then we all laughed.

"This is hush-hush until the DA says otherwise," he said. "First, Bart woke up. And the first thing he asked for was me. Didn't even bother to ask for the doctor. He got one anyway, mind you. When a man returns from the dead twice, people want to be in attendance."

"So how is he?" Ida Belle asked.

"He's decent," Carter said. "I could tell he was still in a lot of pain from the gunshot and the jury is still out on the use of his legs. His upper body is weak but working."

"That's good," I said. "Being immobile isn't ideal, especially in his profession, but it's still workable."

Carter nodded. "I could tell the doctor was nervous about

explaining to him it might be permanent, but he took it in stride. He said the bureau needs the guys sitting at desks analyzing the data as much as they do those in the field."

"That's an incredible attitude to have," Gertie said. "Especially given everything he's just been through."

"You don't know the half of it," Carter said. "So here's the scoop—Bart told me that he'd always thought his mother kept secrets. That she'd go out of town sometimes, especially when his father was on a long fishing trip, and never would say what she was doing. Just 'taking a trip to the city' was all she'd say. He also said that after his father died, sometimes he'd go to check for her in the middle of the night and she wouldn't be anywhere on the property and her car would be gone.

"So not long after his father died, Dinah started fixing up the house and told Bart that if he wanted to go to college, she had the money put back for it," Carter continued. "He didn't think much of it at the time because he figured his father probably had a life insurance policy. But then after he was discharged from the military and came back to Sinful, he heard Dinah talking to Maggie, saying what a horrible husband Bertrand had been and how he hadn't even bothered to insure his boat or himself, so there had been absolutely no money to be gained from his death."

"What about inheritance?" Ally asked.

"None to be had," Carter said. "Dinah's mother died when she was a toddler and her father died when Bart was young. He never met the man. Dinah said he was no good and that was all that was ever said of it."

"Did Bart ever ask her where she got the money?" Gertie asked.

Carter shook his head. "He didn't really start putting it all together until he came back to Sinful after he was discharged. And then, all he knew was that something was off. That Dinah was hiding things, and he was starting to suspect that he'd be better off not knowing what they were."

"Why not?" Gertie asked.

"Because what no one knew, even Dinah, was that Bart was military police," Carter said. "And when he was discharged, he went directly to work for the FBI. His job at the oil company here was an undercover FBI assignment. Company employees were suspected of smuggling drugs through the Gulf. When he wrapped that one up, his next undercover assignment was on the pipeline in Alaska, but he worked it under an assumed name."

"Then something must have changed when he came home for that last visit," I said. "Because he went back and faked his death."

"Yep," Carter said. "Dinah had just sold to Jasper and one night, Jasper caught Bart downtown alone and sidled up to him, saying that he knew all about him and his work, but he could be trusted. Then he said it was better if Dinah didn't know he knew, as she was determined to protect him. Well, Bart did the whole 'what the heck are you talking about' response, but Jasper just smiled and nodded and took off."

"But how did he put that together with Dinah being a burglar?" Gertie asked.

"He didn't right away," Carter said. "But then he got to thinking about all of that and things like his mother doing odd things at home, like climbing up a rope into the top of the barn, claiming it was exercise, or when he caught her crawling out of an air duct and she said it had been clogged and she was fixing it. Some of the drug runners he'd investigated in connection with the oil company employees had been taped complaining about having large sums of money stolen from their homes, and according to the local gossip, this had been going on for years in the criminal community. But they all figured one of the others had done it, so no one branched out in their search and of course, no one called the cops."

Carter took a deep breath, then continued. "Bart said he got a bad feeling about it—you know how we do sometimes— so he got an undercover agent to get him as many dates as possible for those unreported robberies. Turns out, Bart had kept a journal when he was younger and had made a note of the times when he was left home alone. Every one of the journal dates corresponded with a robbery."

"Surely he confronted her then," I said.

"He did," Carter said. "She denied everything and called him crazy, but he's a cop. He knew she was lying. But then he also knew her back issues were real as he'd been with her to doctor's appointments and even seen the lab results. So he figured that would be the end of it, but he knew that he couldn't afford to be in touch with her or he'd keep pushing the issue. And sooner or later he might get her to admit it."

"And then he'd have to turn her in or keep her secret forever," Ally said. "What an awful dilemma."

"Exactly," Carter said. "He wasn't happy about the situation, but she *had* stolen from criminals, so he used that to justify leaving it alone, especially since she'd obviously used the money to improve his life. He was clear with me that his feelings about his mother were ambivalent. He loved her as his mother but also blamed her for his childhood. They had never had a strong bond and as he'd gotten older, it had only gotten worse."

"Too many secrets between them," Ida Belle said.

"So he decided to die," I said. "That way, he never had to be put into the position of knowing for sure and ratting on Dinah, and he never had to address the conflicting emotions about his mother. It wasn't his life anymore."

Carter nodded. "The FBI set the whole thing up—they

were thrilled, of course, because he was the perfect undercover man. No ties. But after some time passed, he realized he couldn't let it go. Not completely. So he watched from a distance, so to speak. He knew when Jasper retired and sold the business, but that didn't raise any eyebrows. However, when Miles turned up dead and I ran those bills from that bank robbery, he called a contact in NOLA and found out that the robberies that had stopped for a couple years then had started back up."

"So he figured out that Dinah had moved forward with surgery and it had worked," I said.

"He suspected, so he headed this way," Carter said. "He approached her house one evening from the woods and saw her walking toward the barn, just as easily as any normal person. He said she had a slight limp when she returned, but nothing compared to the show she put on when a delivery guy arrived a few minutes later."

"It's just as I suspected," I said. "The surgery didn't last. They often don't. She's starting to have problems again and she knows where it's headed. So how did he get to her house and the dry cleaner's? You looked for unclaimed vehicles around town and couldn't find any."

"He had a rental," Carter said. "The night he was shot, he parked it at one of the marinas outside of town and hoofed it the rest of the way. Since they have offshore fishing tours, they didn't think anything of a strange vehicle being there for several days. By that time, Bart had gotten background on Miles and knew he was suspect, and figured since Ally had been attacked there, that the dry cleaner's was at the center of everything. So he went there that night to take a look around and see if he could figure out what was going on before confronting Dinah."

"And Dirk shot him," Gertie said.

Carter shook his head. "No. Dinah did."

"What?"

"No way!"

"You're kidding me!"

"I can't believe it!"

We all spoke at once.

"How in the world did you figure that out?" I asked. "Did Bart see her?"

"No," Carter said. "Dinah confessed but that's for later. When Bart finished telling me his story, he said he'd tried to locate Jasper after he saw his mother walking, but couldn't find a trace of him anywhere since he supposedly retired. Then he started to wonder if his mother had killed both men to cover up her secrets."

"But Dirk killed Miles," Gertie said. "I'm so confused."

"Yes, but Bart didn't know Dirk killed Miles when he talked to me," Carter said. "I told him afterward but his intuition had been so spot-on for the rest of it that he got me to thinking. So I got a team with ground-penetrating radar and sent them out to Dinah's farm. I had them concentrate first on the area where she used to have her garden and her flower beds, and guess what they found under the roses?"

"Jasper," I said.

He nodded. "I have to get a formal match, of course, but the watch he was wearing had his name engraved on the back."

"Unbelievable," I said. "So I assume you took all of this to Dinah?"

"I did," he said. "She knew it was all over and said since it appears Bart is going to live, she didn't want to force him to testify against her. She asked for a plea deal, and the DA was more than happy to comply."

"Convicting a disabled senior would be a rough one, regardless of the crime," Ida Belle said. "You never know where sympathies might lie. And then add the potential for a mentally incapacitated plea due to the abusive husband and she might have gotten off."

"She'll do time," Carter said. "But it's probably going to be under medical supervision. Fortune was right about her back. The surgery lasted for a while, but the problem's returning and the doctors are saying another surgery won't help. She can only manage mobility so long before the pain gets too much for her to handle, and she says some days are better than others. Fortunately for everyone, she was having a good round when she caught Dirk hauling Miles's body out to his truck."

"So Dinah was the anonymous source," I said. "That makes sense."

"How does that make sense?" Gertie asked. "Very little of this makes sense to me."

Ally nodded. "I'm still confused."

"You've got the missing pieces from Dinah," I said, and gestured to Carter to continue. "Tell it."

"Well, I will start with the fact that Dinah's father was a burglar," Carter said. "Apparently, he taught her his tricks young and started using her in jobs when she was six years old, which was shortly after her mother died. Her father was also an abusive man who'd wanted a son and never forgot to tell her how useless and frail women were."

"Kids fit a lot of places that adults don't," Gertie said. "But man, that's horrible."

"And exactly why she married Bertrand to get away," Carter said. "But like a lot of abuse victims seem to do, she picked a man just like her father. Not from the criminal angle, but the abuse and disdain for women were the same. She said he used to tell her that she wasn't intelligent enough to do more than iron clothes and stuff them in plastic bags. That she wasn't strong enough to do physical work all day to provide for her family."

"I'd like to have seen that butthole work in a dry cleaner's all day," Gertie said. "And if Bertrand was such a good provider, then why did she have to work?"

Ida Belle grumbled a choice word or two and we all nodded.

"So after years of taking his abuse and listening to him put her down, she started thieving again," Carter said. "She said the first time was just to prove to herself that Bertrand and her father were wrong. But every time she got away with it, she looked for a bigger and more dangerous score."

"So she started stealing from criminals," I said.

"Sounds like any other thrill-seeking addiction," Ida Belle said. "They just keep upping the ante."

Carter nodded. "The criminals were the perfect targets for her—not going to call the cops but risky enough to up the thrill factor. When she finally thought she was ready for anything, she pulled the Bayou Bank & Trust robbery."

"But why go back mainstream?" Gertie asked.

"Because according to her, robbing a bank was the ulti-mate," Carter said. "And something her own father had never even attempted. It was a surefire way to prove that she was better than her father and not remotely the weak, stupid person her father and her husband thought she was. She knew she couldn't launder the money through the dry cleaner's like she'd been slowly doing the other scores because the tracking systems were coming online, so she stashed it until she could figure out how to clean it. After that, she started having peri-odic back issues and over the years, they got worse. She knew that not only was she going to have to stop the robberies, but she was also going to have to stop working at the dry cleaner's. But she still had a pile of money to clean, so she started looking for someone to take over the business—someone who had no problem taking care of the underlying business as well."

"And she found Jasper," Ida Belle said.

"I have my suspicions that Jasper found her," I said.

"I'm sure that's exactly what happened," Carter said. "Dinah said she consulted with Dirk about appraising the building when she thought she'd need to sell. He sent her to the trade show to see if she came across any potential investors. But Dirk already knew it was the perfect setup to handle the under-the-table money he was getting from his shady real estate clients."

"So Dinah just *happened* to meet Jasper at the trade show," Ida Belle said.

Carter nodded. "She told me that during her surveillance of the criminals she'd robbed, she'd heard Jasper's name mentioned in association with cleaning money, so she knew she'd found her guy. But she didn't tell him she was the thief. She told him she was the cleaner and she still had one client who wanted to continue business with the dry cleaner's with her serving as the middleman."

"Which is why Jasper told Bart he knew all about him and his work," I said. "He thought Bart was the thief and Dinah was cleaning for him."

"That's my guess as well," Carter said. "But eventually, Jasper figured out it was Dinah, not Bart. In the meantime, Dinah started to suspect Jasper was cleaning for Dirk and poked around and found out what Fortune did—that Jasper and Dirk had been in bed together for a long time. There was a lot of heat at that time on suspect commercial real estate deals in NOLA, and the investigations were looking for the cleaners as well. Dinah was worried that if Dirk went down, so would Jasper."

"And Jasper would give them both up to save his own hide," Ida Belle said.

"Without a doubt," Carter said. "So she told Jasper her client was out of the business and she needed Jasper to clear town since the heat was turning up on laundering. Since Jasper knew that was the case, he agreed to take the bonus she promised him and get out of dodge."

"But what happened to the bank robbery money?" Ally asked.

"Jasper had cleaned some of the money in Mexico, but he couldn't go often without drawing the wrong kind of attention. After about a year of that, Dinah said it wasn't worth it and to just destroy the money, which he obviously didn't do."

I shook my head. "No, he hid it in the walls of the dry cleaner's, maybe because he couldn't bring himself to destroy it or maybe because he thought that perhaps one day, he'd figure out a way to clean it."

"But why sell the cleaner's with it still in the walls?" Gertie said.

"Because he still hadn't found a way to clean it and he didn't want to risk getting caught with it," I said. "He was about to get that big bonus from Dinah and disappear. Complications were to be avoided."

"So did Dinah know that Miles was cleaning for Dirk too?" Gertie asked.

"I'm sure she suspected," Carter said. "But as long as Miles didn't know about her, and she had no connection to him, it didn't matter. Even if Dirk suspected Jasper had cleaned for Dinah, he had no proof. Jasper was the only one who could connect her to the laundering, and Jasper was dead."

"I'm surprised Dirk was okay with Jasper leaving," Gertie said.

"He probably figured Jasper was just going to change locations, which he'd done before," I said. "They just had to find another good business to use."

"But since Jasper was dead, he would have never contacted Dirk again," Ida Belle said. "I wonder what Dirk thought then."

"He probably wasn't happy about it," Carter said, "but as the months, then years, passed and Jasper never surfaced, he probably figured he'd either left the country or gotten popped by the wrong person. He thought he was in the clear."

"Then Miles turned up with thirty-year-old bank robbery bills," I said.

Carter nodded. "I get the impression that Miles was no Jasper. I'm sure Dirk knew that if Miles got caught, he wouldn't even make an attempt to cover."

"So Dirk closed the dry cleaner's deal and waited until the night before Miles was supposed to leave and killed him," Ida Belle said. "But how did Dinah know about it?"

"Because she went to Miles's house that night to kill him herself," Carter said.

"I assume it was because Miles had found the money," Gertie said. "But how did Dinah know?"

"My guess was that Miles paid for that painting of hers that he wanted with some of the old bills," I said. "Not realizing, of course, that Dinah was the thief."

"That's right," Carter said. "Dinah said she went there to kill Miles and to find the money and destroy it."

"But Dirk beat her to it," Gertie said. "And she figured that Dirk was making sure Miles couldn't ever come back to haunt him. That's convenient."

"It would have been," Carter said, "but then someone broke into the old dry cleaner's building and assaulted Ally and trashed the rental home that Miles had lived in, and she decided that Dirk must have found out about the money as well and was looking for it."

"So she thought she was in the clear and realized Dirk was the last remaining thread that could unravel if he found that money," Ida Belle said.

"Which is still missing, right?" Gertie asked.

"Yes," Carter said. "We figure Miles had it in his house the night Dirk killed him, preparing to leave with it the next day. Dirk would have taken it, but whether he destroyed it or stashed it, we may never know."

I shook my head. "So Dinah staked out the dry cleaner's the night Bart turned up, thinking she was going to shoot Dirk."

Carter nodded. "She had no idea she'd shot her own son until I showed up the next day at her house."

"So her reaction *was* real," Gertie said.

"Definitely," Carter said. "And then when Bart woke up and said, 'I had no choice...you made me,' she knew he wasn't talking about faking his death."

"And so she tried to kill her own son," Ally said. "I still can't wrap my mind around that one."

"She claims that she knew what it was like to live immobile and in pain and she didn't want that for him," Carter said. "But I don't think that's all there was to it."

"Me either," I said. "But I think it has many layers and all of them complicated. Have you told Bart yet?"

"No," Carter said. "I want to wait until he's stronger. There's no reason for him to know yet. Maybe in a couple days if he remains stable."

Ida Belle nodded. "I think that's smart. Clearly, Dinah and Bart didn't have the kind of relationship you'd hope for between mother and son, but this is a far cry from basic relationship issues. It's going to hit him hard, especially with everything else he's dealing with."

"I imagine so," Carter said. "The whole thing is tragic in so many ways, but the good news is we're getting rid of a money laundering dry cleaner's and gaining a bakery."

"That's a huge improvement," Gertie said. "I'm thinking no one will be murdered over a bakery."

"Good Lord," Ally said. "I hope no one is murdered. That would be the worst bakery ever."

Gertie patted her arm. "Don't worry, dear. You can kill us all slowly with diabetes."

We all laughed.

All in all, it was a good day.

CHAPTER TWENTY-NINE

A MONTH LATER, WE ALL GATHERED IN THE BAKERY AGAIN, but this time was different. It was the official opening for Sinfully Delicious. Dinah had gotten ten years, which would be considered a heck of a deal considering second-degree murder was an automatic life sentence in Louisiana, but no one figured she'd make the ten, so it was likely a life sentence anyway. Dirk still refused to talk but the evidence against him was extensive, and the DA was practically salivating waiting for the trial.

I'd gotten a surprise phone call from Spice, who had taken a server job at a popular restaurant in the French Quarter and had enrolled in school again. She'd seen news coverage of the whole sordid mess and wanted to thank me again for saving her. It was somewhat sobering to think that if Ida Belle, Gertie, and I hadn't gone to NOLA that day to pursue the weakest lead ever, Spice might have been another one of Dirk's victims.

Everyone at the opening was dressed up and smiling as if they'd won the lottery, and as far as I was concerned, Ally opening her bakery was even better. All my favorite people ere—Carter, Ida Belle, Gertie, Walter, Emmaline, ane, and a host of others.

"I don't see Celia," Gertie said. "Don't tell me she opted out of her own niece's opening."

I grinned. "She wasn't invited."

Gertie's eyes widened and Ida Belle chuckled.

"No!" Gertie said. "Seriously?"

"Yep," I said. "Ally said she didn't want any negativity tonight and that's all Celia would bring."

"Good Lord, that girl is really developing a backbone," Gertie said. "I'm proud of her."

"Me too," I said, and Ida Belle nodded in agreement.

The subject of our discussion approached, looking so pretty in a bright blue dress with silver sparkles.

"Fancy," Gertie said to Ally as she took a champagne glass off the offered tray.

"The Heberts sent me a case of champagne with their regrets that they couldn't attend and well wishes for the future," Ally said. "And they sent the good stuff. Three hundred dollars apiece. I spilled some opening the first bottle and had to stop myself from licking it off my hand."

We all laughed.

"I also see a beautiful bouquet of colored roses on the counter," Gertie said. "Who might those be from?"

Ally blushed. "Mannie sent them. I...I've talked to him a couple times over the last month and then he was here to do the permanent install of the cameras."

"Is that *all* he was here to do?" Gertie asked.

She blushed even harder. "He might have asked me to dinner."

Gertie grinned. "And you might have said yes?"

Before Ally could respond, Carter whistled to get every-one's attention. The crowd settled down as he motioned to

Ally. She stepped forward into the middle of the crowd, her smile enormous and her expression one of sheer joy.

"I want to thank you all for coming to my launch," Ally said. "This bakery has been a dream of mine since I baked my first batch of cookies. They were horrible, by the way, but I loved the process so much that I was determined to get it right."

"You darn sure did that!" someone in the crowd yelled, and we all laughed.

Ally blushed. "None of this would be possible without my mother, who was a tough woman but raised me with a solid work ethic and who made sure I was taken care of when she passed. And a special thanks to my friends Fortune, Ida Belle, and Gertie, who take care of Sinful in their own ways."

She held up her glass of champagne. "To many years of baked goods for the fine people of Sinful!"

"Cheers!" the entire room responded.

More investigations with Swamp Team 3 coming in 2022!

Have you tried out Jana's women's fiction/romantic suspense series? The first book in the Tempest Island series is available now. For more information on BACKRUSH, visit her website janadeleon.com/books/ tempest-island-series/backrush/.

To check out other books by Jana DeLeon, visit her website janadeleon.com.

CPSIA information can be obtained
at www.ICGtesting.com
Printed in the USA
LVHW081657251021
701495LV00012B/402